Catalysts

The novels of Stanley Middleton

A Short Answer
Harris's Requiem
A Serious Woman
The Just Exchange
Two's Company
Him They Compelled
Terms of Reference
The Golden Evening
Wages of Virtue
Apple of the Eye
Brazen Prison
Cold Gradations
A Man Made of Smoke
Holiday
Distractions
Still Waters
Ends and Means
Two Brothers
In a Strange Land
The Other Side
Blind Understanding
Entry into Jerusalem
The Daysman
Valley of Decision
An After-Dinner's Sleep
After a Fashion
Recovery
Vacant Places
Changes and Chances
Beginning to End
A Place to Stand
Married Past Redemption

Catalysts

STANLEY MIDDLETON

Hutchinson
London

© Stanley Middleton 1994

The right of Stanley Middleton to be
identified as Author of this work has been asserted
by Stanley Middleton in accordance with the
Copyright, Designs and Patents Act, 1988

2 4 6 8 9 7 5 3 1

This edition first published in 1994 by
Hutchinson

Random House (UK) Ltd
20 Vauxhall Bridge Road, London SW1V 2SA

Random House Australia (Pty) Ltd
20 Alfred Street, Milsons Point, Sydney, NSW 2061, Australia

Random House New Zealand Ltd
18 Poland Road, Glenfield, Auckland 10, New Zealand

Random House South Africa (Pty) Ltd
PO Box 337, Bergvlei, 2012, South Africa

A CiP catalogue record for this book is available from
the British Library

ISBN: 0 09178494 8

Set in Plantin by Pure Tech Corporation, Pondicherry, India

Printed and bound in Great Britain by
Mackays of Chatham PLC, Chatham, Kent

To Jane Davis

O change beyond report, thought or belief!
Milton: *Samson Agonistes*

1

Bravado and nostalgia clashed for the last time. The soloist rose to his feet, cello in his left hand, bow in the right. He made deep obeisance into the rising storm of applause, twice, before transferring the bow to the hand that held his instrument, then embraced the conductor, formally shook hands with the leader, put his feet together and lowered his sleekly combed head in graceful humility. The audience, many on their feet, clapped and shouted.

John Taylor clapped with the rest.

The people standing in front of him prevented him from seeing the soloist, but that mattered little. He regarded their behaviour as odd; they were not young, older than he, perhaps in their late thirties, but they banged their hands together from a yard wide, stamped their feet and grinned, two men, two women, at each other as if to encourage further demonstration, or to compete in enthusiasm. Taylor, applauding moderately, deemed their expression of pleasure more suitable for the football stand than the concert hall. At the end of the Elgar concerto he wanted to edge off, crouch in a corner, be quiet until he had recovered himself.

The soloist and conductor reappeared, were rapturously acknowledged, returned again, and that was over. The four in front made for the aisle, for ice-cream or the bar, their faces and limbs still in a flurry of delight. One was shaking the forefinger of his left hand as if he lectured madly, made certain that his companion, a woman with flat, raven-black hair, understood to the last detail.

Taylor allowed his row to clear before he stood.

Glad to be on his feet, he found his way to the wide spaces of the gallery foyer, crowded now, and loud with social talk. Groups had formed, tight circles of animated heads. He listened. Those near him at least, were not discussing the concert. 'I didn't think you'd want to know about her goings-on,' one woman shrilled. 'I saw him only last week,' a man gravely informed. 'You would have thought he'd have had more sense.' 'No, it's by no means expensive. Not for these days.'

John Taylor stood alone in the middle of it all.

He was amazed at the number of people he did not know. The usual score of recognisable faces were regularly flooded out by a new wave of listeners, here as if by right, occupying seats with propriety or panache. He nodded to a passing couple who acknowledged him, but did not stay.

'Well, John.'

A hand gently touched his elbow. He knew that voice, and turned. A grey man in his late fifties, early sixties, hair plastered above the sharp, sallow face, held out both his hands. Taylor took one, diffidently.

'Mr Alexander.'

Michael Alexander was the music master at his old school, and furthermore the father of the soloist in this evening's concerto.

'I'd have thought you'd be round the back congratulating your son.'

Alexander shook his head, dazed but rational.

'There'll be plenty there without me.' He examined his fingernails.

'Isn't he staying with you, then?'

The father shook his head, lips pursed.

'No. He prefers to drive back to London tonight. Or, at least, I expect so.'

'He's busy?'

'Yes, well occupied.' Alexander's voice dwelt ironically on his chosen word. 'They gave this concert in Glasgow three days ago, Leeds last night, and they'll do it again on Friday, for a broadcast, in the Festival Hall.'

'He plays marvellously.'

'Yes, I suppose he does.' This time one could not guess his intention, whether he praised or blamed.

2

'He has astonishing tone. So big. What's his instrument?'

'Tonight he used a modern one. It's about six years old. Stapleton of Sheffield. Lovely strong piece of work.' Alexander licked his lips. 'Suits his style. He's going to use it for his recording of the Bach suites.'

'He lets you know that sort of thing, then?'

'No. I read it in one of the music magazines.'

John Taylor remembered Sebastian Alexander, five years his senior, at the school. They were in the same house, and those powerful fingers which had won such telling plangency from the Elgar had often pointed first-former Taylor into his place in morning assembly. Alexander had played in all the concerts, on speech days, but had been admired as a cross-country runner, and holder of the school record for the mile. He ran as he played, with rapt concentration, shoving the world aside, intense, his pale face flushing on the cheekbones, his thin frame taut.

'He's certainly making a name for himself,' Taylor said.

'We don't quarrel,' the father answered, ignoring the remark. 'He called in to see me once, a Sunday, by chance, earlier this year. February, perhaps. He had a sandwich and a piece of cake.' Alexander laughed. 'He stayed a couple of hours. Was in no hurry to go. He'd played in Manchester the night before and had stopped overnight with some friends in Derbyshire somewhere. I don't know what made him call in on me. He didn't want anything.'

'Not to ask your advice?'

Alexander grinned with yellow teeth, genuinely amused.

'To him I'm a provincial music-teacher. My opinion is not very valuable.'

'Is there any truth in that?'

'If you've been to the Academy, then Juilliard, studied with Tortelier, had lessons from Rostropovich, actually spoken to Britten, to Tippett, had music written for you by Maxwell Davies and Goehr and Birtwistle and Robin Holloway, then you won't want to hear what I think.'

'He'd be quite young when he met Britten?'

'First-year student. Went up to him at Aldeburgh. After a concert. Asked him a question. The great man actually took time to answer it. And came back a minute later with some rider.'

Michael Alexander's face gleamed, with a fierce liveliness, both mocking and appreciative.

'Don't ask me what the question was,' he said, baring his teeth again.

'He lives in London still?'

'Yes. They moved house again a couple of years ago. Very pleasant. NW something or other. Have you a family these days?'

'No.'

'By choice?'

'My wife and I have split up. Six months ago.'

Alexander shrugged, like a stage foreigner.

'Par for the course,' he said.

They stood, awkwardly, hands deep in trouser pockets, Alexander swaying from side to side at the hips.

'So you won't be going round to see him?' John asked, cheerfully, knowing the answer.

'No. Will you?'

'He wouldn't remember me.'

'In any case. He'll be packing up, and as soon as the second half begins he'll be off.' He coughed. 'He won't wait for Brahms.'

'Does he get that from you?'

'I've more respect for my elders and betters.'

They were both laughing now. A tall woman backed into Alexander. It seemed deliberate. She seemed affronted, but finally broke into apology.

'Pardon me for living,' Michael Alexander muttered.

The woman's expression cracked into dismay or fear, but Alexander smiled at her. She sidled away. He turned towards Taylor.

'I suppose I'd better get back, and prepare my face for Brahms Four. Due seriousness, you know, due seriousness.'

A small man with jacket unbuttoned and a rumpled mop of wavy hair pushed up importantly towards Alexander, pawed his forearm.

4

'Mr Alexander, Mr Alexander, I'm glad I've caught you. Sebastian would like to see you after the concert.'

'How did he know I was here?'

'Eric Smithers told him. He happened to see you coming in.'

'What does he want?'

'I don't know that. They asked me if I could find you. I've done so.' The man broke away, and down the stairs. He did not explain his use of 'they'. Sebastian and Smithers? The concert-promoters?

'There,' Alexander said. 'A turn-up for the book. I tell you what, you come along with me. I shall need some support.'

'Shan't I be in the way?'

'Not mine. I'll see you here once the concert's finished. Here. This very spot.' He bared his teeth and pointed ironically at the ground beneath his feet.

John Taylor listened to the Brahms Fourth, but uncomfortably. He saw no sense in being hanger-on to Alexander, a moody man, a capricious companion, quite capable of wanting a witness to his quarrel with his son. These thoughts did not spoil Brahms for him, but he found himself drifting away into discontent which had no connection with the music. Sir John Waite had now conducted his orchestra through the passacaglia and nodded his satisfaction to the players. He had not used a score the whole night and his baton appeared no more than six inches long. He bowed stiffly.

The audience, on the whole, John noticed, left their seats quietly, bottled their conversation until they had mounted the stairs and passed the foyer door. John made no attempt at haste, but found Alexander had not yet arrived. He watched the buttoning of coats, the donning of light scarves, the deference to women companions, the bustle towards stairways and doors. A young couple, eighteen, nineteen perhaps, came out hand in hand, the boy's hair thick, and combed roughly back from his forehead, the girl striding out but on tiptoe, swinging her lover's arm in pleasure. Taylor's solicitor raised a finger in his direction. A pretty matron waved enticingly, but not to him.

5

'Ready for the royal command?'

Alexander appeared from behind, his tweed overcoat open. Perhaps he needed a lift back home. The two trotted downstairs together.

'You and Brahms in agreement?' the older man asked.

'Of course.'

'Not always the case, was it?'

'And you?'

'For me there is no God but Beethoven.'

'Not always so?' John spoke sarcastically, establishing status.

They made their way through the ground-floor auditorium where a few dawdled still, unwilling to tear themselves away from the place of benediction. A woman checked them, congratulated Alexander on his son's performance, asked if they were going through to see him.

'He looked so well,' she shrieked. 'It must be a life of constant stress and tension.'

'Well, yes.' Alexander sounded like a bishop. 'And boredom.'

The woman seemed unwilling to let them go, but Alexander pushed on, none too politely.

Outside the auditorium, they found themselves in a corridor, one of a series. Men and women in mufti walked purposefully about, presumably orchestral players already changed for their journey home.

'Do you know your way about back here?' John asked.

'I've brought the school choir down for a concert or two.'

Alexander rapped on a door marked 'Private'. Nobody answered. He tried the handle. Locked. He knocked at the next door. They could hear the sound of voices. In the end a young man opened the door a cautious foot.

'Could we see Sebastian Alexander, please?'

The man opened the door widely as if in relief, stepped out into the corridor, pointed at a door further down on the other side.

'That's his room. If he's there. He may have gone.'

'He asked me to call.'

'That's all right then.'

6

The man slipped away from them. Alexander pulled a wry face, walked ahead, and rapped, was invited in. Three men turned to face him.

'Oh, hello, Dad.'

Sebastian Alexander wore a track-suit of green, with a white collar. Taller than his father but as thin he brushed rapidly at his thick, red-brown hair with a flat hand. The two shook hands. Nobody seemed surprised at Alexander's introduction of Taylor into the room, nor commented on it.

'This is John Taylor,' Alexander said. 'You'll recall him from school.'

Sebastian frowned as if trying to remember, or give the appearance of so doing, and held out a limp hand.

'I was in your house,' John murmured. Sebastian nodded as if that explained all.

'I'll bring the car round,' one of the men said. 'How long will you be?'

'Ten minutes. Is that . . . ? Does that give you long enough?'

'Perfect. You wait here, Edward. Help carry the gear out.'

He left officiously.

'Well, Dad,' Sebastian said. 'Sit down. And you, Mr . . . er . . . Sit down.'

They obeyed, and the other man moved out of their way.

Sebastian enquired about his father's health and received a non-committal answer. At this he smiled most pleasantly.

'Somebody mentioned that he had seen you here, and I thought, as I was staying overnight, we might exchange a word or two.'

'About what?' Alexander yielded nothing. His companion felt uncomfortable. Sebastian crossed olive-green legs, relaxed.

'Nothing in particular. I like to check up on you from time to time. With my own eyes.' He clasped his hands quite violently. 'How did you like the Elgar, then?'

'Very good. Very good.' Alexander moved in his chair, forcing it to creak. 'A work of broken lights.'

7

Edward carried two cases nearer the door. Sebastian observed the move. ' "They are but broken lights of thee, And thou, O Lord, art more than they." I did *In Memoriam* for A level.'

His father nodded.

'Where are you staying?'

'With the Parrishes, out at Edwalton. That was their son . . .' He waved in the direction of the door.

'Is Lise not with you?'

'No. She's plenty on. She'll hear this concert on Saturday in London.'

The two men talked trivialities, but while the son sat at his ease, legs crossed, arms draped without tension, the father held himself stiffly, alert for a blow or insult. At the end of small talk, Sebastian turned his head towards John.

'You were at school with me, Mr . . . er . . . Mr . . . ?'

'Taylor. John Taylor. I was considerably junior to you.'

Sebastian nodded thoughtfully.

'Why not spend a day or two with us?' he said to his father. 'Lise would enjoy having you to play for her.'

'It's difficult. Choirs. Church organ. Even in the holidays. Besides, you're never at home.'

'True, true. But give us a ring. I'll talk it over with Lise. She'd enjoy your company. I leave her on her own too often.'

The door opened; yet another man cheerfully announced the car was outside.

'Marvellous to see you,' Sebastian told his father, shaking hands. As he held out long fingers to John Taylor he said, 'Next week, now. One day next week. And we'll fix it.' Over his shoulder.

'Um.' Alexander seemed less than enthusiastic. 'I'll see.'

'Do as you're told, my man.'

Sebastian carried his own heavy, wooden cello case. The acolytes managed the portmanteaux. The visitors brought up the rear, found themselves outside on a small concrete road. They watched the loading of the car, waved farewells.

'Do you know where we are?' John asked.

8

'Not an inkling.' If we walk out and round we'll soon recognise something.

A breeze swooped on them from the October night as they passed a low, wrought-iron gate.

'It's not cold,' John ventured.

'Thank God.'

'Left or right?'

'Left.'

They marched smartly in step. Inside forty yards both knew exactly where they were.

2

John Taylor was surprised, a fortnight later, to receive a phone message from Michael Alexander asking if he could call. Michael arrived exactly on time.

'I came by bus. I usually do. Parking's so uncertain, and then the vandals and joy-riders are on the prowl.'

'This is a very respectable neighbourhood,' Taylor mocked.

Alexander, seated with coffee, did not appear at ease. He spoke briskly, waved fingers about, but looked uncomfortable.

'I've been to see Sebastian and Lise.'

'And all's well there?'

'They rang last week to invite me. I was surprised. She said Sebastian had enjoyed the quarter of an hour in Beechnall, and had instructed her to give me a buzz. I accepted the invitation and went Saturday, came back Monday.' Today was Wednesday. 'It's my half-term.'

'And you enjoyed yourself?'

'Yes. I did. I asked myself what it was they wanted from me. But I never found out. It seemed just as they said it was. They thought they ought to see me, enquire about me. They'd never felt the need before.'

'How did you occupy yourself?'

'We sat around and talked. I played a sonata or two with Sebastian, and had two long sessions with Lise.'

'Is she singing a great deal?'

'Apparently. But they both had a few days off. She's nothing like as busy as he is, but she does a fair amount.'

'And teaches?'

'And teaches.'

They sat, playing with their coffee cups; Alexander had refused alcohol.

'And you're asking yourself,' Alexander continued, 'what's the old sod doing imposing himself on me. And to tell you the truth, I don't know. Perhaps I now connect you with Sebastian, because of the meeting, and I thought you'd be the man to help me sort the visit out. Or that it would explain itself as I poured it into your sympathetic ear.'

'Has it?'

'There's nothing to explain. The more I think about it, the more the mystery dissolves. They're both occupied doing what they want to do, and happy with it. And they had this benevolent urge in my direction. They probably didn't expect me to take them up on their invitation. But I did, and had a perfectly enjoyable time.' Alexander stroked his face. 'He had to go off early on Monday morning. He was playing the Dvořák that night in Cardiff. Lise and I spent the forenoon and a second session going through songs.'

'You enjoy that?'

'I don't often have the opportunity to accompany anybody of their standard. It kept me up to the mark, I can tell you. And my eyesight's not as good as it was. I'm sixty, y'know. Birthday last week.'

'That's no age these days.'

'They've a very decent house. Victorian detached in Kentish Town. Three storeys, but not too big. Plenty of space for a practice room each. Three pianos. They're not short of money.'

'The life style? Isn't constant travelling a pain?'

'In Sebastian's case it's pretty bad. He has to go abroad a fair amount. Lise's work's mostly in England. But it's what he chose to do. And he's young and energetic. They're always away from one another long enough not to quarrel.'

'I know what you mean.'

'Oh, yes. I'd forgotten you'd had your matrimonial troubles. You're divorced now, are you?'

'No.'

Alexander did not pursue the question, but frowned, as if preoccupied.

11

'Perhaps I'm lonely,' he pronounced after a pause. 'That's why I accepted their invitation and looked you out.'

'I'm pleased to see you.'

'Yes, but what would you be doing if I wasn't here?'

'I've a piece of work to look at. I could probably complete it this evening. But there's no hurry. I might read. I might play the piano. I might take a walk down to the pub. Most likely I'd just look at telly.'

'Not very exciting.'

'No. But I've been very busy this last fortnight.' John Taylor was an accountant.

'Is your work interesting?'

'Not in itself. No. But it occupies me, and is well recompensed.'

'I thought the recession had hit accountancy. I read in the papers about large numbers of newly qualified accountants failing to find employment. Is that so?'

'Yes. But that doesn't mean that there's no work about. My firm has as much as it can handle.'

'And your firm is?'

'Benton and Wilkes.'

Alexander looked round the room.

'You seem well settled here. Nicely got up. Do you do your own cleaning?'

'Not entirely. One of these firms descends once a fortnight.'

'It doesn't sound much of a life to me.'

'Go on,' John said, unpleasantly.

'At your age we had Sebastian and the girls, all growing up, all starting music. We were busy. When I look back at it I'm amazed at all we managed. With my job and church and pupils and music school.'

'I'm approaching it slowly.'

They talked for an hour and Alexander suggested out of the blue that they played piano duets together, Brahms then Schubert. Each had a glass of whisky at his end of the piano.

'You've not forgotten how to play,' Alexander praised him.

12

'Well-taught,' John laughed.

At ten-thirty Alexander jumped up, saying excitedly he'd miss the last bus, swilled his drink, and shouting thanks from outside the house, ran down the dark street.

Three minutes later when the efficient Taylor had started to wash cups and glasses the front doorbell rang.

'What's he forgotten now?' John asked the tea-towel. He dried his hands. If Alexander had missed his bus, it seemed likely John would have to take him home.

He opened the front door with a flourish, ready with a sarcasm. A dark, female figure occupied the porch.

'Oh, John.'

His wife. He had not seen her since she had left him in the spring.

'Come in.' Grimly.

'I know it's late. I've been sitting in the car.'

He led her to the sitting room where she took the chair Alexander had vacated. She unbuttoned her coat from her neck.

'What can I do for you?' he asked, not friendly.

'I came round about half-past nine. I've been making up my mind all day to do it, all week. But I heard the piano, and I could see the two of you. You hadn't drawn the side curtain properly. You and your visitor. So I went back in the car and waited for him to leave.'

'You must have been there for an hour.'

'It seemed a long time.'

Stella held her head very slightly to one side, as she often did. It meant nothing. The small, oval face showed no vestige of stress. The wide eyes were clear, the pale skin healthy, unmarred. She wore, strangely, a hat over her dark hair. The white shapely hands were clasped easily in her lap. She sat quite still, shoes together, like a doll. He noticed engagement- and wedding-rings.

'Can I get you a drink?' he asked.

'No, thanks. I'm driving.'

'Coffee? Tea?'

'No, thank you. Not just now.'

It seemed necessary for him to observe these small verbal

13

courtesies for he was shaken by the woman's arrival. Stella had left in April, again to his surprise. They had been at loggerheads for a period of three months; she had seemed not only depressed, but unwilling to be pleased. He could not, at first, understand her trouble. They had been married for four years almost to the day when she left. He had thought her unhappy in her work, (she taught at a sixth-form college) but she had denied this. Then he had wondered if she preferred some other man to him, for one evening by chance he saw her walking along a street in the city hand in hand with a tall, bearded fellow in an anorak. She had been to a well advertised lecture on 'An Introduction to Structuralism', and this colleague had brought her back home. She must have been on the way to the car-park when John, seated in his Rover, outside the main post office where he had dispatched a report he had worked on all that evening, spotted them. Not only did the two swing arms as they walked, Stella seemed to be laughing, quite at odds with her glum behaviour at home.

'I saw you on Queen Street,' he had said, 'with a young man.'

'Jon Burrows. He gave me a lift home.'

'Was the lecture good?'

'No. Unintelligible and dull.'

She did not mention her companion. Nor their laughing progress.

Both had been busy in the New Year, and both made few concessions. Stella often went upstairs to her books, leaving him to wash up the dishes after a meal he had cooked. She did not excuse her behaviour, merely walked away.

On the occasions he suggested they go out to a restaurant, or on a visit to the theatre, or to attend a concert, she refused with barely a word of thanks. He went to a dramatic performance of a Shaw play at her college in February, and there she deserted him after the first act, leaving him to sit on his own. She vaguely excused herself on the way home, claiming she had found some kind of crisis backstage which had needed her presence. She had made no attempt to appear plausible.

14

He had dragged himself miserably about at this period, but had attempted reconciliation, tried to elicit explanations from her, without success. Household duties were neglected, especially hers. There'd be no meal prepared, and he had to rush round at the last minute to cook, and then more often than not, she'd push her plate away after a few mouthfuls. Sex was rare, perfunctory, wordless and grudging on her part. He consoled himself with whisky, she with solitude. He hated the drawn little face, the dull voice, the hesitant movements, the tears and dark volatility, so that the one or two occasions when they had blazed into open quarrels were almost welcome.

He could not understand her unhappiness; she would not explain.

'Leave me alone,' she would snap, snivel, and edge away.

'Look, this won't do.'

'I'm not pleased either.'

'What can I say?' he'd ask. 'Suggest what I can . . .'

'If you don't know, it's useless telling you.'

'But, Stella, what's wrong? We're living like zombies. At Christmas we were right as rain.'

'You mean you were drunk.'

'If only you'd tell me what's wrong, then I could . . .'

'You can't.'

These bursts of sullen conversation and long periods of silence crippled their pleasure in company. They invited no one to visit them, repulsed friends, turned down parties, even a dinner. Work became an excuse for late or irregular arrival at home.

Now as John Taylor watched his wife, infinitely puzzled, he tried to make sense of her appearance. She did not seem troubled; she had, hat apart, not made any great effort with clothes. She was neat, sat still, seemed in no hurry, waited for his invitation.

'Well, then,' he rubbed his hands shopkeeper fashion, 'What can I do for you?'

As soon as he spoke he regretted his half-jovial manner. She had come to demand a legal separation or to set in motion proceedings leading to divorce. He did not want to

15

face such decisions without preparation. Though he paid the mortgage, the house belonged to them both. He wasn't sure that he would stay in the place once they were legally parted. Perhaps she had already chosen her new partner, moved on to the next phase of her life, wanted to make it clear to him.

As he covertly glanced at her, he could read none of this in her behaviour. She sat still, head on one side, pretty, unassertive, feet together. Her eyes were wide.

'I've been thinking,' she said.

'Yes?'

'I've been wondering if we should . . . try again.' The one hesitation seemed without deliberation, unpractised.

'I see. Has anything happened to make you change your mind?'

Stella had been sharing a flat, he knew, with a colleague. Since her first note announcing her departure which had surprised him at the time, but seemed inevitable afterwards, she had written one more message announcing a further change and a permanent address, asking him to forward her mail, saying plainly that she did not want to see him. The letter had sounded neutral, demanding from him the one favour, and warning him to leave her alone. There were no threats and certainly no promises. Her own state of health, and mind, went unmentioned. She made no enquiries about his.

Now he felt shock.

When she had left him, his damaged pride lacerated him, but there was relief. He came home to silence, but it was not shared, not caused by unease between two people. Within a month he had accepted the situation, announced it without qualms to his parents, his friends and colleagues. Three times he had taken out one of the girls in his office; five days ago after an office dinner she had shared his bed. Samantha had made him laugh, was grateful for his attention, but he was in no way serious about her. He was certainly not her first lover.

'Not really. Not in that sense,' Stella said. 'But I have been thinking. I've said so. I am much better. Mentally.'

16

She flashed a mischievously brilliant smile. Her teeth were excellent. 'And it seemed a shame that after four years we should just throw it all away.'

'We weren't happy,' he said, heavily.

'That's true. I was nearly desperate. But now I'm more settled.'

'Is there any reason to believe we'd do any better this time round?'

'I'd be willing to try,' Stella said. 'I think I am different.'

'Thank you.' He breathed deeply, sat solemnly, hands on knees. He needed help, somebody to advise him. No inspiration arrived. He genuinely could not understand what was happening, had never envisaged it. Again, he forced himself to lift his head, examine Stella's features, as she sat, apparently in patience, waiting for his answer. 'Thank you,' he repeated. 'You've taken me by surprise.'

'It's the end of the day,' she answered pacifically, 'and you've been whacking those Brahms waltzes. We tried to play them at one time. I couldn't manage them. I could have written to you, I suppose, with my proposition.' She wagged her head at the word. 'But it's so easy to put words down on paper instead of actually making yourself speak them, face to face. And in the same way it would have been equally simple for you to screw a letter up and throw it in the waste-paper basket.'

'You would sooner have written?'

'It would have been much easier.'

'I see that.'

John fell to thinking, groping about in his head. In the six or seven months since she had deserted him he had beaten off the original shock to his pride, accepted the situation, managed the necessary modifications, and was almost ready, had his wife or her solicitor so indicated, to make their separation legal. Fortunately they had not fixed a holiday together, so that he had arranged without complication a somewhat unsatisfactory fortnight, as it turned out, on the Côte d'Azure. What puzzled him was Stella's balance, coolness, utter reasonableness. The unbiddable, depressed, awkward woman, with her silences or outbursts,

17

now sat in front of him calmly pretty, a well-organised schoolma'am much in control of her class. He could make out no trace of embarrassment. This seemed, in view of his own uncertainty, somehow wrong.

'I hardly know what to say,' he began again, speaking very slowly, 'because this is all unexpected.'

'I should have given you warning?'

'No. I appreciate it that you've come in person. But I feel quite shaken. We were not doing well together for something like three or four months, from the New Year onwards, and I could not make out for myself what was wrong. It was as if you'd changed, or I'd committed some horrible outrage that you couldn't possibly forgive. But you'd never discuss any of this. You spoke as if the fault lay in me, but that I was too stupid to see it, and that such obtuseness meant that any discussion was automatically ruled out.'

'I don't doubt that there were bad errors on both sides.' She spoke from the touchline.

'I'm sorry to bring this up, Stella,' he'd spoken her name, 'but we, I, can't ignore what happened.'

'That's right. So I take it that under no circumstance at all would you consider reconciliation.'

'No. I've not said that. No. I'd need to think.'

'Then I'd do better to come and see you again when you've had the chance to mull it over?' She spoke without rancour, without ill-temper.

'If that's possible. I'm in no position to lay down conditions. If somebody had told me this morning that we should be sitting here, in this room, like this, I'd have dismissed it as impossible. But it's left me, well, wordless.'

She smiled as in agreement.

'What do you suggest?' she asked.

'That I get you a cup of coffee, or a G and T, and . . .'

'I'm driving. Coffee, please.'

'And we'll arrange a second meeting.'

They drank together, without discussion. He gave her an account of his meeting with Alexander at Sebastian's concert; she described a conference on teaching method held in a stately home.

18

'Did you learn anything?' he asked.

'Not really. The best parts were two of the demonstration lessons. These were superb, but done in a way that didn't suit me. I mean, I couldn't copy them, not in a thousand years. But they were marvellous.'

'Do you go with friends to these conferences?'

'Sometimes. Not this one. I knew nobody there. But people are sociable.'

'You had a disco or a dance?'

'We did. On the Saturday night. Women teachers wear too much scent.'

She had made him laugh.

They arranged to meet in two days. She stood, thanked him, made smartly to the front door, like a not quite satisfied salesman. He washed the cups and saucers, uncertain of his feelings.

3

On the next evening, John took Samantha Oldham out to dinner. The arrangement had been made before Stella's visit, and he saw no reason to cancel it. Samantha amused him with her chatter, mainly about the office and her workmates. He learnt what the girls said of their bosses; that Roderick Fielding, his immediate superior, was unpopular and prized himself too highly by a mile. She let out their nicknames; he was 'Trotty' Taylor because of his walk; Fielding 'Bumfluff', no one knew why; and the principal of the firm, Keith Wilkes, 'Crumble' because of his messy eating of the eleven o'clock biscuits. As he listened to Samantha, he concluded that her work, like that of her colleagues, was one uproarious round of surprises, foolishness, sexual harassment and competitive scoring by the girls off their immediate superiors.

'I'm amazed you come out with me,' he said, half-seriously.

'Why?'

'If we're such a set of dunderheads and gropers.'

'You're one of the nice ones. You're quiet. You can be sarky and strict if something isn't done right, but we don't mind that.'

Later, warmed by the wine, he had confessed.

'I'm married. Did you know that?'

'Yes, I did. Your wife left you, didn't she? I remember when it was first going round (I hadn't been there long), Denise Docherty said, "Some women don't know when they're lucky," and Tracey Sammonds, she wasn't doing any too well with her husband at the time, grumbled that men were quite different at home from at work.'

He would fail to recognise Mrs Docherty, if he met her, he thought.

'What does Mr Sammonds do, then?' he asked.

'He manages the Keyhole, the club, you know, on Old Church Street.'

'I went last week. They had a comedian.' He named him.

'Was he good?'

'If you like that sort of humour.'

'And you don't?'

'There's a bit too much about religion and God in it for me. And too much swearing.'

'My father was a Catholic,' she said, 'once. Not now.'

'And your mother?'

'She's not anything. Never has been.'

'What's she interested in?' John asked.

'Holidays. Money. Clothes. She goes to work. She's a doctor's receptionist.'

'And your father?'

'He's a teacher.'

'Where do they go for holidays, then?'

'Singapore, last year. Los Angeles, this.'

'Enterprising. Who's the driving force?'

'Oh, my mother. My dad has to do as he's told. He'd go to Mablethorpe or the Lake District every year, and be quite satisfied.'

John looked with undisguised pleasure at Samantha; her fair hair was bobbed into a shining modern neatness which suited her short polka-dotted dress. She carted round a large white handbag. Her appearance presented bright cleanliness, polish, quick gold so that heads turned; people smiled in approbation. A kind of art-deco novelty, sprightliness, upright mischief pervaded shape and movement. She seemed just to have stepped out of a scented bath as in the advertisements, into exiguous, delicious underwear, modestly naughty. Golden shoes matched the hair. Her nails, manicured to perfection, were plum-dark red, like her lipstick. One took instant delight in her appearance, eye-catching but not vulgar.

The girl knew how to dress, how to present herself, and invariably spoke easily, without show, in a local accent. She talked to John mainly about day-to-day concerns at Benton

21

and Wilkes, which presented endless anecdote, and more rarely of her family, father, mother, older sisters and a brother who was at university. She had been twice engaged to be married but had broken off both engagements, the second not a month before the wedding ceremony. Taylor had heard this before from office tittle-tattle, not from Samantha herself. She wore no rings on her splendid fingers. She could chatter, almost thoughtlessly sometimes, and yet listened carefully, eyes alert, to his dullish conversation. He felt bucked by her company, a somebody in her attractive presence, slightly amazed that she had accepted his invitations. She ate delicately, without hurry, knew what she liked, emptied her plate, drank moderately. She had joined the firm last year just before the Christmas party where he had noticed her, and had been promoted as his personal assistant – not quite so important a position as the title suggested, in that she had to help out with the typing elsewhere – about the time Stella left him. He had appeared a morose boss, he guessed, but she put up with his moods, his temper, worked efficiently, made no nuisance of herself, no demands of him.

Only a month ago he had taken her out for the first time, on a visit to the theatre, to see a version of *The Phantom of the Opera*. He had asked her, almost obliquely; she had been plain in her acceptance, but never gave the impression that she had expected it. She had enjoyed the performance as he had not, and was clearly much more experienced a theatre-goer than he. They had called in at his house afterwards, but there had been no sexual exchanges because he feared that such might endanger their relationship at work. He had driven her back home and she had sounded grateful and chipper. Next day at the office she had acted decorously. He was pleased. Even their last evening together, which had ended nakedly in his bed, had not altered her efficiency in the morning. They were on first-name terms, but kept at a distance in public. It would be known in the typing pool that Sam and Trotty 'went out', a verb of moderation, 'together' from time to time, and this was regarded, he hoped, as a reward of virtue; two decent people, both good at their jobs and pleasant with it, rewarding each other socially, as was proper. How far beyond this speculation expanded, he could not guess.

Now as they slowly ate their way through Pot Roast Chicken with apples and garlic, suitable for October, he claimed, having read the Sunday food columns, Samantha talked while he sat silently.

'You're very quiet tonight,' she chaffed.

'I'm not usually the life and soul of the party,' he answered, truly enough.

'You're not worried about that Steelbright account, are you?'

She did not usually ask questions like this. Though never short of subject matter, and though free and lively in manner, he had never known her talk seriously to him about personal matters. Conversation was to her like her clothes, adding glamour to an occasion, or propriety, an addition to her social persona, but covering the nakedness of her real self.

'Not really.'

'There's no Fraud Squad hanky-pank this time?'

Six months or so ago John had been seconded for a few weeks to the Serious Fraud Office to help an investigation. It had enormously added to his prestige and glamour in the office.

'No. There's been some carelessness, but we'll sort it out in the end.'

'So you're not worried?'

'Preoccupied,' he drawled.

'What's that mean?'

'Lost in thought.'

'Yes, but what about?'

These questions and answers flowed slowly, with mouthfuls in between, like moves in a difficult game.

'Not very interesting,' John answered. She nodded smilingly, willing to pursue the topic no longer. 'It's my wife.' Again Samantha kept an uncharacteristic silence, concentrating on knife and fork. 'She came to see me.'

'Is that unusual?'

23

'The first time since she left.'

He put his cutlery on his plate, and gripped the edge of the table with the fingers of both hands.

'It's worrying,' he said, at length.

'In what way?' That seemed a daft question to both.

'Oh, never mind.'

They finished the meal with apple sorbets, and then coffee, all without haste. Conversation proved desultory and after they left the restaurant they drank halves of lager in the Rose of England, listening in bemused discomfort to a man playing 'Forties Favourites' on an electronic organ. Two or three elderly women near them sang without much interest, but the organist, wearing a bucolic trilby, which he lifted, squashed and waved, announced his items with aplomb through a deafening microphone.

'It sounds like grandparents' night,' Sam said in one of the blessed oases of silence.

They did not stay for long but sidled out during a vocal solo from the organist of 'Room 504'. They closed the door on a thundering line, 'But who could bargain over paradise?' and stepped into October chill under sodium lights.

Back in Taylor's house, Samantha seemed to have caught the plague of dullness, and sat with a straight face, refusing alcohol, sipping a small cup of milky tea. When he kissed her she responded with tenderness, but made it clear that it was 'her time of the month'. She sat briefly on his lap while he stroked her hair and her breasts. Both lacked enthusiasm.

'Would you like me to take you home?' he asked at eleven. 'I'm not very good company.'

She accepted with alacrity, adding sombrely, 'I don't like to see you like this.'

'Nor me. I don't know how I stand. She wants to come back.'

'And will it be awkward if you say "no".'

'Shouldn't think so. You mean financially or legally? I can handle that. No, I don't understand it.'

'Do you want her back?'

'I never even thought about it.' His voice dropped, glum.

24

'She went. Of her own accord. Upped and left. And now. It's "Please may I come back? Please? Please?" '

'You're angry, John.'

Samantha pulled him to her; he bent, sagged, so that his head lay awkwardly on her breast. Her right hand played in his hair, roughly comforting.

'You should have told me,' she said. 'I wouldn't have minded scrapping the date. I've had a few late nights out.'

'No. You cheer me up.'

'It doesn't feel like it.'

He kissed her hard on the mouth, then stood upright, lifting her two feet from the floor. She laughed out loud.

'Samantha Dawn Oldham, you're a good girl.'

When he returned and had garaged his car, he threw himself down in one of his fireside armchairs, and turned on the television set. He flicked through the channels, found nothing to his liking, rose, snapped the power off at a point on the wall, and stood, surprised at his discomfort. Still on his feet and glowering at the fireplace, he began, to his amazement, to cry.

Taken aback, he allowed himself to sob; the bout quickly ended. He wiped his wet cheeks with a handkerchief, dashed out to the cloakroom, and washed hands and face with the vigour and thoroughness of a surgeon. He now regarded himself with suspicion. Perhaps the absence of a sexual culmination to the evening had disappointed him. He had probably been working too hard; this Steelbright audit had been more complicated than he had made out to Samantha. He needed at least two more whole days on it, and then he was not certain he could put up to the In- land Revenue the sort of case the Nicholson brothers, the directors, wanted. They had been inordinately careless, but not criminally so, but it would cost them more money than they could afford. They knew this, he supposed, but pathetically hoped he'd play Santa Claus for them. He liked them; they worked twelve hours a day, but had expanded beyond their means, and had been cutting corners. The tax inspector was a reasonable man, approved of compromise, would listen to an accountant's schemes of clearing the debt, but

25

he had his rule-book, could not budge beyond certain limits. The accountant the Nicholsons had employed before had not bothered them, or himself, had been feckless, and ill. He had now retired, was dying. John Taylor would have to straighten out what he could, and then throw himself on the mercy of the Inland Revenue pundits. In the most optimistic scenario the Nicholsons were due for a lean two years at least. And in a recession. Tomorrow would decide. There'd be plain speaking, and the possibility of redundancies.

John bit the fleshy bottom of his index finger, and swore. He turned on the telly again, out of habit, and as suddenly dismissed it. He opened the drinks cupboard, closed it, pulled it open, banged it shut twice.

He locked the house carefully, by habit, stumbled up to bed. Turning his mind to Stella he realised that he had no idea what he wanted there. He supposed he'd hear his wife out, but he lacked mental energy. He knew, constantly redrew, the lines he'd adopt in the Steelbright business, had planned approaches or withdrawals, visualised obstacles and their conquest, but about Stella's request he was barren. He had only just accustomed himself to her disappearance.

Yawning widely, he decided against a bath, pulled off his glad-rags and took to his cold bed.

He slept badly, hated himself when the seven o'clock alarm roused him to a raw world.

4

John Taylor spent the next day with the Nicholson brothers at Steelbright.

Though their sick accountant was in some measure to blame for the muddle, the brothers had not acted sensibly, had taken up options without circumspection.

Taylor laid figures before them. For the first twenty minutes they argued, but soon gave up. He had done his work too well. They paused for lunch, dry sandwiches and tasteless coffee, which lasted less than half an hour, taken in the directors' office in laconic mistrust. Outside they could hear the whirr of machines, the shouts and footsteps of workmen.

Once the Spartan meal was over, they washed hands and separately found their way back to the office they had opened to John for his investigations. He set out the line he would take with the Inland Revenue and the bank, listened to their objections, which sounded feeble enough, obtained their permission to begin the campaign and rang tax inspector and bank representative from their office. Both officials agreed to call in at the firm, nominated certain documents they wanted to see and demanded that both brothers should be present. 'Inland Revenue, tomorrow,' he intoned. 'Bank, Friday. Both nine o'clock. Early birds.' The rest of the fraught afternoon he spent setting out the necessary papers for instant access. Over the four o'clock cup of tea, he asked the Nicholson brothers about their plans for the next year. Chastened, they answered sensibly. When he left at five-thirty he felt almost optimistic.

He had not once thought about his interview this evening with Stella.

On his way home he had called in at a drivers' cafe he knew, and had eaten, though slowly, a large mixed grill.

27

Then he recognised how tired he was, but he had shaved again, bathed and dressed carefully for his wife's arrival at seven-thirty.

Stella rang the front doorbell ten minutes late.

She had taken trouble over her appearance. A dark green skirt, white blouse, expensive shoes and tights suited the neat, dark hair, the pale face. The skin under her eyes was shadowed as if she had not slept well either.

She refused refreshment, but opened the conversation by enquiring about his work, as if to get him used to talking to her. She listened with attention as he described his week's struggles at Steelbright.

'And the real hassle starts tomorrow?' she enquired.

'You could say so.'

'How will you do?'

'Don't know. At least I've done my homework, sorted it all out at the factory, given the owners an organised account of what's happening to their money. Whether the tax-man or the listening bank pay any attention depends on policy from on high. A decision to support businesses such as this only so far and no further may have been taken in London by the directors, let's say, last week, and that will tie hands all round.'

'I often wondered whether the fact that one of these decision men is suffering from a hangover or bad news, some worries of his own, will make any difference.'

'Slightly, I suppose. They might draw the lines a bit more rigorously because they feel like it, but, no, they'll look and see what they can do inside the framework of rules they're given. If the bank thinks, for instance, that you're likely to continue manufacturing, because you're efficient and there's a market or prospective market for your product, then they're likely to let your loans run on. I mean, that's common sense. To extend your credit. They've more possibility of getting all their money back with a fat slab of interest if in a year's time you're really thriving, than by closing you down now when things are sticky, even though they have first stab at what's left, over the heads of all the other creditors.'

'And will this firm survive?'

'I think so.'

'What do they make?'

'Garden implements. High-grade spades and forks. That sort of thing. A goodish market, I'd guess, but shrinking a bit with the recession. If the economic climate improves we'll all rush out and buy the first-class stainless-steel trowels they make as presents for grandma. Gardening's big business these days. Look at the number of nurseries opening up.'

'Plants die,' Stella said. 'Well-made spades last a life-time.'

'That's not their only line.'

'No.'

Stella watched her husband now, judging whether the time to address serious business had arrived. She sat straighter. He looked relaxed, she thought, but weary, defensive and puzzled.

'Well,' she said.

'Yes?' Gently enough.

'I don't know if you've had the chance to think about what I said to you the other night.'

'Go on.'

'It's October now. We've been apart since April. That's nearly seven months. I put it plainly to you. I wondered . . . if we should try again.'

'What made you change your mind, Stella?'

'It wasn't a sudden conversion.'

'I'm not suggesting it was.'

'Over this past, oh, six weeks, two months, I used, began to ask myself about the time we were married, and whether we should throw it all away. We started well enough, didn't we?'

'I don't deny it.'

Stella looked up sharply. His answers, though softly delivered, seemed unsympathetic.

'You don't see it like that?' she asked.

'Those first three months of this year were hell. In your eyes I could do nothing right. If I tried to enquire what was

29

amiss you either lost your temper or refused to answer. You'd hide yourself away. You made no attempt to give a hand with . . . . We can't close our eyes to that.'

'No,' she answered, humbly nodding.

'Something went badly wrong, and I couldn't tell what it was. You seemed as if you could barely put up with the sight of me. I didn't know why. You wouldn't say. You seemed desperately unhappy, and on my account, even though I seemed to myself much the same man I'd always been. I'm sorry to be blunt about this, Stella, but we might just as well be honest as not.'

'Go on.' His tone and words now.

'To me, and I may have been mistaken, or exaggerating, it was as if you'd had enough of me. I couldn't do anything right for you.'

'Were you faultless?' she pressed.

'I'm not saying I'm without blame. If I'd had more about me, then perhaps I'd have got it out of you what was wrong. I appeared, to myself, to be no worse than I'd ever been, but that you had changed in some radical way or other and were no longer willing to put up with me.'

'That's not quite as I saw it.'

'I'm sure.'

'I was depressed,' Stella continued. 'Things weren't going well at school for one reason and another. You didn't seem to care, or notice. You were more interested in your work than in me. I was nearly desperate, and you didn't even try to understand.'

'Why didn't you sit me down and tell me how you felt?'

'How could I? To my twisted mind you were the cause, or one of the main causes. We were no good in bed; we were hopeless in company; we couldn't talk.'

'And what makes you think that in six months' time we shan't be just as bad?'

'We've had a period apart. That makes a difference. We've thought about it. I have. Night after night. Besides, I've straightened myself out at school. I've had treatment for my depression.'

'Drugs?'

30

'Yes, drugs. But I'm not on them now. And once I began to be nearer to myself, if you know what I mean, I began to see how unfair I'd been to you and to remember what it was like when we first met, or when we were first married.'

'But I failed you when you needed help?'

'Well . . .'

'And you packed your bags, and got out.'

'Yes, but . . .'

'One minute. If you will allow me to be rude and interrupt you. I want to get this straight. In my mind. If it's possible. You just upped and out without any explanation. That convinced me that the rift was final. Look, Stella, I'm struggling a bit here in that I'm trying to put things neutrally. I don't want to upset you with anything I say this evening. But I don't want things left unsaid. Does that seem right?'

'No. Accountant's talk. Income and expenditure.' She laughed out loud, genuinely amused by her summary, without irony. He saw the girl he had married.

'I don't want to upset you,' he continued staidly, 'by saying something out of turn, because too many things were already wrong. You say you've sorted your problems out at school, and you've consulted doctors and they've helped you over depression. That's good. Because I know it takes some courage to pull yourself up by your own bootstraps and tell a psychiatrist all about it. You always seemed an independent sort of woman, with some confidence in yourself. That's why I'm all admiration for you coming here to beard me.'

He broke off.

'But you need convincing that we shan't be just as badly off in six months' time? That's it, is it?' She spoke calmly.

'Exactly.'

'I'm willing to try,' she said. 'Are you?'

He paused, head sunk on chest, before answering.

'I'm not sure,' he said, grudgingly. He held up a hand, gesturing that he had not yet finished. 'I'm suspicious. I was badly knocked about by that three months.'

'But what about the three years? Three good years?'

31

'They weren't much help. Not to you, were they?'

Now she paused, head to one side.

'John,' she asked. 'There isn't someone else, is there?'

'Someone else?' He stupidly repeated the phrase.

'You've not fallen in love with some other woman?'

'Oh, I see.' He coughed at enlightenment. 'I've been out a few times with my secretary.'

'What's her name?'

'Samantha Oldham.'

Stella shook her head.

'That wasn't the name of . . . Is this one new?'

'Yes.'

'Is she married?'

He shook his head.

'Is it serious? What I'm getting at is this: is she a reason against reconciliation?'

'It's not serious.'

'Isn't that what everybody says? What does the girl think? Is she considering marriage? You're a good catch, John.'

'We have enjoyed ourselves. No more than that. At least on my part.'

'Sex?'

She delivered the word with such strength that in his dazed state it seemed to bounce off him so that he did not immediately grasp the meaning.

'Look, Stella, that's between Samantha and me. I've said we've been out together. For all I know, somebody's already reported it to you. People talk. But I'm not serious about it, if by that you mean contemplating marriage. Nor do I think I've misled her in any way about my intentions.'

'How old is she?'

'Twenty-two. Twenty-third birthday next month.'

He had sent neither card nor present to Stella in August on her twenty-ninth birthday.

'Are we getting anywhere?' Stella asked, surprising him.

'We're talking. We haven't lost our tempers yet. I don't know that I'm altogether in favour of sudden off-the-cuff decisions. I'm not sure that I know what I want because I don't know quite what it is you're after.'

'I've offered to come back,' she said, without rancour or emphasis.

'I know that. And I realise that if I thought anything of it, rated you . . . no, that sounds arrogant, mean-minded and I don't intend it like that. I'm moved, touched by your offer, and I don't consider that you're acting from material motives. No. But . . . Can I ask you something?' Neither spoke. Stella looked candidly up, ready to face his question. 'If I appear reluctant, not counting tonight, but after a week or two, are you going to propose divorce?'

'It hadn't entered my head.'

'Oh.'

'I came back here,' she answered, 'because I wanted to try again.'

'But if I refused?'

'You think I might fling divorce proceedings at you as a threat? Because you're comfortable here, and don't want to change, because the division of the spoils and the disruption might cause you problems? Is that it?'

He smiled, neither complacent nor grim.

'No, Stella,' he said. 'I'm an accountant. I know pretty well what a divorce would cost financially.'

'So you've considered it?'

'You might have wanted it. So it was as well to work out how I stood.'

'You wouldn't have minded it? Or contested it?'

'I'd have two different answers to your two questions. But as I feel at present, I wouldn't have instituted proceedings myself. I don't know why. Perhaps because I hadn't considered it carefully enough. If somebody, some friend had questioned me in the street or in the pub on whether I expected you back I should have said, "No". Perhaps that's my lethargy or conservatism. I don't poke sleeping tigers to see if they're still alive.'

She frowned, perhaps at his metaphor.

'Shall I make you coffee . . . ?' John asked.

'No, thanks. We're sorting things out. I'll be off soon. But go on with what you were saying.'

'That I was content to paddle along, at least for the

present. That's true. I've been pretty busy, including one or two periods away. I was shaken for a start, but it didn't impair my efficiency. I slogged on. To tell you the truth I expected you to want a divorce, and that's why I worked out a reasonable financial settlement, so that I wouldn't have any trouble with your lawyers when it came to court.'

'You would have sold this house?'

'Yes. That would have been sensible. Dependent on the market. Though I could have afforded to keep it.'

'You'd no sentimental regard for it?' Stella asked. 'It meant nothing to you?'

'No more than it had for you when you left.'

For the first time he sounded riled or rattled, making his debating point.

'We won't quarrel about that,' she said. 'I can see that I haven't given you very long. That's fair enough. But we've said a few things that needed saying.'

'I'm not sure that discussion as such does much good in cases like this.'

'As such?' she queried sharply. 'You mean I'd have done better to fling my arms round you and said I wanted to come back more than anything in the world.'

'Something like that.'

'I felt as awkward and embarrassed as you when I made my offer. But it was worth the effort. Or so I thought. How long do you want? A week?'

He did not answer.

'Isn't that enough?'

Again he was silent. Her mouth twitched.

'Or have you made up your mind already? You don't want me back?'

He shook his head, blindly, as if not understanding her question.

'I don't know what's wrong with me,' he said.

'Are you ill?'

'No. Busy. Tired.' He forced the words out.

Stella sat rather sternly, face pale, fingers laced in lap, feet together.

'Shall I come back for an answer?' she asked. 'And

34

when?' Her lips had set thin. 'Or would you prefer to write?'

'Why should I?'

'You may find it easier to put it on paper. That's up to you.'

'Which would you prefer?'

'Face to face.'

John took out his diary, played with it without reason, suggested a week ahead.

'That's Bonfire Night,' she ventured. He waited for mention of fireworks, but none came. Stella thanked him, marked her own diary, stood and within a minute had left the house. He returned to the room to turn out the lights, and stared at the chair she had occupied. He picked at his left thumbnail with his teeth, dissatisfied with himself.

5

Michael Alexander telephoned.

'I've been talking to Sebastian,' he confided, once the exchanges about health had been dashed through, 'and he's made a suggestion.'

John Taylor turned this over in his mind. Idly.

'A week on Friday I'm going up to stay the weekend with them, and he suggests that you go along with me.'

This sounded unlikely, so Taylor made no answer, merely humming his puzzlement. 'It's like this, John. He wants you to cast a critical eye over his financial affairs. He's not altogether satisfied with his own accountant. I had mentioned to him that you had worked for the Serious Fraud Office, and perhaps that put the idea in his head.' Again an awkward pause. 'What do you think? He'd be willing to pay your fee.'

'Look. There are two reasons against it. He'd do better to employ somebody locally. It costs less. Subsequent phone calls, for instance. Visits. Speed. Fax doesn't solve all problems. That's the first thing.'

'He'd like somebody from the outside.'

'Is there something radically wrong then with his accounts?'

'I don't think so. He's just not satisfied he's getting good advice, value for money from his man.'

'Why does he think that?'

'Don't ask me. He's a suspicious devil, I can tell you. You mentioned a second reason against it.'

'I could think of a dozen. But it was that my fiddling with his papers might quite well ruin your weekend together. I'd need him there if there are any difficulties. Especially if there's been hanky-pank.'

'I'm not saying that at all.'

'Then what are you saying?'

'Jesus Christ.' Michael sounded off his exasperation. 'That makes two of you. Suspicious bastards. I don't think there's anything criminal about Sebastian's financial affairs, or his accountant's examination of them. I expect they're a bit higgledy-piggledy, and perhaps his accountant's careless or doesn't turn up when he's asked to, or gives advice that Sebastian doesn't want to hear. So here's a chance to get somebody from the outside. Somebody from the Midlands, all common sense and moral virtue.' Michael laughed at himself with a hacking cackle. 'He's not short of a bob or two. So he'll pay for a check-up.'

'But what leads him to think it's necessary?'

'I don't know, but I didn't get the idea that it was anything serious. Shall I try to guess how his mind worked?'

'Right.'

'He thought you were friendly with me since I took you to see him after the concert. And I suppose I've mentioned you a time or two since. Probably he thinks we're closer than we actually are. So you'll be company for me on the way up, and the way back. Moreover, the pair of them won't be saddled with my boring company for two whole days. You'll be there. With cunning variations.'

'He doesn't know me. I might be dull as ditch-water.'

'But not so bad as Dad.' He cackled again, *sotto voce*. 'Have I convinced you?'

'It's not exactly as I should choose to spend a weekend, I can tell you. If his affairs are in a bit of a muddle, they'll need time spending on them. Perhaps the whole two days.'

'But you'll be comfortable, and well fed, and they're good company, quite apart from any music you'll hear. Will you go?'

John took out his diary, wrote into it.

'Train or car?' he asked.

'Which do you prefer?'

'To drive. That's what I usually do.'

'Even in London?'

'Yes.'

They arranged a time of meeting, and Michael Alexander

37

rang off, pleased with himself. John, slightly flattered, tried to make sense of the invitation. He concluded that Michael was at the bottom of it all, wanting to show off his successful son and his daughter-in-law to a gawping provincial who had, however, just about enough intelligence to grasp what a favour was being granted to him. John laughed out loud at his fancy.

At the weekend he rang Samantha and drove her out into the country, and then to Southwell Minster for a performance of Haydn's *The Creation*. She was a clever girl, and musical. She had never heard the oratorio, but had sung 'The Heavens are telling' at school. The bright weather struck cold, but trees were still profusely hung with yellow leaves. They ate an excellent lunch, a bucolic tea with thick cups and thicker, delicious scones, and enjoyed a lively performance. Samantha surprised him by wondering in the interval what this great Norman nave must have looked like at this time of night and year when the only illumination flickered from candles.

'And the cold,' she said, shuddering.

John returned her to his house, where they drank coffee and pleasured each other. Delighted, he wanted to meet her again the next day – the same day, for he took her home at one in the morning – but she had arranged to attend some family anniversary in Newark which she refused to forgo. Her determination to stand by domestic arrangements was both polite and impressive. His commerce with the girl had the wholesome, low-key beauty of a wash with scented soap. He could love her, he decided. This conclusion seemed precarious, based on a foundation of non-commitment. He shook his head at himself.

He constantly thought forward to Stella's visit. His present content with Samantha's company led him to decide on a refusal of his wife's proposition, but this he could not regard as anything but churlish to both women. He opted for his own enjoyment and that seemed unsatisfactory.

Stella arrived in red, strikingly smart. Outside, fireworks exploded, and he had stood at his bedroom window after he had changed into jeans and T-shirt, watching the violent flames of a neighbour's bonfire, leaping with danger. Small figures, dark against the glare, then redly lit, shifted about like ghosts. The sky prickled with rockets. He was on his way down when she rang the doorbell.

Again she refused his offer to drink.

'You're not on your way to a bonfire party?' he asked, nodding at the scarlet clothes.

'No. I shouldn't dress like this to stand about in a garden. Nor to eat sooty potatoes and toffee.'

He asked if she remembered a display of fireworks they had enjoyed in Paris during the first year of their marriage. She unenthusiastically agreed that it had been brilliant, the best.

'Have you thought about what I said?' she asked, crudely. Stella was not here to discuss *feux d'artifice*. He had been given a reasonable time, and now he should answer. Stella's voice spoke plain, not loud, without harmonics, white, inflexible.

'Yes. I have.' Pseudo-parsonical.

'And?'

'I can't give you an answer, Stella.'

'Why not?'

'I can't commit myself to inviting you back. I'm not ready. I know this sounds mean, but I've just about re-gained equilibrium, am beginning to enjoy myself once more.'

'With your secretary?'

'Now and again. But this next weekend, for example, I'm going to London with Michael Alexander to stay with his son, the cellist, and his wife. I can accept invitations of this sort.' He looked long at his feet. 'On the other hand, I realise that it can't have been easy for you to come along here.'

'That was my problem, not yours,' she said dismissively.

'And I don't,' he ignored her interruption, 'therefore want to answer with a direct "no".'

'Why not? If "no" is your answer, it's your answer.'

'Only for the present. That's what I'm saying. I admire you for coming here. I don't think I could have done it, even if I'd puzzled out and decided, as you have, that that was how I stood. I dither. I haven't the courage of my convictions. I can't help admiring what you've done.'

'Thank you. But your answer is "no"?'

'Well. A modified "no".' He started violently from his chair, then settled himself. 'I don't want you to think I'm fooling about with you. It's just that I can't honestly accept your offer. I don't know why this is. But emotionally I'm knocked sideways when I consider what your return entails. I haven't come to terms with our trouble, and your leaving, as you have. I'm not in any way blaming you for this. It's my fault because I probably haven't mulled it over and over as you clearly have done.' He waved his hands in front of his chest, and watched the movements as if he had no control. 'This sounds feeble. You don't think I'm serious.'

He broke off, but she did not speak, merely watched him, neither malevolently nor compassionately, as a doctor watching a patient for a symptom.

'I'm sorry, Stella.'

'The answer is still "no"?'

'Yes. I'm afraid so.'

Stella immediately rose, nodded to end the interview, and made for the door.

'Can't I get you a drink?' he asked, too boisterously.

'No, thank you.'

'You could tell me what you think.'

'John, I'm not here to try to convince you.'

She opened the door into the hall passageway, knowing her way about this house. Efficiently she lifted her brilliant cloak from the coat-hanger where he had hung it. With a swirl of red movement, a bullfighter's, she swung it over her shoulders, chained it about her throat, and using two hands, one on lock, one on brass knob, opened the front door.

'Thank you,' she called, not looking back. 'Good-night.' She closed the heavy door lightly behind her, leaving him to his own devices, in stupefaction.

He stood in the hall wondering what he had done. Given the right answer for one thing. Why then did he feel so

40

shabby? He'd consulted his own interest first. Why had he not more generously accepted her offer, and begun again from there? Simple. He did not want to do it. He stepped along the passage, opened the front door, walked along the path to the gate. If she sat in her car, would he invite her back? He need not have troubled himself; she had disappeared.

Above the houses, stars of fireworks sporadically burst and scattered. An explosion from close by punctured his ear-drums so that he jumped in alarm. A revolver shot from a yard or two away would have been no louder. How did he know that? He didn't.

Sighing, he shut, locked and bolted the door against a world celebrating with gunpowder.

By Friday he had come to terms with his decision and, finishing work early, had picked up Michael Alexander from his home. They settled to travel in opposite moods. John spoke cheerfully in spite of awkward traffic; Michael sounded gloomy. They made excellent time on the motorway, stopping twice to allow the older man visits to the urinals. By the time they were in the Home Counties, Michael talked more comfortably.

'Good car, this,' Michael admitted.

'Granada. The firm's.'

'Plenty of legroom. Support in the seats. And fast.'

'An accountant's car. We have to show the clients we're up to date, with it, snazzy but reliable.'

'And they deduce this from your car?'

'That's the story.'

On Sebastian's road, Michael produced a torch and parking instructions. They edged into a lane forty yards back from the house, did a right turn, eventually found a widely open gate, the number heavily marked in white on a garage door behind, and there they backed in.

'It looks as if we'll have to walk right round to the front,' Michael said. The width of the garden was completely blocked off by a double garage, both doors solidly fastened against them. They emptied the boot of their cases, closed the gate, and set out in the unfriendly darkness. The surface of the lane was hard, unmuddy, and the only light filtered from curtained windows in the backs of two rows of houses and high stars ahead.

'Ideal place for robbery,' Michael said. He lugged two smallish cases.

'Hit 'em with your bags.'

'If they stand still long enough.'

They emerged into the smudgy, brighter lighting of the street and tramped on to their destination over uneven paving slabs.

'Five steps up,' Michael grumbled on arrival. 'By God, they make you welcome here.'

The lack of illumination in the front bow-window and the stained glass of the door did nothing to cheer them. Michael, cases at feet, searched with his torch, then leaned on an old-fashioned bell, the word 'Press' almost erased. They heard the peal.

'It works.'

'It's more like an organ stop,' John said. No hospitable light, sound or movement from within. Michael began on an anecdote about Sir Arthur Sullivan and friend, who had forgotten the address of the house they were calling at, walking up and down the street kicking the boot-scrapers because Sullivan could remember the pitch.

'Which was?' Taylor, sharply.

'God knows. D flat.'

Michael poked the bell again at furious length.

'I hope we've come on the right night,' he muttered. 'To the right house.'

A door was opened inside with a consequent small diminution of darkness, and then suddenly the hall blazed with light, even the small porch where they stood. Michael Alexander's trilby, John noticed, was perched askew on the back of his head.

A woman opened the heavy door, wiping her hands on an apron.

'I'm sorry,' she said. 'I'm cooking. I thought his lordship was out of the bath.'

'But he wasn't.' Michael, exasperated. 'He was not.'

42

'Come in. I thought you might be later than this. You've obviously made better headway through the traffic than I do.' Hands were shaken.

They left their cases, at her orders, in the hall and followed her into the brilliance of bar-lights in the kitchen.

'Smells delicious,' Michael said. 'I hope you're not putting yourself out catering for us.'

'I love cooking,' the woman answered.

Sebastian's wife, Lise Martin, was recognisable from her photographs, but bigger than John expected. As his grandfather used to chuckle: 'A back-hander from her 'uld flatten a donkey.' About five feet eight and broad, she held herself well, bosom high, hair whipped roughly up into a knot on the top of her head. Her features were Slavic, with high cheek-bones, and the large eyes dark, very handsome. She spoke with a vaguely transatlantic accent as she ordered them on to stools.

'Tea or coffee?' she asked. Her voice seemed battened down. They chose coffee; the pot was on, she said.

Lise made them welcome without affectation; she seemed genuinely glad to see them, apologising for her husband's absence.

'He's a lunatic once you show him a bath. Some Sunday mornings when there's no need to travel or go out, he'll lie there two or three hours.'

'Doesn't the water get cold?' Michael asked.

'He has refined the topping-up process to an art.' She continued with her culinary exercises. 'I don't know why it is.'

'He's not rheumatic or arthritic, is he?' Michael enquired.

'No. Do you lie in the bath for hours, John?' She used his first name easily.

'Not really.'

'Has he a thing about cleanliness?' Michael continued.

'No more than anyone else. I guess he finds it the most convenient way to relax.'

'You can practise that in airport terminals,' Michael said, as if in the know.

43

'I can't. But he's very laid-back these days. Except when he's playing.'

'And that's often?'

'And that must be often?' Taylor asked, at exactly the same moment.

'He did over a hundred last year. And that's not counting recording sessions. I don't do half that. I'd be dead.'

'Aren't you starting work on a new opera? I think Sebastian said something.'

'Yes. Nicholas Webb's *Oedipus*.'

'You sing?' Taylor.

'Jocasta.'

'When does it open?' John again.

'March the first. I've started work but Nicky keeps making alterations.'

'Have you sung it to him?' Michael.

'Several times. With James Parkin, the conductor.'

'Is it difficult?' John asked.

'Yes. Hard and with a wide tessitura. But not impossible. He's very gifted. He's made the alterations since he heard my voice. He says that's proper. It's better to write with a real voice in mind.'

'I doubt that,' Michael pronounced, with authority.

'How old is he?' Taylor asked, to avoid argument.

'Thirty-nine, forty perhaps. He's a bit older than Sebastian. I could look it up for you.'

'Impressive?'

'Yes. He's rather squat. And quiet. But intense. Keyed-up.'

At that moment Sebastian entered the kitchen. Without ostentation. He was oddly dressed in an open-necked striped shirt without a collar, grey corduroy trousers held up by a cricket tie, and grey suede shoes. His hair shone; his face was newly shaved, pinkly clean.

'Welcome,' he called out, and shook hands with the visitors.

'Ablutions complete?' his father asked.

Sebastian, sidling round the room, poured himself a mug of coffee and began to explain that both he and Lise had three days together, days of complete rest.

'And you're wasting them on us?'

'Father, father. O ye of little faith. No, we didn't want to go out much, nor to receive chance visitors. So we ask you to come. And John, here, will look into my finances. After all, he's an old boy of the school, so . . .'

'I tell you what else he is,' Michael croaked.

'What's that?'

'Suspicious. It's not usual to employ one accountant, and then set another to watch him. Not unless somebody's up to something.'

'He'll soon see. All open and above board. There's nothing untoward. But my man seems very casual, and I don't want trouble.'

'Why didn't you bring in somebody local?' Michael, sitting lordly, holding up his yellow mug.

'You recommended him. Keen-eyed. Fraud Squad man.'

'So there is something up?'

'There is not. I might be missing a few perks, that's all. And I thought you might like John's company on the way down. And he can look at the papers, all laid out here, while I'm actually in the house, and not intending to go out. So I can answer any questions. It seemed convenient. I'm sorry if I made it look questionable or suspicious.'

'What your father doesn't understand, I think,' Lise said, 'is how rarely we are both at home together, unrushed, unharassed, kicking our heels. This,' she turned to John Taylor, 'doesn't happen often. We always have to catch up on hospitality, because we've been away so much. And more often than not we're preparing for tours or concerts or recordings, practising really hard.'

'So you've not played or sung today?' Taylor asked.

'Yes, I did an hour or so, this afternoon. Exercising my fingers. I don't like to take an unnecessary day off. That happens only when I'm travelling. But I wasn't exerting myself.'

'In fact we went down to the pub at lunch-time,' Lise said.

'That's not usual?' John asked.

'It must be six months at least. In spring. Blossom on the

45

flowering cherries if I remember rightly?' He glanced affectionately at Lise.

'And did you enjoy it?' Michael. 'The boozer?'

'It was a change. I drank a pint and a chaser, and watched a darts game. Lise sipped a ladylike sherry. Inherent interest to me was nil. It had the same sort of fusty, solemn atmosphere as church.'

'But better-attended?'

'I don't know about that. It wasn't busy. Perhaps Friday lunch-time's always slack. And there was no music, muzak, anything. I saw a telly on at the far end of the bar, but the sound was turned down. Odd to have a news-reader's head, but no words.'

'And the darts-players?'

'They played. And chalked scores. Like robots. It didn't seem to matter.'

'Now,' Lise said, 'I'd like the kitchen to myself for an hour. So take them away, Sebastiano, and entertain them. Otherwise I won't be answerable for what appears on the table.'

Obediently they trooped out.

Sebastian carried the tray of coffee-making equipment with him, and they settled themselves to talk. John sat alert, much immersed in the musician's account of his travels.

'I think I'd hate hotel rooms,' he said.

'Better than army barrack-blocks.' Michael surprised John.

'But late at night, all on your own. After you've been the centre of attention, people fussing over you all evening.'

'Fussing?' Sebastian stroked his chin. 'That's a variable, I can tell you. Some are all over you. Some have arranged nothing for you. Some want to entertain you all night long. Others prefer you to turn up, play and shove off.'

'Are you not dealing with professional handlers? People used to dealing with visiting celebrities?'

'Who know how to deal with eccentric geniuses?' Michael, tartly.

'No. Not really. I sometimes am asked whether I prefer a hotel, or wish to stay with a family.'

46

'That has its dangers?' John asked.

'Sure. They want another concert. Just invite a few friends in, and have you playing or talking to the small hours. Though I like that sometimes, I must confess. After some concerts I feel exhilarated, can't sleep, so an hour or two in good company is just what I need. At other times I'm whacked, and want nothing more than a bath, a stiff whisky and a warm bed.'

'Does this add up to a life you recommend to your pupils?'

'I don't teach a great deal. I've too much on. Consultations and master-classes if they can be fitted in. I think I'd like more.' Michael screwed his face. 'I know. I might see it quite differently if I had to do it. But this playing and travelling, and knocking about odd corners of the world, is what I wanted to do from the word go. If you're a first-rate player, you need to fly the air-routes and demonstrate how good you are. It's all right for your Sviatoslav Richters to play now and then when they think fit. He's an old man. He's signed his name upon the vivid air. But here am I, thirty-six, and just beginning to make a decent living out of it. Well, for the past three years.'

Michael rubbed his hands like a bad Shylock.

'Look at my father. He's just as good a musician as I am, if not better. But he couldn't have afforded those ten or dozen lean years I had. He'd married, begotten me and Maria and José. He had to tie himself down as a schoolmaster. I did what I could as a solo instrumentalist. It wasn't always good. But I stuck at it. I think back to those days often now. No money. Not much work. By God, I must have been determined. And not afraid to cadge.'

'What about Aunt Anne?' Michael intervened.

'My great-aunt, God bless her. She died just at the right time.' He and his father laughed coarsely together. 'Left me her all. A substantial house and contents to sell and some money in the bank. Kept me going for four or five years. I might not have made it without that slice of luck.'

'I couldn't have supported you,' Michael said, solemnly. 'And Annie, poor old soul, she'd had precious little out of

47

life. A pious fraud for a husband. No children. Next to no pleasure. Do you believe in providence?' He turned fiercely with the question on John.

'Oh, well . . . I'm . . .'

'I sometimes think she was put on earth just to accrue enough money to make a successful cellist of his nibs here.'

'Was she interested in music?'

'God knows what she was interested in. Penny-pinching.'

'No, Dad, no. She wrote me some good letters. Saying things about concerts, and asking shrewd questions. And always with a bit enclosed. I'm not sure she quite approved of a relative of hers racketing about the world. That was best left to Russkis and Jews. But she had enjoyed music, concerts, at one time.'

'And she died just at the right minute for you. That's certain. I thought she'd live to be a hundred.'

Conversation faded into complacent smiles all round.

'Those ten lean years of yours,' John asked, keen scholar in the class, 'did they, do they make any difference to your playing?'

'Almost certain to. They affected my personality. And that affects the playing. I practised like blazes, I can tell you. I think I could easily have lost heart, and become an orchestral player or even changed professions. But I worked like a madman.'

'You're the complete cellist now?' Michael asked.

'No, you sarcastic sod, I'm not, as well you know. But I've served a hard apprenticeship. And I suppose I had just enough success to keep me going.' He suddenly stroked, then gripped his chin with violence. 'It's left me suspicious.'

'Suspicious?' John.

'Uncertain. We're doing nicely, thank you, the pair of us now. In fact Lise did, was doing, rather better than I was when we first married six years ago. Just after the great-aunt Anne's bequest. Now, I make more than she does. But I'm looking over my shoulder all the time. Fashions change. Even in cellists. There's no telling how much work I shall be getting in ten years' time. Even if I'm fit and well enough to continue with this sort of life.'

48

'But the actual notes you play. Are they different because of your struggles?'

'Must be. But I'd be pushed to say how. Look at old Elgar. You heard me play him in Beechnall. There'd been a war. His wife was ill, soon to die. And though he didn't know it, the rest of his life would be downhill all the way. His music out of fashion, his appearance against him . . .'

'And young fly-by-nights with not a tenth of his talent pissing all over him from a great height,' Michael said.

'But he didn't compose any more?' John mused.

'No. Poor sod. Not much. Lady Elgar, she dead. He needed her for all his roving eye towards the pretty titled ladies.'

'He had about thirty years of success, and that's enough to show your mettle. Purcell or Mozart didn't get that.' Michael pedantically.

Gloomy silence dropped. Uncomfortably. They fidgeted. Michael roused himself, wrestling himself up from the chair.

John looked from one to the other. Father and son sat as if ashamed, one examining fingernails, the other his shoes.

Lise burst in, pulled a face over their silence and ordered them to make such preparations as they deemed necessary, for she'd serve the meal in ten minutes. She left in a hurry. They collected suitcases from the hall and trundled them to bedrooms. Michael brilliantly whistled a Rossini overture to which John Taylor could not put a name.

49

6

Next morning they were all up and about earlier than John expected, and were finishing a leisurely breakfast by nine o'clock.

'We don't stay in bed when we're at home,' Lise told her visitors, 'unless we're really whacked. We want daylight. Once the clocks have been put back, we're chasing the sun. That's when time's our own.'

'And that's not often.' Sebastian.

They took a turn round the small square of garden, hurrying in the raw cold. Sebastian led Taylor to his study where the papers were laid out on a huge office table.

'I shall be downstairs if you need information. Use the internal phone.'

He seemed loth to leave.

'Is there something you want to tell me?' Taylor asked. 'Or some instruction? Something you particularly want me to look out for?'

'Won't you see if there's anything wrong?'

'I've no idea until I've made a start.'

Sebastian explained how he had laid the papers out. John sat down. Nine-fifteen.

At ten-thirty, Lise interrupted him with coffee and biscuits, said they'd be out for the next hour, but that they'd lunch at one o'clock.

'Is all going well?' she asked.

'Yes, I think so.' It seemed utterly straightforward, but he would never commit himself so early.

She backed smilingly out.

John Taylor worked without trouble. The papers were complete and conveniently arranged, presumably by the local accountant, so that by lunch-time he was certain

50

nothing was wrong. He said as much when Sebastian fetched him downstairs.

'I'll need an hour or two more, but there's no problem. Your accountant's a sensible man. All his suggestions are good. He's doing you well.'

'I know that.' Sebastian waited for a question that did not come. 'But I'm willing to listen to ways of improvement.'

'All accountants are much of a muchness.'

'That's their beauty and worth, is it?' In Michael's rough tone.

As he washed his hands, John Taylor considered why he had been called in, and decided that Sebastian had chosen this roundabout mode of publicising his success. Certainly he was making a great deal of money, and before the weekend was out would give John ready permission to quote exact figures to Michael. Then his father could not accuse the boy of boasting; here lay the accounts, certified by a professional. Music paid handsome dividends. For all you had said.

The atmosphere in the dining room grew genial. Lise presented them with great plates full of some foreign ragout, and the men did it justice. Each had second helpings. John found himself surprised that these thin musicians could eat with such verve. Fruit salad and thick cream followed, and almost immediately the three Alexanders set out to visit a friend of Michael's in Belsize Park, taking it for granted that Taylor would retire upstairs to his accountancy. Lise pointed out the coffee and tea-making equipment, the tins of biscuits and home-made shortbread.

'When are you due back?' he asked. 'Next Tuesday?'

She showed him the packed drinks cabinet. They had not, he noticed, drunk wine at lunch, perhaps to keep his head clear.

'No later than five. We're going out this evening. Just after seven. No more cooking today. Short commons and culture.'

He heard them drive off though there had been talk of walking. By four o'clock he had completed his report, restored the papers to their original order and sat for a

51

moment, contemplating his work. There had been no real reason to bring him in; he had made one suggestion, half-hearted, about tax, and one about travel claims. At best these would save Sebastian only a few pounds. He closed the study door, washed his hands, and went into the dining room. It was warm, if rather dark; he picked up a book from a nest of tables, and began to read. He did little enough of this these days: sections of the *Financial Times* and the *Sunday Times* sufficed. He went along the lines carefully, sometimes going back over a whole sentence although there was no obscurity in the text. Though he understood, he wanted to make sure he savoured every word, wrung from it in this house, a new place, a fullness of meaning that would be denied him elsewhere. He surprised himself.

The book, substantial in a yellow cover, began with the description of the fag-end of a funeral, the gravedigger shovelling earth, as the hero, the only mourner, exchanged words with the clergyman. He seemed bright, pointing out to the parson a fault in his understanding of the comforting sentence he had quoted. Taylor liked that. It pleased him that some people knew what they were about; he himself would not have noticed the error in the cleric's reasoning. On a third perusal he was not so sure that the objector had scored anything but a debating point. Still, it was good, to leave him there, watchful for every word as he reread the first side and a half again. He had enjoyed himself as he had not expected. He looked about the room, at the polished furniture, great table, strong chairs, sideboard wide enough for a banquet. No books, though the drawing room had two walls floor to ceiling with shelves, but here hung a mirror and two pictures, all in ornate frames, snakily golden. One, nearest to him, was a print, greenish black, of a piece of lifting tackle, over a half-covered trench, a stone ball, man-made ballast, but all without chain or rope, presumably deserted in a wood. Shapes of cloud pasted themselves on the irregular sky, this side of very distant hills. Brown patches, of growing or faded plants, sprouted near the ball; he had not noticed these at first. He looked for a name among the paint splashes, was successful in the end, finding on a curving slope the word Paul and an 'N', the rest cut off by the frame. Why hadn't the man written straight across his paper? John switched on more lights, studied the composition again, walked across and stared into the darkened back-garden. How would he or Paul N, deal with these bushes splashed with light from the window? He couldn't paint. Well, no. But he could look, and come to no decision. Paul N could simplify these thousands of shapes of sheen and blackness. London was doing him proud.

He restored the lights to their original dimness, and hitching his trousers, picked up his book.

This time the hero chatted up a girl and though this seemed nearer his own condition than the cold comfort of the graveyard, John felt less concerned, and was pleased to hear the doors rattle as the family returned.

Lise found him eventually.

'Put the lights on,' she called. 'We can afford a dazzle.' She splashed the room with brightness from a chandelier, wall-lamps, two standards, bars over the pictures. *'Fiat lux.'*

'Don't forget,' Sebastian warned smilingly, 'he's been going over my accounts. Perhaps he's breaking it gently to us that one small reading lamp is about our limit.'

'Oh,' Lise jovially groaned. 'Oooh.'

John, now standing, asked, pointing, 'Who painted that?'

'Paul Nash.' Sebastian walked across, tapped the glass in the bottom corner where the signature declined. 'Do you like it?'

'What's the ball?'

'I've no idea. A counterweight of some sort?'

'Man-made?'

'Yes. Concrete, d'you think, not stone? I just don't know.'

'Will that be a gin-pit?'

'I've never heard of that. Gin-fizz. Gin-sling, now.'

'Gin-rummy,' Lise added. They both seemed delighted.

'Little hand-dug pits, as opposed to deep mines.'

'First page of *Sons and Lovers*,' Lise said.

'What erudition. It's called the Forest of Dean. Was that a coal-mining area?'

Nobody knew.

From some way above they could hear Michael Alexander singing. His voice rang true, hard-hitting tenor.

' "Farewell and adieu to you fair Spanish ladies." '

'Somebody's happy,' John grinned.

'We had a good hour or so with his friend. They didn't like each other much, but they argued like blazes. About money and Brahms. Both were the causes of half the tribulations of the world, according to Jim Huntingdon. Michael had to argue. They bit and snarled and enjoyed every minute.'

'Who is this man?'

'He was at the university with Dad.'

'A musician?'

'No. Not professionally. He's a lawyer, I think, but in insurance.'

'He wrote a month or two ago out of the blue to Sebastian to ask if he was Michael's son. And telephoned.' Lise spoke with a slow beauty of expression as if she were about to set the dull words to music. 'And when we arranged for Michael to come here, we fixed up the visit.'

'Not telling Dad,' Sebastian glossed. 'You never know with him. He might have refused to go.'

'They hadn't kept in touch?'

'No. Not for forty years,' Lise said. 'This is one of the small side-effects of Sebastian's fame.'

'Notoriety.'

Both laughed, quietly, delighted.

'Jim's a widower. Has a divorced daughter living there with her children. We didn't see anything of them. The two were very cagey for a start, but then thoroughly enjoyed themselves.'

'Reminiscing?'

'Oddly not. Arguing. Putting each other straight. We weren't needed. Jim was worse than Dad, and that's saying something. It was great.'

' "Farewell and adieu to you ladies of Spain",' they heard from upstairs.

'Perhaps you'd give me half an hour on my finances.' Sebastian spoke in a low voice, as if he found the topic shameful. 'I take it I'm solvent.'

'Very much so.'

'Well done.' Sebastian patted his arm and marched immediately towards the door. 'Tomorrow, perhaps,' he said as he shut himself out.

Lise looked up, smiled as if excusing her husband.

'You know we're all going out this evening, don't you? We haven't said much. For one thing we weren't sure about this afternoon's jaunt, and for another we thought you might be tangled up all day with these accounts.'

'I'm at your service.'

'Sebastian's money is all right?' She asked hesitantly.

'Yes. He, his agent and his accountant have all done the job properly. There was no need for me.'

She moved around, touching the table with an elegant left hand, staring out into the dark garden, holding on to an undrawn curtain.

'I think,' she began, broke off. 'Does this bore you?'

'Not at all.' He laid his book back on the tables, uncertain of her topic.

'He can't believe he's making so much money. Perhaps it isn't surprising, because he had a long stint of poverty. So it seems fool's gold.' She turned. 'There's no chance of somebody dropping on him and snatching it all back?'

'Who, for instance?'

'The tax authorities.'

'No. They agreed last year's computations. They'll accept this.'

'I think we shall move house again. He just about understands that property can have value, but money in the bank, or in shares, seems unsafe.'

'Property's losing its charm.'

She smiled at his layman's words and stood, still by the window, looking troubled.

'He's off to Australia in the new year,' she said. 'With the Philharmonic. And then on to Japan.'

'Will he be back in time for your opera?'

'We hope so. He's a bit at the mercy of the tour-organisers.'

'You'd like him here?'

'I'd like him to hear it. Especially early on. He has good judgement. He's looked at the part with me a bit. He's a marvellous accompanist on the piano, like Rostropovich.'

She came back towards him.

'Thanks, anyway, for coming. If you can settle his mind, it'll make this little break of ours perfect. You know what we're doing this evening, do you?'

'Not really.'

'We're going to listen to music. The Delkar Quartet. Have you heard them?'

'Yes. At our music club. They played Haydn, Mozart and Debussy.'

John waited for her. She stood both with dignity, and yet uncertain, like a new judge pronouncing a heavy sentence.

'We're going to hear them privately, at the house of a mutual friend.'

'That's the high life. A string quartet at home.'

'They're adding Shostakovich's last, his fifteenth, to their repertoire, and they're not quite sure what they're up to.'

'Is this unusual with them?'

'I shouldn't think so. They're young, and pretty confident I'd have thought. They've done some very modernist works, tapping glasses, wrapping the fiddles round their necks, whacking gongs, aleatory coughing bouts, the lot. But this has caught them napping on two grounds. One, how to play it, and then, two, whether audiences will want to hear it.'

'Have they not done any Shostakovich before?'

'Oh, yes. I heard them do the famous one, the Dresden, No. 8 is it? That was last season, and they were good. But . . . So they asked the Watsons to collect musical friends to try it out on. Or perhaps the other way about. Caroline Watson loves organising and she probably suggested the idea to them. They'd like Sebastian to hear it. That's part of the draw.'

'Does he know that?'

'Oh, yes. He doesn't mind. He's no expert. His father will give a more balanced opinion, judgement, he thinks. We haven't told you anything about this because he doesn't want Michael looking things up. His virgin opinion's what we're after. A concert-goer who's spent his life on music.'

'That won't be common.'

'No. I expect Michael has heard if not studied Shostakovich, even if he's never taught him. He must have.'

'So Michael doesn't know what we're doing tonight?'

'No. He knows we're going out. That there'll be plenty of booze.'

'You didn't tell him where he was bound this afternoon till the last moment.'

'No,' Lise answered, winningly. 'And look how successful that was.'

She answered his questions about dress. No, he could wear what he liked. A suit, collar and tie if he wished. Jeans and T-shirt. Seb would probably wear a suit, 'to put him in a judicial frame of mind'. She gave a little shriek of deflating laughter. 'But you do as you fancy. The bath water's hot. We'll have a cup of tea straight off now and a biscuit. There'll be plenty to eat tonight.'

'I'm still full from lunch.'

'Oh dear, dear, dear.'

At seven-twenty-five the taxi called for the three men in their sober suits, and Lise in an ankle-length, sweeping print dress, bright with autumn colours. She wore a shoulder scarf or poncho, white and gold, and her hair was done up into a high bun, defying gravity.

'We look the part,' Michael mocked. 'The natty gents' outfitters have done their best by us.'

'Never mind the suits,' his son warned. 'You get ready to listen to Shostakovich.' Michael pulled a sour face; Sebastian had obviously set out the object of the exercise.

'I wonder if we shall be the first there,' Lise said.

She need not have worried.

Caroline Tenby-Watson welcomed them, relieved them of scarves and coats, led them upstairs to a large room which had been cleared of all furniture except chairs, which lined the walls, with the exception of the four in the centre with the music stands and a large standard lamp.

'I decided against taking the carpet up,' Caro told Lise as they entered. 'It was possible, it's not fastened down, but Jack wasn't keen.'

Her husband bustled up to provide drinks from outside; introductions were made to the half-dozen people standing around. They shook hands gravely as if this were a funeral. John Taylor recognised one name, that of a young man in admirable jeans and sweater, as one of *The Times* critics. Everyone treated Sebastian with some awe, or circumspection. He had become very quiet, introspective, hardly speaking. He stood and listened, cruelly handsome, frightening people. When an aristocratic lady asked him about his future tours, he answered politely, and with slow accuracy, but distantly as if he had more important considerations on his mind. A young woman with prominent teeth, hearing his plans, assured him that he'd enjoy Australia as she had done. He nodded, graciously enough, but left the impression that he went there to play the cello and the people and country round about made little difference. A couple discussed the staging of the last act of *Don Giovanni*; *The Times* man spoke about the connection of the libretto of Haydn's *The Creation* with Handel. He never raised his voice; he might have been conducting an Oxbridge seminar. The next time Taylor listened in to him, not two minutes later, he was explaining in the same tone, in shaped complex sentences, just what he understood by post-modernism in music. A bald man, head down and fierce, made some quietly furious point to Michael Alexander, who, noting Taylor's approach, signalled him closer. The fierce man complained about the transport system, the Channel Tunnel, the crass stupidity of politicians. Lise caught up with John before he could become involved, introducing him to a thin young woman in green. Emma Somemumble. Though her legs were beautiful she had an extraordinarily flat chest.

'Are you a professional?' she asked.

'Not musician.'

'What are you, then?'

'An accountant.'

'Don't talk to me about accountants.'

'I had no intention of doing so.'

She laughed at that and pointed a long, bony hand at his heart. She was nearly as tall as he was, and her hair was beautifully bobbed, like that of a flapper of the Twenties. Its economical lines suited her thin features.

'And what do you make of tonight's *tamasha*?' she asked

'Tonight's . . .?'

'Oh, *tamasha*. It's one of my grandfather's Indian words. A show. A performance.'

'It hasn't started yet.'

'No.' Emma sounded annoyed at his incapacity. 'The idea. Roderick Delkar questioning us, I ask you.'

'Why shouldn't he?'

'Because he's a know-all. If anybody knows his mind he does.'

'Perhaps he needs a run-through with an audience. You can practise and practise until you lose your hold on what you are playing. You get into certain habits and before long you can't see any other way to do it. So perhaps they hope that giving it a performance will make them think harder.'

'A discriminating audience?' the young woman said.

'Of course.'

'What's so good about us? There's Sebastian Alexander and Lise. And Caro said Sebastian's father was sharp. And there's Tom,' she pointed at *The Times* man, and Hetty Braithwaite's a powerful pianist, but what about the rest of us?'

'We represent the concert-going public,' John said.

'Oh, do we? Do we, by God?'

Her long face, John decided, was attractive, well made, chiselled. The eyes gleamed large and the teeth were excellent. Her skin, hardly made up, had a smooth beauty about it. She attracted, without artifice.

'What's so tricky about this quartet?' he asked.

'It's his last.'

'Is it difficult? Technically?'

59

'I don't think so. I'm not sure. I've only heard it once, on a gramophone record. They weren't playing together all the time. Perhaps that's the snag. To make one bit fit in with another. All the movements, all six, are marked "Adagio". You knew that?'

'No, I didn't.'

'He wrote it in the last year of his life. He was very ill. Obsessed by death, my record-sleeve said.'

Mrs Tenby-Watson clapped her hands and shouted out to them to take their seats. The quartet had followed her in, and now fussed with their chairs, their light, the music, the stands. They had dressed casually. Delkar was a hard-faced man with sleeked-back black hair; the second violin looked like a Raphael Jesus Transfigured with long fair locks and soft beard. The Jewish viola plumply wore glasses; the cello had shaved his head and held his shoulders powerfully braced. They retuned their instruments and fidgeted. When they sat, poised, ready, Roderick Delkar politely said, facing Caroline, 'We'll play the whole work through, and then after a break, do it again, movement by movement.'

'How many movements are there?' the bald man asked.

Delkar turned over a page of his score as if the question had thrown him. He bared his teeth, drew in breath.

'Six,' he said at length. 'The first's called "Elegy". It's quite long.' As if that was the difficulty. The chubby violist grinned at the cello-player who used his bow to make little épée-thrusts. Delkar looked questioningly again at Caroline, accusingly perhaps. 'Well, we'll play it for you.' He waited. 'All of it. All.'

He sighed.

The single line falteringly opened, E flat, repeated without confidence before it expanded into a snatch of theme. Played without pressure, struggling, unnatural.

During the time, slightly under half an hour, that the quartet performed, John Taylor tried to concentrate. With so small an audience each person must be important, he decided, out to prove the necessity of his or her presence. But the music baffled, not by an inconsequentiality of

notes, not by desperation of cross-rhythm, nor by unfamil-
iarly hateful harmonies. Sometimes the audience caught a
popular snatch, twice a flourish of speed as if to show the
instrumentalists had lost none of their virtuosity, once he
heard an echo of the Volga Boat Song, but the work seemed
to limp. Its strangenesses appealed, the long single wide-
ning notes which snapped off, at the beginning of the
second movement; the refusal to continue with combined
performance in the funeral march as if the majority of the
marchers dropped out, leaving the forward momentum to a
single, ghastly player. Odd, and puzzling, he decided and
watched the faces of the instrumentalists for clues. They sat
intensely, but without the shoulder-charging that they'd
show in, say, Brahms. They did not seem disturbed,
troubled, out-of-element; they pursued their lines with a
kind of impassive doggedness. John learnt nothing there.

When they had completed the work, Caroline Watson led
the scatter of applause.

'Well, that's it,' Delkar said. 'Tell us about it.'

'Over food,' Caroline ordered. 'Next door. Help yourself.'

The players packed their instruments and moved out
smartly.

'You find something to eat first,' Caroline instructed the
retreating backs. 'You've been working.' She then approached John, not the experts. 'What did you make of
that, then?'

'Odd,' he said. 'Frightening.' Certain he needed to give
more.

'Do you think the composer intended to scare you?' She
laughed at her own question.

'He didn't seem much concerned with his audience.'

'That's about it,' *The Times* man said. John felt gratified.

In the next room a middle-aged woman helped them to
choose an ample buffet-supper. Watson, all teeth and black
moustache, lavishly filled glasses, tempted them to champagne.

Taylor, near the end of the queue, found that when he
had helped himself most of the rest had returned to the

61

music room and that discussion, in spite of eager eating, had begun. The quartet, Sebastian and Michael, *The Times* man, Emma and a small, dark, ferocious lady, led the talk. The rest sat a short distance away, listening. Taylor joined the inactive participants, parking himself next to Lise.

The dark lady stabbing the air with her fork, revealed Death as the *fons et origo* of the music. Her face worked, her voice pierced; inside her black dress her whole body boiled, angrily galvanised.

'Shostakovich at this time was obsessed by death. He knew he hadn't long to live, and tried to express this.'

'Life-in-death?' Emma queried.

'You can say that if you like, but this music looks death full in the face and then describes the experience.'

'Is he saying something about death itself?' Sebastian queried. 'Or merely expressing his fear of it?'

'Both,' the dark lady snapped. 'I guess he feared it as everybody does. But saw it as a disruptive force, splitting sensibility, taking away the order and continuity we should find in music.'

The dark lady lectured; the players ate and drank copiously; they were strong young men.

'Who's she?' John asked Lise.

'I was introduced, but I've forgotten her name. Both she and her husband are journalists. They have musically gifted children. I think I've got the right woman. Said to be a good pianist. Helen Somebody.'

When the dark woman had finally decided to concentrate on her food, Delkar, his plate almost empty, challenged Sebastian for an opinion. People looked up.

Carefully clearing his mouth, Sebastian waited, nodding.

'I don't know,' he said in the end. 'I'm puzzled. I don't know whose fault that is. Perhaps Shostakovich was trying to write un-alive music.' He shrugged. 'If he did, he succeeded with me. I didn't find it very interesting music-ally. If some student had written it, who'd see much to praise?'

'Isn't that the point?' Emma asked. 'To compare this with the quartets of his strength and maturity?'

62

'I'm not enough of an expert on his quartets.' Sebastian sat, holding the audience to silence with his left hand. 'Quiz my father here. He's good on explanations.'

Delkar turned to Michael courteously.

'If you ask me,' Michael completed his mastication and laid plate and fork at his feet, 'it's his life, not his death, that's responsible for the music. He was obviously very ill. He'd had some sort of paralytic attack that had stopped him playing the piano, and then he'd been involved in a serious car accident, and had had a stroke. And heart attacks. He was obviously very ill indeed.' Michael spoke more slowly than usual. 'Dying perhaps. But he was highly regarded. And the one thing he had done all his life was compose. And so he dragged himself to his desk and wrote music, thin music, desperate music, but all he could manage in the scarecrow physical state he was in.'

'Was he frightened?' The dark lady, snappy.

'I expect so. I would be, in such weakness.'

'Hadn't he been frightened all his life?' A man from the audience end. 'What with Stalin and his criticisms?'

'Yes. I guess so. Terrified.' Michael shook his head. 'And yet I can't help thinking this constant pressure from Stalin or his minions was good for him. It kept him in touch with his audience. It gave him a – let's put it vulgarly – a popular touch. That's necessary. It's only this century that composers have deliberately staggered away from musical listeners. Music, orchestral, chamber, opera, has always been a minority art, but that minority has been counted in thousands not dozens.'

This led to argument, broken finally by a trek to find pudding.

On their return, John Taylor, again near the end, found that this time the seating order was different, with no division into principals and non-participants. Most were standing to eat. Taylor found himself next to Delkar and Michael.

'I think what you said is about right,' the quartet-leader said. 'The question is, how shall we play it?'

'That's it,' Michael warned. 'How should you play music

written in chains? I take it that you admire Shostakovich, see his efforts to continue as heroic. He was here to compose and though he's half-dead he still writes his music. Should you play it heroically? Should you, a powerful young man, healthily robust, play tribute to his heroism by giving these faltering utterances a heroic strength, or should you play them as if you had as much difficulty as he had, make the audiences understand how battered, debilitated, the man was. I mean, you can always pitch into the one or two manic bursts he wrote. No. Play it feebly, low-key, as if virtue had gone out of you.'

'Sebastian said he didn't find the music very interesting musically,' Delkar growled, 'and if we play it as if we're half-paralyzed, won't people be even less likely to want to hear it?'

'Then they'll have to learn. If you come to Chopin expecting Bach, you'll be disappointed. If you expect earlier Shostakovich, it won't be there. Look at the last Britten quartet. It shows the composer's physical weakness.'

'If a pianist', Roderick Delkar argued, 'lost the use of let's say, his right hand . . . .'

'Like Paul Wittgenstein?'

'Yes. Would you expect him to play the great two-handed classics of his instrument? And if he did, however much you admired his courage, the result would be a failure.'

'But Ravel could write good music for the left hand only. Part of the attraction of art is the way it surmounts obstacles. And here we have a great composer, as I believe Shostakovich was, left only half a man. And what he wrote is interesting. Don't you think so, John?'

Taylor jumped, not expecting to be included.

'It is certainly interesting humanly. I'm not sure about musically.'

The other two looked at him with respect.

In the event, the quartet played only the first movement again, as the violist had to leave. Their performance lacked force, deliberately. When they had packed away their instruments, only Delkar and the cellist returned.

The rest of the evening was crammed with talk. Some

drank heavily. Sebastian seemed cut off from the rest of the company. He spoke, like a ghost, only when addressed first. Taylor asked Lise about it.

'He doesn't like to talk about illness and death,' she said.

'Why did he come, then?'

'You mean he'd know what they'd discuss? Yes, I suppose he did. But he can't resist a challenge. Especially an unpleasant one. Now he's fighting this one over in his mind.'

The Alexanders and John Taylor left soon after midnight. They seemed tired, Michael especially, and went straight to bed.

7

They rose late, took coffee and cereal at eleven, lunched at two-thirty.

Sebastian called Taylor aside, and they spent half an hour on financial affairs. Sebastian expressed his satisfaction.

'You won't understand why I called you in,' he said pleasantly. 'But I just wanted to be sure. That, for instance, I shouldn't be whacked down by an enormous tax-demand. Something of that sort. So I bring somebody in from outside. To buy peace of mind. I'm not used yet to all this money. And yet I suppose it's chicken-feed to that of some pop-stars or financiers.'

'Or conductors.'

'Some. So they say. Anyway, my mind's at rest. I can be happy for the remainder of my break, today and tomorrow. Send me your account.'

'There'll be none. I've had a fascinating weekend that more than makes up for any trouble I've taken.'

'That's very kind of you. But I'd sooner pay.'

'You don't charge me for meals and accommodation.'

'You ferried my father up. Anyhow, thanks very much. My mind's settled. And we've still tomorrow by way of holiday. We've enjoyed your company. Lise's chatting to my father, getting to know him. He's been here before, but too infrequently. He's delighted with last night. He likes having to sort himself out.'

The provincials left early at about five, found the motorway uncrowded, made good time. Michael invited John in for a drink, but he refused.

'Good weekend,' Michael said. 'Different world.'

'I wonder.' John felt argumentative, but Michael Alexander didn't find the dark street the place for polemics. They shook hands heartily.

66

Back at home John idly read Saturday morning's mail, ate a sandwich, altered the central-heating clock, walked the cold darkness of the garden. He checked the answer-phone: Samantha Oldham asked him to ring urgently.

He glanced at his watch. It was now past nine on a Sunday evening. He wondered what the girl wanted, dialled her number. A dull-voiced woman answered, found Samantha.

'You asked me to ring.'

'Yes. I didn't . . . Well . . . John, it's my father. He's dead.' She began to cry.

He mouthed clichés of sorrow into the mouthpiece to give the girl time to recover. It had happened, a heart-attack, in the early hours of Saturday morning. It had been unexpected, yes, though he'd had trouble with his heart. Two years, now. He was only fifty-one, had been perfectly well the day before, had gone to work and bed perfectly happy, but had woken her mother, asked for his pills, said how bad he felt. By the time Mrs Oldham had fetched medicine and water, he was dead. She could not believe such things happened so quickly. They'd rung an ambulance. No, it hadn't been too long. Mother and an older sister had gone to the hospital. But he was dead. Hilary, the sister, was a nurse, knew about these things.

He gently drew the story from the girl. She talked occasionally with a subdued violence and fluency, while at other times he had to coax her into answering.

'How is your mother?' he asked.

'She's marvellous, really. My sister's very efficient.'

'Is there anyone else at home?'

'Peter, my brother, has come back from university. He was at Birmingham.' She seemed to choke. 'My other sister's in New Zealand.'

'You've been in touch with her?'

'Yes.'

Samantha seemed more settled, as if her announcement to him had comforted her in some oblique way.

'What is it now?' he asked. 'Nearly half-past nine. Would you like to come round for an hour? And your mother and the rest of the family, if they'd like it? It gets them out of the house. To have a cup of coffee and see a different face.'

'I don't think they would, John.'

'Go and ask them.'

'Are you sure? It's late.'

He could hear voices in the distance over the sound of television. She returned.

'My mother thanks you very much, but she won't come. But I will if I may. I shan't be at work tomorrow.'

'Right. I'll fetch you.'

John stepped inside Samantha's house, solemnly shook hands with the mother and sister. He did not see the brother. When he spoke his sympathy, he saw how easy Mrs Oldham made it for him. She talked quietly, but with sense, never deviating into overt grief, and yet not frozen. She explained what had happened, what they needed to do, mustered a smile on her white face. Neither she nor the sister resembled Samantha.

'Come round for an hour,' he asked.

'No, thank you. I shall be going to bed soon. Take Sam for a bit. She needs new places. She's young.'

When Samantha stepped into his car, she sat calmly, but by the time they reached his home she wept. They had exchanged very few words. She told him the probable place and time of the funeral, how they had woken her on Saturday morning, how she had seen her father slumped on the bed.

He led her indoors where she stood at the entrance to his drawingroom. He put his arms about her, and she responded hugging him. As he held her close, his sex stirred, and he drew back ashamed. Samantha did not seem to have noticed and clung to him the harder. Her eye make-up was comically spoilt. He kissed her, and she lifted her mouth, like a child, for more.

'Sit down,' he ordered. 'It's quite warm in here. What would you like to drink? Tea? Coffee? Something stronger?' She chose coffee tremblingly.'

When he came back he found her in front of a mirror repairing her face.

68

'I look a mess,' she said.

'No, you don't.'

He took her again into his arms, kissed her cheek, lowered her back down into her chair, dragged up a stool on which he laid her feet as if she was an invalid. She enquired about his weekend in London. It seemed long enough ago.

'I rang you on Saturday morning. Twice. And then after lunch. It wasn't until then I remembered where you were. It must have been shock.'

John described his visit. She, listening, sipped her coffee, ate two chocolate biscuits, asked questions, talked and sat normally. While he had chatted at Sebastian's breakfast table, the Oldham family had groped madly to handle this unexpected devastation. He ventured a query or two, hesitantly, but now she sat eager to talk.

Mother and elder daughter followed the ambulance; Sam had crept back to bed, had dropped off. Two or three hours later they had returned. She had woken and run downstairs. Both were like statues, she said. She had cried so that they had to comfort her. Her sister knew what to do. They put their mother to bed in the place where her father had died, and Samantha had crept in with her. They had hugged and she had fallen asleep again. Her sister had roused her with a cup of tea. Now her mother cried, and her hands shook so violently she could not hold her cup; it bounced in the saucer. They all got up, had a breakfast which was awful. Then they'd started on the phone calls, to Peter, to the grandparents, to uncles and aunts. Samantha had been sent by her sister in to tell the neighbours.

'I didn't know what to say. The Wylies hadn't heard anything, but then they're old. The Todds had seen the ambulance, but didn't know what it was for. They thought my dad had had a fall or something. They were very good. Came in, took my mother back for a bit in the morning. She made no fuss. She looked dignified, not like herself. And she wouldn't let us draw the front curtains. "Not these days," she said. "People don't go in for show these days. Anyway, Arthur wouldn't have wanted it." My sister went out to do the official things. And they asked me to go up to tell some old friends of my father's. The Rileys. They weren't on the phone. They'd hardly got started, though they'd finished their breakfast. The house was upside-down. Reg Riley was making the fire, things topsy-turvy all over the place. And I had to tell them. I didn't know how to do it. I said I had bad news and then came straight out with it. They both cried, and I did. And Edna kept saying, "I only seen him on Thursday, and he looked well. I only seen him on Thursday." I felt awful having to tell them. But when I got out of the house, everything was just, well, normal. People doing their Saturday shopping, and shouting and all the rest.'

'And back at home?'

'Terrible. Except Hilary's so good. She knows what's to be done. And she gave us all little jobs. My mother cooked the dinner. I had to do more ringing-round. I tried twice for you. Then I left a message when I remembered.'

Samantha sat more freely now.

'It seems so peaceful here,' she said. 'I mean, we're not making a great hoo-ha at home. If we want a quiet sniffle, we get off out of the way. But all the time it's as if there's some bogey, black and horrible, waiting to jump out on you. I know it isn't so. My mother says, "Your dad would want more salt on this," while we're eating, and suddenly we're all crying.'

At eleven, Samantha said she must go, before the rest of the family locked up. John took her in his arms, let her lean heavily on him, as he kissed her face, stroked her hair. He felt no sexual desire for her; little, in fact. He could not set her right and she therefore seemed not to make demands on him. A strong young woman she occupied space rather than lived. Her face lacked intelligence.

He drove her home, steadily, talking; the car was warm, the streets free from traffic.

'Oh, they're still up,' she said. True, the downstairs lights burned.

'Good. Now let me know if . . .'

'Yes.'

She leaned across, kissed him clumsily on the mouth,

70

made her way to the front door. He leapt out, it seemed appropriate, and stood by the car door until she let herself in. He heard nothing, no voices. Merely the closing of wood on wood. He wondered if the Wylies were watching him. From some way up the street the bass of a music centre greyly thumped. He scuttled in, drove off, saddened.

Four days later, he attended the funeral service, a lugubrious affair at the crematorium. The parson, not Catholic, who clearly did not know Oldham, read and spoke without attempt at drama or involvement; the mother and Samantha wept. Hilary and Peter sat silently. A fair sprinkling of neighbours or colleagues occupied the chairs but made no attempt to sing 'Crimond'. The man next to John Taylor wriggled, thrusting his hands in and out of anorak pockets as if frustration or embarrassment did not allow immobility. The mourners assembled outside in the cold, stood in mist round the wreaths, talking awkwardly. John shook hands with Mrs Oldham, exchanged banalities with Samantha and Hilary. The brother, Peter, looked as if he was wearing a suit, someone else's, for the first time in his life. John knew no one, wondered who were Wylies or Rileys or Todds amongst the sober suits. He noticed few black ties and one or two cloth caps. The tower of the crematorium chapel on its hill loomed dimly, cut off by fog from the rest of the world. John walked sedately back to his car, glad to be away from it.

Two days later he asked Samantha out to a meal. Oddly, she refused.

'I'll come round to your house,' she said. 'But I don't think my mother would like it if I went out gaddervantering, not this week.' He looked the word up at home but could not find it. A mixture of 'gad' and 'gallivanter', he concluded, a local, even a family, variant.

Samantha made her own way to his house.

'How are things?' he asked.

'My mother's very upset. She seems to be getting worse. Hilary told me I had to go out and enjoy myself. "She'll spoil your life," she said, "given half a chance. I know it's hard for her, but she's got to fight her own way out of it.

She'll try to cling to you if you'll let her, but don't you allow it." '

'This sister of yours seems sensible.'

'She is.'

'How old is she?'

'Twenty-eight now.'

'Has she ever married?'

'She married as soon as she qualified, but it didn't last. He was a self-employed builder, very hard-working, but all he wanted was to make a slave of her, she said, and she wasn't having that. It lasted less than a year. He was free with his fists when he'd had one or two.'

'She came back home?'

'No. She had a flat in the nurses' home. She only came back a month or two ago, after Peter had gone to the university. I don't know why.'

'She hasn't married again?'

'No. More sense, she says. She fancied the look of you.'

'How do you know that?'

'She said so.'

'I'm flattered.'

Samantha kissed him, enthusiastically. She sipped gin and tonic, bloomed.

'I was glad to get back to work. You don't know what to do at home. It was like being at church or somewhere. And my mother complains. "Oh, our Samantha, you might have *thought*." I could have hit her. It's not as if she thought so highly of my dad when she'd got him.'

Talk came easily to her; she laughed, lay on him, began on blatant advances. He wondered if she had been drinking before she came. They made love, she squealing with pleasure.

'That was it,' she said when they had finished. 'I needed that.'

She lay naked on the floor, arms outstretched in Rubensesque beauty, palely wholesome, the summer's tan almost unnoticeable. He knelt, kissed her lips and she pulled his head down roughly.

'Oh, you man,' she said, nuzzling. 'You big man.

72

He dragged his clothes on, marched up to the bathroom delighted with himself, pleased at her pleasure. When he returned she had just begun to dress. They embraced again, rolled on each other.

'Do you know what?' she asked him in the end. 'I'm hungry.'

John laughed. Samantha seemed natural, unaffected, free.

'I'm peckish myself. Get yourself dressed and I'll make a Taylor special.'

'What's that?'

'A sandwich too big to get your mouth round.'

She picked up her clothes and flounced upstairs near-naked. Whistling, he made coffee, cut and shaped cold gammon and salad sandwiches. Samantha took to an armchair, lifted her plate with delight.

'You certainly know what a girl needs,' she said. She spoke unlike her humdrum, polite self, mistress of the scene, ready to issue orders. She bit into her sandwich, chewed.

'What's it like? Suitable?'

'I can taste apple in it,' she answered. 'If I told my mother that she wouldn't believe it. Her idea's a scrape of margarine and marmite, or cottage cheese.'

'She's thinking of your figure.'

'Aren't you?'

She poked a finger of derision at him, danced shapely legs on the carpet before her, waving oriental hands by her head as she sat. This girl had lost her father a week ago. She had barely mentioned him, even when he was alive. Her mother ruled the roost. He had no idea whether Samantha approved of this state of affairs or not, nor what she thought of her father. Her present enjoyment was almost palpable.

'Would you like another?' he asked, as she picked up her last crumb.

She frowned, comically, fondled her belly. 'Oh, my sylph-like shape. Yes, please. But only half-size, please.'

'Same ingredients?'

73

'Oh, yes. You're a genius at fillings.'

Samantha had not taken her first bite when the front doorbell rang.

'Who's that, I wonder?' John, surprised.

'You're not expecting anyone?'

'No.'

'It's a good job it wasn't an hour ago.' Samantha laughed, but immediately appeared uncertain, a shadow of apprehension on her face. Straightening his face, he went out from the room.

His wife, Stella, stood at the front door.

'Is this inconvenient?' she said. 'I saw your car outside so I knew you'd be at home.'

'I have a visitor.'

'I won't come in, then. It isn't important. I was just passing. I wondered if you'd had any second thoughts about . . . about our . . .'

'Come in,' he said. He had to challenge himself, though he could not understand why. 'Please come in.'

When he showed Stella into the drawingroom, Samantha seemed much at ease, mouth full, eyes beaming.

'This is Samantha.' He made the introduction carefully. 'My secretary. And,' he waved a hand, 'Stella, my wife.'

The women nodded but did not shake hands. Samantha now seemed embarrassed to be caught eating.

'Sit down. I'll get you coffee. And would you like a sandwich?'

'I recommend them,' Samantha said, mouth now clear. 'They really are something. But you'll know.'

'No.' Stella shook her head, bemused.

'What does that mean?' John asked.

'No, thank you. Eating's over for the day.'

He sauntered out to the kitchen, dawdled over the making of coffee, wondering what the women were talking about. He could hear no sounds. He tiptoed in with Stella's coffee.

'Is it Instant?' Samantha asked.

'It is not.'

He settled himself again. Stella had opened her coat, had removed a small turquoise silk scarf.

74

'Samantha's been telling me about her father,' she said to her husband. 'You've been very kind to her.'

'Wasn't he always?' Samantha's question and the tense of the verb seemed mischievously conceived.

'I hope so.' Stella answered with tact.

John looked at the two women. The fair and the dark. Stella was smaller-boned, would keep her figure beyond middle age. Samantha would spread. He recalled the ample, pale beauty of her buttocks as she'd flounced upstairs earlier in the evening. Her skirt was six inches shorter than Stella's, but she sat chastely enough, a plate with its half-eaten sandwich held steadily on her lap. The women showed no animosity towards each other. Stella would guess that he had just had sex with Samantha, who knew, because he had told her, that his wife wanted to come back here. But both sat politely, waiting for him.

He remembered his recent meetings with Stella.

They had been courteous enough, but lacking tenderness. That he judged was his fault. He had set the tone at the beginning by rejecting her advances, refusing to yield.

Stella, glad she could play with her coffee cup and thus hide her face, could not decide why her husband had brought her indoors. To allow him to parade Samantha in front of her, to demonstrate that he did not need her, that his life was fulfilled without her? That seemed unlikely. John, to her mind, was not malicious. Perhaps it was to show, without putting the message in blunt words, that he had no intention of having her back.

Samantha, the half-eaten sandwich still on the plate, looked with some admiration at her rival. Stella was dark, neat, pretty, well dressed, well spoken, with nothing of the slattern about her. The voice sounded quiet, but made every word clear. The hands were slim, beautiful, cared for. She had poise, made an impression without trying so that Samantha felt abashed, vulgarly comforting herself with the thought that she and this proud woman's husband had been rolling in ecstatic sex in the very place which Stella occupied. Yet there was no pride about the wife. She sat

75

quietly, deftly raising and lowering her cup, never setting it down.

Stella asked a few, sympathetic questions about the Oldham family. These Samantha answered without constraint. John, slightly out of character, began to describe the Delkar Quartet's performance. Stella kept him talking with strategically apt questions. Samantha, more at ease, finished her sandwich. This was friendly: a stranger would have been in difficulty deciding which woman was the wife. John Taylor seemed determined to impress Stella, but did not exclude Samantha.

After half an hour Stella said she must go, and immediately stood up, resumed her scarf, buttoned her coat. She held out a hand in friendly formality to Samantha, and made for the door. John followed obediently. She said she would call again if he had no objection. He had none. The night outside struck bitterly cold so that he shivered as he returned.

'I liked your wife,' Samantha confessed.

'What's good about her?' He asked only half in earnest.

'She's clever. And ladylike.' The word was unusual enough to ring true.

After Stella's departure, the other two sat less comfortably, talked more hesitantly. Samantha perched herself on his knee, but she was too heavy and soon heaved herself off. At the tail of several questions about Stella's age, occupation and temperament, Samantha asked, 'Do you never want her back?'

'Not really. I never think about it.'

'But didn't she ask you?'

'Yes. I don't think about it.' He repeated the sentence more angrily than he meant.

'Are you serious?' she asked.

'Don't I sound it?'

They hung about, touching, kissing, but enthusiasm had waned. Samantha demanded, almost childishly, to be taken home, a quite different being from the sexually electric body of two hours earlier. Now she was lumpish, not quite sullen, but tired, or with mind elsewhere. He blamed the

76

change of atmosphere on himself rather than on the woman, but was surprised, disappointed.

He drove her dully back.

On the last day of November Michael Alexander rang, quoting Housman inaptly as the weather outside was mild and wet. John Taylor, relieved to be interrupted in some work he had brought home, asked after Sebastian and Lise.

'Haven't heard anything. Have you?' Michael answered.

'No. I dropped them a note of thanks.'

'I ought to have, but didn't.' Michael coughed. 'Are you busy tonight? Can you give me an hour? I'm depressed.'

'What about?'

'Never mind what about. The world. Is there a good pub near you?'

'I rarely use 'em. The Lord Nelson's all right.'

'Quiet enough to talk in.'

'If it's quiet you want, why not come round here?'

'I'd like to talk, but to see a few faces at the same time. No canned music. No telly.'

'Anything else?' John enquired.

They met at the Lord Nelson an hour later, and sat in the lounge-bar drinking half-pints of a much-advertised lager. The large room had few clients. Both men had walked the hill to the place, Michael from a bus-stop, John from his home.

'Are you busy?' John asked.

'Just beginning on the Christmas stuff. Nothing complicated this year.'

'A carol concert?'

'Yes. I don't know why I bother.'

Michael took a sour mouthful from his glass, then yawned.

'I'm getting old, John. Over sixty. Time I retired. Sebastian now, he's playing the Dvořák concerto four times this week in different cities, and has a great bag of recitals in the weeks before Christmas, and here am I, you can't ask me to transpose a hymn-tune without my feeling exhausted. I wrote a new carol for my church choir, and damned if they can learn it, or I can teach it to them.'

'Is it difficult?'

'Not really. Rhythm odd once or twice. And the occasional out of the way note-cluster. But if they put their minds to it, they could do it. But they can't be bothered. "Away in a manger" and all go home.'

John watched the other man, whose eyes sparked malice from a face which was still, thinly, sarcastically handsome. His body moved, lively, as if to sit quietly would betray him.

'It's no joke getting old.'

'Sixty's nothing these days.'

'It's not twenty nor thirty. Not forty.' Michael frowned lofty disdain. 'You – I, rather – feel the weakness. The onset. The beginning of the end.'

'Like Shostakovich.'

'He was older. And much more of an invalid. But, yes, there's a parallel. And yet he continued to work on. He was highly regarded you know. Worshipped in some quarters. It makes a difference. Though I'm not sure in his case. He'd been terrified too often. I guess he was always on the look-out for the next blow. When Stalin had finished with him, God or his body took over. But that's the beauty. There must be some composers who write when they are physically humiliated, not themselves, whereas others need to be strong, optimistic.'

'What sort are you?'

'A nobody. A performer not a writer. A teacher. An expounder. What I say disappears.'

'As is the case with most music.'

'I grant you, I grant you. My trouble is that I'm on my own too much. The people I see, my pupils, choir-members I'm no longer interested in. I've no intimate life with another. My wife, Seb's mother,' he rarely used the diminutive, 'left me fifteen years ago.'

'Had you been married long?'

'Twenty-two years.' He rattled a left-hand scale across

79

the table. 'Sebastian was still at the Academy. The girls were at or about to go to university. They all upped sticks and went. I wasn't displeased.'

'You still see them?'

'Yes. From time to time. Sebastian least. Until our last little trip. And I'm expecting a large hiatus now. He's off on tour.'

'Will you go and see Lise's opera?'

'Yes. I hope to. And in fact she suggested that she came up here to spend a day or two practising with me.'

'That's flattering,' John said.

'Is it? I never thought about it. She knows I can tell her whether she's singing the right notes, and we can discuss what she's making of the part, and all a long way from the rehearsal rooms. Sebastian'll be in Oz or Japan or wherever, so he can't do it for her.'

'Would he?'

'Yes. She says he's a first-rate coach.'

'Then why, may I ask, are you so down?'

'It's the end of the year. The nights are darker and colder. The end of the term. And I'm doing a job I've lost interest in. And when you get to my time of life, people you know keep dropping off, many of them no older than I am. And I'm making nothing of it.'

'Making nothing of? "Understanding", do you mean?'

'Could do, be. But not creating anything as well. I've been thinking about that Shostakovich quartet. At first I admired him, and that was about the length and breadth of it. Weak and ill and frightened and old as he was, he still sat down and wrote music. That's admirable. I approve of courage of that sort. But that was about as far as it went.'

Michael dipped into his glass and failed to continue.

'Go on, man,' John encouraged. 'It's just becoming interesting.'

Michael sipped again, looked quizzically at the contents of his glass.

'I thought,' Michael spoke solemnly, pausing often, 'that his incapacities, his feebleness made, in spite of his heroic efforts, his production worthless. It seemed like', he waved

80

the left hand, 'putting a footballer who had lost a leg back on the field. His efforts might be superhuman, but he's deprived of the means which made him outstanding. He'd show a touch, here and there, heading the ball, for instance, if he happened to be in the right place.'

Again the lacuna.

'But,' John said, laughing. 'But, but, but?'

'Now I'm not so sure. Ours is an ageing society. More and more old people about. And this sort of music from the dying soul, is perhaps what we need to hear. What do you think of that as a theory?'

'Not much,' John, bluntly.

Michael grinned, exhibiting large teeth.

'Why not? A receptive audience is necessary.'

'I'd have thought that music was like football in so far that it was best when the practitioners, the creators and performers, were at the height of their powers.'

'I'm talking about the listeners.'

'Shouldn't they be powerfully strong and receptive?'

'Probably. Music had a frightening and yet uplifting effect on me during my late teens. But what I'm saying is that the audience of elderly, enfeebled, crippled listeners is, on account of modern medicine, very much larger.'

'Not altogether convincing.'

'What isn't?' Michael snapped.

'Your argument. If the number of blind people became larger, then football matches, to use your example, or paintings or telly wouldn't be much use, as entertainments or means of instruction or consolation. They'd have to seek another form. To do with hearing or touch or smell or taste.'

'Except . . .' Michael, grinning again.

'Except what?'

'They have not always been blind. They can remember matches from the days when they could see.'

This seemed an interesting conceit to John, but just as his companion changed direction and was five minutes into a winding critique of a book on Cambridge, a university about which Michael confessed to knowing nothing, they were interrupted by a large man who sat at the next table not a yard from Michael. He had deliberately chosen his position since the rest of the room stretched empty. He opened with the weather, warning them not to grumble.

The two replied without enthusiasm, though Michael made no further attempt to resume his topic. The big man folded his hands across his paunch and politely waited for them to continue conversation. Michael obliged.

'There aren't many people in tonight.'

That proved sufficient. The man lectured them on shortage of money, the recession, the stupidity of the banks. They learnt little they did not know. Then the man leaned towards them, a pudgy index finger straightened in their direction.

'But do you know what strikes me as most remarkable?'

'No.' Michael's air of innocence seemed satirical.

'The disappearance of cherished beliefs.' They raised eyebrows compliantly. 'No, I'm not talking about God or religion. Something nearer home. Owning your own house.' He outlined his case: high interest rates, sudden redundancies, paying mortgages in the end for something not worth the price, negative equity. 'I would have said that it was the most popular belief amongst people with a respectable wage. You could buy the place where you lived, and when you died, leave your children a nice little nest-egg in bricks and mortar. And it's gone. Within a year. Disappeared like morning dew.'

'Are you one of the property-owning democracy?' Michael asked.

'Yes. And mortgage pretty well paid off.' The man laid his hands on the table. Clearly he had not come here for alcohol, but company. 'And still in work. I'm lucky.'

He raised his hand suddenly in a Hitler salute, and staggered to his feet. They realised he was greeting the arrival of a woman, in a hat with a wide feather, who minced across the floor. She was much the man's age, perhaps fifty, but heavily made up, cheeks rouged, eyebrows drawn, long excellently shaped fingernails, blood-red. She had opened her coat so that her breasts swung as she waddled across the room. Approaching, she drenched them with perfume.

'Welcome, welcome,' the large man shouted, beaming, waving his arms.

'George,' she answered, in a deep voice, mannish and cultured. 'I'm nearly on time.'

'What will you drink?' George asked.

'Something innocuous.'

'Will you gentlemen join us?'

'No, thank you,' John said. 'I've barely begun.' Michael placed the hand of refusal flat over his glass. The man cheerfully started away for the bar while the woman sat at their table.

'Not busy tonight,' she told them, but did not wait for their opinion. 'The trouble with this place is that nothing happens, they say.' They waited. For nothing.

'This pub?'

'I don't know about that. This town. This city.'

'Is it true?' Michael did not keep the sarcastic edge from his voice.

The woman turned to stare straight at him, challenging him. He stared gently back.

'It is not.'

George returned. Her drink shone bright red, to match her lipstick.

'We live,' she continued once she had eyed her companion into his seat, 'in a very respectable street.'

'Though we are the least respectable of its inhabitants.'

'But,' she ignored him, 'we have our share of goings-on.' She looked up as if expecting criticism, of vocabulary or sense, put two fingers to the stem of her glass, then let it go. 'This week. The police. In full force. At the dead of night.'

'Eleven o'clock,' George amended.

'Such banging and bawling and to-ing and fro-ing.'

'And the cause?' Michael spoke coldly.

'What you could call a domestic altercation in the first place,' George said. 'Man and wife at words and blows. She rings her family and they arrive with an axe, and when the husband won't let them in, they set about the front door.'

83

'He escaped through the back,' the woman said.

'And the wife?'

'Stood screaming in her nightgown in the front garden once the door was open.' She pointed a crude finger at Michael. 'You're going to ask me why, aren't you?'

'No. Not really.'

'Some people have to perform in public. There was no need for it. And her brothers seemed in no hurry to fetch her back in. There was quite a crowd by the time the police arrived.'

'Amongst whom I was numbered,' George admitted, with a satisfactory, large mouthful of beer.

'And what was the outcome?'

'Anti-climax,' the woman said. 'All ushered indoors. The family sent on its way. And two days after, I see the man and woman arm-in-arming it down the street as if it was their wedding day.'

'I blame drink.' George held his glass up to the light. 'They have one or two, and can't control themselves.'

'What do they do for a living?' John Taylor asked.

'He's in computers, so I was told. But that means anything these days, from the expert to the man who dusts the screens.'

'How old are they?'

'Rising forty,' the woman said. 'Well dressed. Not short of money. A car each. House well looked after, at least on the outside.'

'Is the door back on?' Michael.

'Yes. Workmen round next day. Replaced. Repainted. Good as new.'

'And this sort of behaviour is frequent?' John.

'I wouldn't say that. We see the tip of the iceberg. Though only two months ago the police shot and killed a man two streets away. He'd taken part in an armed robbery.'

'Served him right,' the woman said. 'He holed up in some high-rise flats they've just built. Took a young woman hostage. And was waving a shotgun at the police. They tried to talk him out, but he wouldn't hear sense. He had a pot-shot from the window, and so the marksman killed him. He deserved what he got.'

'And the young woman? The hostage?'

'Unharmed. He'd tied her up in a chair. Had no connection with the man or the robbery or anything else. She just happened unluckily to be about and he dragged her in. She's none the worse for it.'

'As far as we know,' George amended, and began a glum disquisition on compensation for injury or misfortune of this sort. His sister standing at a bus-stop had been hit, together with the rest of the queue, by the skidding car of a joy-rider aged fourteen, already in care, already condemned for driving without a licence in a stolen vehicle. Nobody had been seriously injured, but some had lost days off from work. All had been shocked. Society, it appeared, had no way of recompensing them for their hurt. The large man outlined the story with force, but without anger. He might have been leading a seminar.

The woman, who had now announced her name as Rowena, described a stabbing outside a pub near where she had lived as a girl. She spoke with relish, piling bloody detail on detail until the strangers wondered if she had been an eyewitness. George suddenly interrupted her flow.

'May I ask what you gentlemen do for a living?'

Rowena did not appear to mind this interruption, feeling perhaps that she had contributed sufficiently to the gaiety of the evening.

'Guess,' Michael ordered.

George looked them up and down.

'A teacher,' he said in the end.

'No.' Rowena, with emphasis, startlingly.

'Yes,' Michael answered. 'And my friend?'

'The same.'

'I'm an accountant,' John said.

'Um. Do you know what I am?' George now, genially. He had barely smiled since conversation started.

'No.' Michael, firmly.

'I'm a musician. You wouldn't think that, would you?'

85

He addressed himself to John. 'Except whacking the big bass drum? Or cuddling the tuba?'

'What do you play?'

'The clarinet.'

'Full-time?'

'Not now. Started with the Liverpool, then the LPO, then the BBC. Not now, though. It's no sort of life for a man of my age.'

'What do you do, then?' Michael.

'Play for various local orchestras. Teach a bit. Peripatetic. Saxophone twice a week with a jazz band.'

'They were on telly last week,' Rowena said. 'Pebble Mill.' John noticed that she barely touched her drink. The mention of television animated her. John imagined she might stand to dance some exotic tango.

'But mainly,' George drew in a breath to spread his wide lungs, 'we keep a boarding house.'

'A select clientele,' Rowena elucidated.

'Single men. Banks and libraries and the law. Dull and interesting.' George lifted his glass. 'You may wonder I say that. What I mean by "dull" is "respectable". They have professional jobs with regular hours done in suits with collars and ties. Yet once you get to know them they all have something tucked away behind the façade.'

'Such as what?' Michael.

'Broken marriages, romances, affairs. Odd hobbies. Out-of-the-way ambitions. One of them wants to live in Egypt. He's a solicitor, an Oxford graduate, but he wants to live in Cairo.'

'Has he been there?' Michael, again.

'Several times. And he reads about it. He's a homosexual.'

'Has that anything to do with it?'

'Not past belief, no,' George answered. 'Shouldn't be surprised. I might learn in time. He's only been with us two years. And I tend to meet him casually on the stairs, or pick up snippets as I serve the evening meal. We have dinner, soup, main course, pudding, cheese, Monday to Friday, at six. I can help Rowena to get it ready before evening

86

if I'm due out, and it gives them plenty of leisure time if they want it.'

'We were lucky,' Rowena said. She spoke always as if surprised at her conversational intrepidity. 'An aunt died, left me this big house in Mapperley. George said it was a millstone round my neck. I thought differently.'

'Sometimes,' he said gloomily.

'We had to make alterations. Fire-doors and God knows what. And it was hard work. Compared with my work as a PA. Have to be up early. Though they are all crying off big English breakfasts these days. But I don't have to go out. And I've a settled population now. And I can get help about the place easily enough.' She straightened. 'Mount Vernon. That's the house. Princess Drive. And George joined me as a partner.'

'Sleeping,' he sneered.

'Sometimes,' Rowena said stonily, 'he lets his tongue run away with him.'

George visibly expanded at the rebuke. Michael rose to replenish glasses. The woman refused, looking at her drink as if trying to fathom its provenance. Michael returned with the three jars on a round tray, which he cleared, then tramped fifteen yards of carpet to return.

'Your friend tells me you're a musician,' George said when all had settled again.

'That's so.'

'And would you tell me your name?'

'Alexander. Michael Alexander.'

'You're the organist at St Paul's, aren't you? And the father of the cellist, Sebastian Alexander.' George looked the other up and down as if deciding how to continue. 'You're a bit of a bastard, aren't you?'

'George,' Rowena gasped, ladylike.

'Well, he knows what I mean. He chases his choir. Doesn't let them idle about. You took the Bach Society's orchestra for rehearsal when Anthony Saltburn was ill, and you didn't half shake them up. It's a wonder we've never met.'

'Oh.' Michael, apparently displeased.

'I did nearly play for you once. At your school. But there was some snag. And your friend? Are you musical?'

'I play the piano,' John said, 'a bit.'

'We all do that.'

From that time on George Paxton plied them with incidents from his life, with anecdotes about conductors and soloists. Rowena encouraged him. John enjoyed himself, but Michael sat tight-lipped, and finally said he must go. Paxton's offer of further drinks was refused. Rowena presented Michael with the Mount Vernon card. Hands were shaken.

'I heard your son play the Elgar here just recently,' George Paxton told Michael as he walked away. 'Gorgeous tone, gorgeous. And enormous. Quite unique. Elgar, now.'

But the two had marched beyond earshot.

9

Michael Alexander in his Christmas card to John, posted early, wrote that he'd met 'that big man', Paxton, again by chance. 'He's a bit of a rogue, I'd guess.' The two had run through a Brahms sonata at Mount Vernon, and Paxton had then invited Alexander to play with him in three evening recitals in the spring. 'I agreed. I don't know why. Perhaps because Mount Vernon was so interesting.'

Christmas passed quietly for John.

He'd seen less of Samantha away from the office. She had refused his invitations out, politely and with adequate reasons, but she seemed changed, as if her father's death had made a different woman of her. He did not quite understand this because she worked cheerfully with him, was infinitely friendly, sometimes laying a hand on his sleeve or shoulder, but seemed not to want more intimate contact outside. Whether this was the result of bereavement or her meeting with his wife, John could not guess. He, by chance, found himself extremely busy up to the New Year, and the girl had spent the whole Christmas break with her mother and sister at a relative's house in the Lake District. John had been uncertain whether he felt disappointed.

Stella, his wife, had sent a present, an excellent silk scarf and tie, by post with a non-committal message. This meant he had to rush to the shops, where he failed to make his mind up and decided on book-tokens. His gift to Samantha, a huge box of continental chocolates, he presented on Christmas Eve, marvellously wrapped. It was such an armful, he had to drive her home with it.

'This'll ruin my weight-watching,' she said.

'Can't have too much of a good thing.'

She kissed him, but without fervour. Her mind seemed concentrated on the journey that night up to Penrith. Her sister would drive them immediately they'd eaten the evening meal. Samantha seemed to live in a clearer, more exciting world, like that of a child. Christmas, especially Christmas amongst trees and rocks and mountains, dismissed housework and humdrum wage-earning, even death.

'We shall sit in front of a log fire and gorge ourselves on your chocolates.'

John spent Christmas on his own. He cooked a chicken, had a shot at the trimmings, felt pleased with himself, walked out in the woods at Bestwood Lodge for an hour in the brief afternoon, and returning, rang Stella on impulse to wish her the compliments. She cheerfully said she would be off to a party shortly; but they talked quietly and companionably enough for a quarter of an hour. He turned away from the phone disappointed in himself, believing that had he pressed her she would have come round.

Next he rang Michael Alexander and found nobody at home. Desultorily he looked at television programmes, went to bed sober at ten and slept soundly.

When the postal service reopened he received a card from Michael saying that they had been invited to Mount Vernon to see the New Year in. Half-seven for dinner at eight. Dress informal. Bring a female partner, if he thought fit.

He rang Stella, explained about Alexander and Paxton, extended, he liked the word, the invitation, which she accepted without hesitation. She would drive round to his house or, better, take a taxi.

At seven-forty-five Stella and John Taylor rang the bell of Mount Vernon. Clouds raced across the moon; wind whipped black branches of the shrubs crowding the front garden, rattled them furiously across the wrought-iron railings.

'An imposing pile,' Stella said. She seemed pleased with herself, having driven him up in her car, arguing that she saw no sense in using his, and that it would protect her from temptation to overdo, her words, 'the demon drink'.

'The last thing you'd be prone to.'

'You don't know me now.'

She had giggled; they stood in the porch in front of the stained-glass five-panel front door of Mount Vernon. Stella looked small, infinitely neat and composed, in a dark coat. They could make out the lights of a Christmas tree inside.

Rowena opened the door, peered.

'John Taylor,' he said. He introduced his wife.

'And I thought you were an eligible bachelor,' the woman said.

She took their coats. The wide hall was hung with paper-chains and bells and every picture had its sprig of berried holly. The tall tree at the far end had been lavishly hung with silver baubles, angels of raffia, tinsel loops, assorted garish wooden fruits, coloured globes and reddish smooth distortions of thin metal, hopping birds, and at the top, teetering slightly, a naked female doll, wearing a minuscule, home-cut crown.

'They're upstairs,' Rowena said, having disposed of their coats and bottles. 'In the study.'

'Doing what?'

'Arranging concert programmes, so they say. In reality, drinking themselves silly.'

Rowena's words lacked charity; she frowned, darkly dis-pleased. She breathed in, puffed air loudly from her mouth and said, 'We'll go up and surprise them.'

She led the way, hauling herself up by the substantial balustrade, to the top of the house, the fourth floor. She hammered at the door, flung it open with such violence it banged on the shuddering wall.

The untidiness of the room smacked the visitors in the face; no sense of order existed at all. Even the books which had reached the shelves straggled, while on the floor lay untidy heaps, mainly of music, tattered sheets, ash-trays, cigarette-packets, cups and saucers, a shambles. Muddle and heat.

Paxton and Alexander sat on pine-wood chairs, well apart, without alcohol, both surprised at the violence of the entry.

'Giving us a heart attack, then?' George Paxton asked ungraciously.

'No. Showing your guests in.'

'A shout would have fetched me down.'

George now stood, shook hands with Stella and John, wishing them the compliments of the season pleasantly. Michael, also standing, greeted them.

'That's it, then,' George said to Michael.

'We'll start Friday.' He smiled at the Taylors. 'First recital in a fortnight.'

'Are you going to play for us tonight?' Stella asked.

'I wouldn't dare. I need a day or two of practice.'

'Below,' George ordered. He stepped neatly between the piles in spite of his size. Rowena led the way. They trooped down to the comparative brilliance of the drawing room with its wall- and standard lamps, its patterned carpet, its watercolours. When the host had provided drinks, the choice wide, he said that they had invited their neighbour in for dinner but it was uncertain whether he'd come.

'He's eccentric,' George pronounced.

'He's a musician,' Rowena amended, and scuttled for the kitchen.

'Poor old Row. She hates entertaining. It's no trouble. She cooks for nine every day of the week, but you need talking to, amusing. *I* know you don't, but she doesn't. So she rushes about all day. Now she's gone to have her last look, and then she'll dress up in her Sunday best, and cover the whole shebang with aprons and pinafores so she won't splash herself with gravy. Funny woman.'

The meal, soup, gammon and finally mince-tart proved excellent. The three men drank deeply, and roared with laughter. Paxton helped clear the table, and serve.

'I've not eaten so well for a year,' John said.

'You poor lamb.' They could not decide if Rowena spoke sarcastically.

They all helped carry dishes out to the washing-up machine. Stella was surprised at the size and modernity of Rowena's kitchen.

In the drawing room talk flew. Politics and the arts; the lodgers and their idiosyncrasies; Rowena's first husband who could not bear the change of the old year to the new;

Paxton and the man outside the sex-shop; Stella's views of education, the television and books, Alexander on his army service, his brushes with lawyers, his present headmaster, his son, Lise's new opera, and lengthiest of all, late Shostakovich. He spoke with an ease and mastery, knowing he could hold their interest. At one stage – he had now made some point about Bach – he asked permission to play the piano, and gave them the B flat minor Prelude from Book I of the '48'. This moved him, he said. Soul spoke to soul. He looked straight at Stella and she was amazed at his words.

'Give us the fugue,' Paxton demanded.

'You've had enough of me, haven't you?' Alexander asked Stella.

'Oh, no.'

'Give us the bloody fugue,' George roared jovially, thumping the table.

'Do you want to know what he says?' Rowena asked them. ' "A fugue a day keeps the doctor away." '

'On your heads be it.'

Michael Alexander completed the fugue without slip. They raised their glasses to him so that he seemed bemused and moved his seat, settling himself at the side of Stella. She congratulated and thanked him, and he heard her but seemed caught up still with the music, retrying approvingly Bach's plangent harmonies in his head.

On the other side of the room George Paxton laid down the law. This city, this county, this police authority had the highest incidence of murder per head of population in the country. He had these figures from one of their lawyers.

'What sort of percentage is it?' John asked.

'He did say. I've forgotten. About one in forty thousand. Does that sound right?'

'And why is it so high?' John again.

'It's not by much, he says. The actual first position will change from year to year, but it's the type of district. Most murders are the result of domestic trouble: rows, unfaithfulness. And unemployment can raise the profile of quarrelsomeness. God. I nearly couldn't say that. While on the

93

other hand if you're employed you drink too much, and so you go on.'

'Like us,' Rowena said.

'Bollocks. We're as sober as crows.' Paxton now looked as serious as the judges he'd dismissed from his simile. 'Most murders don't need your Sherlock Holmeses, you know.'

'Nor your Morse nor Wexford,' Rowena added.

'What do you know about it? It's some sort of local dust-up in the home or the pub that gets out of hand, and somebody goes too far. Everybody knows who's done it. It's more a business of deciding if it was intentional, so they can frame the charge.'

George and Rowena now argued about a man they knew who had knifed his mistress to death. They disagreed about time, and names, even motive.

'The cow deserved it,' George said.

'He was no angel,' she answered. 'A womaniser. He made passes at me.'

'A man of taste,' said John.

Later, Rowena lifted the edge of the curtain to report on the street.

'Who's there?' George.

'Nobody.' She sighed. 'But lights in windows all over the place. And,' she rolled her shoulders under the curtain, 'I can see the moon.'

This roused Michael from his rumination.

'It amazes me,' his voice was slurred, 'that we can see the same moon as Aristotle, or Jesus, or Mozart, or even Stone Age men.'

'What's so wonderful about that?' Rowena, laughing.

'It seems to shorten the course of human history, and its importance. These great geniuses, and unknown brutish creatures about whom we know little, must have looked up and seen the same moon as we do.'

'And named it.' Paxton.

'And wondered about it.'

'It drove people mad,' Rowena said, 'when it was full.'

'What's Greek for "moon"?' Paxton asked.

94

'*Selēnē*, I think,' Michael answered.

'Is that a feminine word?' John asked. 'It's masculine in German.'

'And *chand* in Hindustani,' Paxton informed them. 'How about that?'

'Thank you, professors,' Rowena.

Conversation staggered on. Stella again asked Michael and George to play, and this time they agreed. She was strictly sober. Paxton chose the music upstairs, saying they could never perform this in a recital. He did not announce the title, but Stella recognised it at once as the slow movement of Mozart's Clarinet Concerto.

The performance was not immaculate, but all could understand that they were in the presence of good instrumentalists. George Paxton's smooth tone flowed with such strength as to be almost physically unbearable even in this large room. He swayed, directing Mozart's sadness deep into their heads, conjuring it, savouring it. Stella could see Michael's hunched back at the piano, shaping, supporting Mozart's eloquent grief, the dips and swoops, the elegance that still tore heart-strings. Tears stood in John Taylor's eyes; his mouth was open. The world's sorrows and his own met in the music and moved him.

'Play it again,' Rowena asked.

'Eh?'

'Please.'

George looked at Stella, who nodded her confirmation. His face showed surprise at Rowena's request. This time they followed the slow movement with the bounce of the finale, but that took a painful tinge from what had gone before.

At midnight George opened a bottle of champagne, and they drank noisily to their health and prosperity. The front doorbell pealed and a heavy-fisted knocking followed.

'The police,' George said.

'The Gestapo.' Michael.

'Somebody's first-footing it for you,' Stella suggested.

'Are they, by God?'

'Who?' asked Rowena.

95

'Find out, woman. Open up.'

A small, dark neat young man stood framed in the door-way. He held out a piece of coal.

'Mr Temple,' Rowena said. 'I didn't think you were back.'

'I rode over specially to provide you with a dark stranger.'

'From where?'

'The next street.'

That seemed typical. The young man, a lodger, was at a party in the area, and had decided to visit his landlord. He had done the journey on a borrowed bicycle. He presented a piece of coal before he drank a small glass of wine with them, and they trooped out into the front garden to see him off. He made a performance of putting on his clips. The bicycle was an old-fashioned affair, with downturned ram's-horn handlebars.

'Must be ten years,' Temple said, ruefully. He set off with a wide swerve, but thereafter rode straight. Out in the garden, Stella found that Michael Alexander was holding her hand. It seemed simple and innocent, and she wondered if John noticed. Or George. Or Rowena.

The party broke up almost immediately, abruptly. One minute they were in full conversational spate, the next they grouped on the pavement as Stella opened her car. Hand-shakes and kisses were exchanged. Lights shone in many windows. Michael sat at the front with Stella. John in the back seat hummed Mozart's elegant grief clumsily. George now had an arm round Rowena's shoulder.

'They're not married, I take it?' John asked before they had reached the end of the short street.

'You take it wrong.' Michael sounded dismissive, and gloomy with it.

10

Stella delivered Michael home first, then her husband. Both staggered so that she waited until they had opened their front doors.

John invited her in for coffee or another drink.

'No thanks. It will be one o'clock now before I'm home.'

'Are you at work tomorrow?'

'No. Are you?'

'Yes. I shall go in. I can get on when there are no secretaries or phone calls.' He spoke with an appearance of sobriety. 'Come round tomorrow evening. Are you doing anything? Have you arranged anything?'

'No. Tell you what. When will you come back from the office?'

'Five. Perhaps before.'

'Give me a ring at five,' Stella said. 'I shall be in then. And issue the invitation again if you're still of the same mind.'

'Why shouldn't I be?'

'The festive spirit may have drained away.'

'You're a hard woman, Stella.'

'Five. Telephone at five.'

John saluted comically and almost fell over. Alcohol affected his legs rather than his speech, she decided. She made for her car without looking back.

Next day the sun shone as in spring; the sky showed no wisp of cloud and the television forecasters, predicting fog and frost, delivered neat two-sentence, smiling lectures on the effects of high pressure in January. Stella walked after an early lunch for an hour and a half in Papplewick woods, a remnant of Sherwood Forest, with its roads and paths cleared recently and signposted for pedestrians and riders. She followed her colours at great speed, finished the ninety-minute walk in fifty, and immediately repeated it. Smartly dressed couples with dogs passed in their dozens. Few children or people under thirty made any appearance. The sun struck white beauty from silver birches, so that she thought of Russia, Tolstoy, Turgenev. Exhilarated, she drove home to enjoy from the top of the garden of her flat the wide, bright silver-gold of sunset. The air nipped already. As yet, though, no fog.

At five her phone rang, Her husband, on the dot.

She did not pick the instrument up straight away. She had not exactly expected the call, certain he'd forget. Nor was she convinced she wanted it.

'John Taylor,' he said. 'Invitation repeated as per order.' Assumed brusqueness.

'Time, please?' Sweetly.

'I'm still at the office. Give me an hour or so to clear up. Shall we say seven. Would you like to go out?'

'They say it'll be foggy.'

'Bit after seven, then. We'll eat at home. Seven-thirty for eight.'

'Thank you.'

He put the phone down at once to her surprise. She sat, toying with a book, short but already interesting. She forced herself to read slowly at first until she had decided on the quality of the writing. The heat of the room and the afternoon's exertions gave great pleasure. Soon she would make a pot of tea, and when she had drunk it, take a leisurely bath, deciding which clothes she should wear as she lay back soaking. Nobody else moved in the house. She had the world to herself, with both time and inclination to enjoy it.

At five-thirty-five she brewed the tea. At five-forty the telephone rang.

This time Michael Alexander called, to thank her for last night's lift. She answered politely, found him in no hurry to ring off. She sat comfortably back in her armchair, sipping, listening to the clipped voice.

Clearly the man was lonely. Stuck in his house with little to do, nothing to look forward to except the beginning of the next boring term in less than a week's time, he raked over his troubles. Stella reminded him of his daughter-in-law's visit (he had mentioned it to her last evening), their three days together on this important new opera, already being discussed in the quality dailies and magazines with, as yet, not a note heard in public. This must be exciting, she claimed, to be in so early on this new creation.

'One part in itself is limited. We can see that the notes are right, yes. But one needs to know the rest, the conflicts, characters, complexities. The orchestral writing, the placing of climaxes, all decide the pace, the voice of the solos.' The composer, Nicholas Webb, did write instructions on the score, mostly in English, 'with intensity' or 'serenely'. What sort of man was Webb? Michael had never met him, but said Lise described him as both energetic and nervous; he could be rude and inflexible, while at other times he didn't know his mind. No, he was not tall, stocky rather, quite powerfully built, with a black beard and a bush of not very tidy hair.

While all this was discussed, Michael spoke strongly, but he soon dropped back to his lassitude, his lack of resolution. 'I've been dozing all through this lovely afternoon,' he grumbled.

'If I'd have known, you could have come with me to Papplewick.'

'I wish I had.'

'The sun shone really quite warm.'

'It wouldn't have been the sun I'd have appreciated, it would have been you. Last night you did me a power of good. Of course, in my usual way, I spoilt it all by drinking too much, so I wake with a headache, feeling like death. But while I was sober I looked at you, and listened to you . . .'

'I wasn't saying much.'

'There was no need. You were there. Your presence was enough.'

'Are you serious?' she asked, half-joking.

'If I say exactly what I mean, nobody believes me.'

'Why's that?'

'Why?' Michael snarled to himself. 'I've reached an odd time of life. I'm sixty. I've said and done all I'm ever going to manage. Sometimes I've done it with force. But not now. I can give the appearance of energy, but really I'm dependent on experience. People have heard all I've got to do or say. And so they pay little attention. In any case people only hear what they want to, and they expect nothing from me. Rightly. What can I give them?'

'Wisdom?'

'That's the last thing. I'm a musician and music handles emotion. Formally, with order, in perceptible patterns, agreed, but unless a fugue or a canon has power to move, then its intricacies are wasted.'

'Some people are emotionally shaken by intricacy or simplicity or order themselves. Mathematicians see beauty in one equation rather than another.'

Her argument seemed to depress him; he said nothing. Silence over the phone set her on edge. She closed her eyes. In the end it was Michael who spoke first.

'What I can do these days is remember vividly.'

'Things from a long way back?' She felt glad to ask, to include herself.

'Yes. The other day I recalled a Tennyson poem, "The Poet's Song". Do you know it? "The rain had fallen, the Poet arose".' She did not. 'It's not good, or not very good Tennyson. We had to learn it in the elementary school. And I set it as a student. But,' he paused, 'what comes back is the excitement I felt at the age of ten, perhaps, at this. And second the classroom with a fireguard round the fireplace (we had radiators so no one ever lit a fire) and a kind of meaty smell, like poor broth, because there was a tannery right next door to the school.'

'Marvellous,' she said. He demurred. 'Can't you use it? Musically or somehow?'

'Use it?' he snapped. 'No.' He coughed. 'Except to try to interest you.'

'You've succeeded,' Stella said.

'Who's serious now?' he asked.

He talked on gloomily about the world, his neighbours,

the state of education. Anger soon scratched his voice. In the middle of a diatribe about the waste of his life, he stopped and asked if she would walk with him in the Papplewick woods.

'When?' she asked.

'This week. They say the high pressure won't move much.'

'Thursday,' she said. He expressed delight and surprise. 'We'll start about one o'clock.'

'I look forward to it. Where do we meet?'

She issued orders; he thanked her and rang off. Stella uncomfortably wondered what she had let herself in for, and what sort of walker Michael Alexander was. She shrugged. The man was too depressed to be interesting. She remembered the beginning of last year when she could not drag herself out of dejection, when the world seemed set against her. Now she barely understood her paranoia. Wrapped inside the steel, constricting tube of her own concerns, she had seen only disconsolately day after black-grey day without mitigation.

Stella arrived at her husband's house exactly on time.

John was casually dressed, with a tartan open-necked shirt, green corduroy trousers, a plain grey schoolboy pullover which suited his figure. She eyed him, not without appreciation, but wondering why she considered him at his most handsome in his working attire, three-piece suit, white or striped shirt with white starchy collar and plain, silk tie. She had met him so dressed for the first time. At a performance of *The Admirable Crichton*. In the bar. He had nudged her and spilt her drink, insisted on buying another. The orange juice had neither splashed his suit nor her dress. She smiled now at the banality, and stared about her.

'Bacon omelette and salad?' he called out, when she had refused a drink.

'Very small for me, please. I'm fighting Christmas excess.'

The room was much as it was in her time. She had been responsible for the décor. The same furniture occupied usual positions; no one had changed round the pictures on

101

the walls, the Corot and Cézanne prints. The curtains looked clean, recently laundered. Carpets were smart; shelves shone free of dust; the glass of pictures and mirror gleamed.

Stella sat. The last time she had been here Sharon, was it? Samantha? had occupied this chair, a plump, well-scrubbed, perfumed girl, replete with chips, custard and sex.

'What will you drink with your omelette?' John shouted from the kitchen.

'Water will do, thank you.'

That fetched him to the door. He'd donned an apron advertising Martini.

'Oh, come on.' His face had grown ruddy.

'Water suits me.'

'Then it'll suit me.'

They ate their omelettes leisurely. His plate was piled high, so that she wondered how he kept his figure so well. Perhaps he didn't. He had something of a paunch now. No, very little. And with his breadth of shoulder he could carry it off. He drank her health in vin rosé.

'Are you ready to start work?' he wanted to know.

'It has to be done.'

'Do you wish it was something else?'

'No,' she answered. 'Given that I have to earn my living, I'd as sooner do that as anything.'

This time last year she had dreaded the start of term. The principal was unsympathetic, the head of department un-helpful, the syllabuses old-fashioned and dull, the academic pupils idle, the rest stupid. Now she knew she had been at fault, not they. Now she could face them, chase them, stamp her personality on the classroom. It seemed impossible, yet here she sat, in the dark of the year, in the place where twelve months ago will and nerve had slipped, facing her husband, who had been an enemy then, in expectation of a pleasant evening.

It seemed a miracle.

She raised her glass cheerily to John, swilling the inch of water round and round. Stella spoke about Michael Alexander's phone call, and in return her husband gave an expansive account of the visit to the London Alexanders.

'Let's wash up,' she said at the end of the meal. He did not object, and they stood together at the sink, chattering about their work, the new year, holidays. No mention was made of Stella's permanent return.

They sat in armchairs on either side of the hearth. Stella refused alcohol, saying she had to drive.

'It's an invariable rule,' she said.

'You're a puritan.'

'Then I wish everybody else was.'

He nursed his brandy, unsure of himself.

'How are you keeping these days?'

John set his question flatly, so she could misunderstand if she so wished.

'I'm miles better. In a new world, if I can put it like that.'

'How do you mean?'

'It's miraculous. It really is.'

'What is?' John, fidgeting, sounded deliberately uncouth.

'My cure.'

'What was wrong with you?'

'Depression.'

'I see.' Clearly he did not. 'And how were you cured?'

'Drugs and counselling.'

'You didn't say anything about this when you came here before, when you offered to come back.' He could not keep aggression out of his voice.

'No. I didn't. And you, incidentally, didn't ask, either.' Her tone froze. 'When I claim to be cured, that's not exactly it. I had months on end in trouble. Now I can cope. I'm better than I have been for two years. They got me back my confidence at school. I went abroad on my own. But I couldn't help wondering if, some time, I'd have a relapse.'

'Are you still on drugs?'

'No. I didn't want them at all, partly because they're addictive and partly on account of side-effects. But my psychiatrist persuaded me. She's a young woman, not a great deal older than I am. And not afraid to play it rough.

"It's tranquillizers or hospital," she said. "You can take your choice." And she put me on to a counsellor. A man called Derek Jones. I used to go to his house twice a week. To talk.'

'To talk about what?'

'Me. What I felt like. And why I felt as I did. If you're as down as I was then you can't, you won't look outside yourself. You're concentrated on your despair and all the pain.'

'Physical pain?'

'Yes, in my case, physical pain. Headaches, migraines, muscular aches, cramps. Stomach trouble. God.'

'And they cured this?' John had put down his brandy glass.

'They presumably,' Stella spoke quasi-scientifically, without force, 'set the chemical imbalance to rights, removed some of the environmental hazards.'

'Did you have much time off?'

'Not really. Eight days once. That was the longest. And the odd day now and again. I was lucky.'

'In what way?' he asked.

'Isabel, the psychiatrist, hit the right drug from the word go. This was fortunate. She says so. Now. Often they experiment, with dosage or kinds of pills, I guess. But she was on target straight off. Moreover, she says my illness was perhaps not as deep-seated as she feared. So I began to come round, felt the benefit . . .'

'When did the treatment begin? While you were still here?'

'I went several times to Dr McCabe while I was here, and he referred me to Isabel Lennox just after I left. They coincided. Same week.'

'Did you count me as one of the environmental hazards, as you call them?'

'You must have been. You didn't seem to understand what was happening to me. I don't blame you, because I didn't understand either.'

Stella laughed, nervously scratching her forehead. Suddenly she pointed a finger at him with tigerish speed. Then she sat unmoving, still as a stone. John felt unnerved, as though he feared that this small woman would explode.

'When I tell you all this now,' Stella began, and brightly, 'it seems very plain and straightforward. Take the tablets, Stella, talk to me, talk to Mr Jones, try new things if you can. It was ravelled, I can tell you. A tangle, a mess, chaos.'

'But it came together.'

'Yes. Within a month or two. By and large. At the end of the summer holiday I was almost normal. Of course I felt suspicious. I thought there might easily be a relapse, but there wasn't, and every day I felt better and stronger.'

'You were off your drugs by this time?'

'Yes.'

'And haven't gone back on them?'

'No.'

'Do you still see the psychiatrist, and this Jones man?'

'I've finished with Isabel. She has too many patients as it is. I visit Derek once a week now.'

'What for?'

'To talk. It gives me a good opportunity to judge for myself how I'm shaping.'

'Does he give you advice?'

'Yes. But that's not the main idea. But he will tell me what he thinks I should do, if I ask him. He advised me to come here. My first visit. I'd been telling him how guilty I'd begun to feel.'

'And?'

'Well, he's very mild. He asked if I blamed you for my breakdown or if I thought my illness had caused me to treat you badly. I found that almost impossible to answer. But we tried to explore it. Not very successfully in my view, but it made me face what I'd done. In the end he said, "How do you feel about going back to your husband?" This would be, oh, three or four months ago, when we were certain I was coming round.'

'Go on.'

'I didn't feel up to it. So we just discussed it as a possibility for the future. The trouble with my sort of depressive illness is that you withdraw inside yourself. You don't want change, because change means challenge and your lack of will cripples you, and your anxieties are so great you don't, no, you daren't, add to them.'

'Are these anxieties real?' John asked.

'Real? We're all anxious if we're trying something out for the first time. It's an advantage. We take precautions or ask advice or go over the possible snags. It's when these anxieties become so powerful that they stop you doing anything that you're in trouble.'

'And what triggers it off?'

'I don't think anybody knows for certain. Human beings, human consciousnesses, are so complex. I mean it's obvious sometimes: some trauma, a setback, an illness, a bereavement, a disappointment, a desperation makes a beginning. But at other times it's just a chemical, hormonal failure. Something happens, your body, your brain deals with it by giving itself extra doses of this or that – you know, like adrenaline when a bull's chasing you – and when the excitement's over you put the brakes on to this extra spurt, and then they stick, won't come off.'

'What started yours?'

'I don't know. Derek and I have tried, and Isabel, to sort it out. There doesn't seem to be one main cause. Isabel thinks it might date back to childhood. I was worried about my job; I had one or two failures there. Nothing one couldn't get over in the ordinary way. And you and I seemed a bit edgy. I thought that you were worried about your work, the recession and so on. And then I used to wonder whether we ought to start a family. And you were often too busy to talk. And at Christmas you seemed to get drunk so quickly, as if you wanted to protect yourself from the world.'

'Why didn't you say something?' he asked.

'I tried to. Times. But you wouldn't listen. Or that's how it seemed. You were in opposition, uncooperative. And I was busy.'

'That's my trouble: I'm always up to the eyes in work.'

'You should be thankful these days,' she murmured.

'Yes. But work's not the be-all and end-all of life. I ought

106

to have seen that you were ill.' He looked her straight in the face. 'The trouble with you is that you didn't complain until it was too late. If you had been sick all over me, or screaming with pain, I might have understood. But I thought it was just a mood.'

'It lasted rather long for that.'

'The damage was done,' John mused. 'I was used to your unhappiness. It made life at home uncomfortable, unbearable sometimes, but I'd plenty of work, and I occupied myself with that.'

'I see.'

'And what's more, when we were together outside, at your college functions, with other people, you were, more or less, as far as I could judge, normal.'

'I put a good face on it, when I could.'

'I saw you once,' he said, 'walking hand in hand in the street with a young man. A colleague, you said. After a lecture. And you were laughing.'

'You've mentioned this before. There was nothing serious there.'

'I'm not saying there was. But there was precious little hand-holding or smiling going on at home.'

She did not answer. He lifted brandy to his lips and then concentrated on the ground between his feet. The silence was not now awkward, but seemed to each as if the other tried to account for inexplicable behaviour. John spoke first, hesitantly, holding his glass up, as a symbol of truce.

'It seems extremely queer,' he began, 'that you, my wife, living in the same house, should be quite seriously ill, and I didn't notice anything.'

'You noticed all right. You drew the wrong conclusions.' She held up a hand to give herself some time to think. 'I've known people not notice physical symptoms. An aunt of mine died of cancer. She kept it to herself. There was bleeding and sickness and weight loss, but her husband didn't suspect anything out of the ordinary.'

'Was he unsympathetic?'

'I shouldn't have said so. He was a clergyman, rector of a large London parish, and very occupied. He broadcast

107

quite a lot. She struggled on and on. He put her lethargy
down to her time of life. She collapsed in the end, and died
within a month. She was like a sick animal, and kept out of
his way.'

'Had they no children?'

'Yes, but they had left home. Daughters, with their own
families.'

'Had their mother not . . . ?'

'Yes. She talked to the older one. But too late.' Stella
shook her head. 'My uncle blamed himself. He said to me,
"Stella, I'd honestly no idea. And I'd have thought that
Catherine would have got herself down to the doctor. She
seemed so efficient and sensible." '

'Is he still alive?'

'Yes.'

'Has he married again?'

'No.'

John shook his head.

'I suppose that's a kind of parable,' he said. 'For us.
Except there's nothing to be learnt from it. She died. We've
parted.' He made rapid radical alterations to the shape of
his mouth as if clearing his teeth of some obstruction. 'I
don't know. I don't know.'

'Don't know what?'

'What to make of all this. Your explanation's clarity itself,
but I can't grasp it somehow. It doesn't tie up with the way
I remember it all.'

'No,' she said. 'I see that.'

Oddly they re-explored her account of her illness. He
questioned her; the same queries, as if some new words or
glosses could clarify his mind. This time she asked about
his own feelings, his own memories of the time. The double
cross-examination, hectic sometimes, though frequently
softened by side-issues, anecdotes, stories from newspapers
dragged in to keep the adversarial situation within bounds.
John, she noted, did not refill his glass, perhaps remembering her comment on his drunkenness, or perhaps indirectly
informing her, that he, at least, did not need drugs or
alcohol to contain his problems.

108

Suddenly Stella felt exhausted. John seemed to her not to have weakened, to be prepared to press steadily on until a conclusion was reached.

'I'm whacked,' she said.

John stood, sighed, apologised. He squinted at her as if she had puzzled him beyond his reason.

Stella smiled, leaning back.

'You can stay the night here,' he said. It sounded innocent.

'I shall be all right, thanks.'

She yawned, standing.

'That's cleared the air, at least,' John said when, out in the hall, she was putting on her outdoor clothes.

'I'm glad I could talk to you.'

She kissed his cheek and he accompanied her to the car. He seemed subdued, and when she turned at the end of the street, she caught a glimpse of him still standing on the pavement, not sensible on an uncouth January night.

John shuffled indoors, locked up. Back in the sitting room he knelt at the chair she had occupied like a man praying. The cushion smelt of her perfume, but faintly.

He pushed himself violently to his feet as if ashamed of himself. Carefully he cleared away glass and brandy bottle. He rubbed his cheek roughly, swore softly, unfastened his shoes. At the end of the table he sat in his stockinged feet unable to understand himself. He glowered at a white hyacinth.

11

Thursday spread sunny, without fog, a west wind spoiling the mildness.

Stella drove round to Michael Alexander's house to pick him up for the afternoon walk. He was ready, in military topcoat and scarlet scarf, and with him in anorak, jeans and strong shoes, Lise.

'My daughter-in-law.' He introduced them, proudly. Today he seemed chipper.

Stella was surprised that Lise's speaking voice sounded ordinary; she had expected an opera-singer's boom, or unusual harmonics. Perhaps Lise reduced her vocal power for everyday use.

'Is it cold out?' Michael asked.

'Not on the thermometer, but it feels chilly.'

'You're nesh.'

They piled into Stella's car, laughing.

'What sort of woods are these?' Lise wanted to know.

'Pines. Firs. Coniferous. Good for you to breathe in. Plantations.' Michael, full of importance.

All the way he offered a commentary to Lise from the back seat about the buildings, the roads, the signposts, the associations. He sounded utterly confident, as if he'd mugged his subject up.

In the car-park they tightened laces and scarves.

'A sylvan scene,' Michael said. His cheeks were bright. 'Which way?'

Stella led through a spur of woodland on to a road with notices.

'Which walk?' she asked. 'Long or short?'

'Seventy minutes, blue; forty minutes, yellow. You choose, Lise.'

'The blue.'

They set off, swinging their arms. Though they had noticed three other cars in the park, they met no one. Sometimes the road ran darkly into shadows, but almost invariably they could see the sun striking treetops in the distance.

Michael explained that Lise had come a day earlier, and that already they had spent time on her opera.

'It's *Oedipus*, isn't it?' Stella asked.

'Yes. I'm playing Jocasta.'

'Is that difficult?'

'Very. It's written over a very wide range. Nicholas says one must choose the obvious dramatic setting, and make it remarkable, if that's what it's going to be, by means of the music. He wrote his own libretto at first, but handed it over to George Crane, the poet. It's the end of Sophocles, before she hangs herself and he blinds himself. It means the young ones, the sisters, Ismene and Antigone, you know, get more of a part. Not just appearing like two lost children.'

'Is it tiring?' Stella asked.

'Yes.'

'And unusual,' Michael interpreted. 'I think you need perfect pitch.'

'You have it?' Stella.

'Yes. And Sebastian. It's an advantage sometimes. Not always.'

They were walking quickly – had loosened their scarves – up a hill through a clearing. Sunlight dazzled. Not a cloud daubed the high blue. They grew warm. Michael had stuffed his gloves into his pocket.

'This is some January,' he said. 'We reserved it specially for you.' He raised clenched fists above his head.

'Do you know this part of the world?' Stella asked.

'No. Hardly at all. I couldn't even find my way round the city centre.'

'How do you like what you've seen?'

'I'm pretty well all she's seen,' Michael interrupted.

'A good start.'

'I'm surprised how hilly the place is,' Lise said.

'Does your husband talk about it at all?'

111

'Occasionally. But mostly about himself. In various places. School. And going to the Council House to receive a musical bursary. I have pictures of these places, but I don't know how far they correspond to reality.'

'Michael will take you round.'

'I don't know whether I want to go. I'm content.'

Their pace had become furious, a sprint.

'Steady on now,' Michael warned. 'I'm an old man.'

They stopped in a long patch of sunlight. Two horse-women approached and rode slowly past, both touching the peak of their riding-hats with their whips. The three watched in silence, having returned the solemn greeting. Lise spoke first.

'Riding is like speaking the language of angels,' she said.

'Is that a quotation?' Michael asked.

'No. I just made it up.'

All puzzled, they set off again, now in dapple, now in shadow, talking only intermittently. Once or twice, Lise exclaimed her delight out loud.

'But you must have travelled abroad,' Stella said, and seen some of the most beautiful places in the world.'

Lise nodded assent, but added, 'This weather in January, two friends, my present expectations about the opera all make me happy.'

'She's got rid of her husband,' Michael gibed.

'Well, that may be part of it. I feel the difference. I'm not responsible for him, though he'd claim I never am. I suppose his absence makes a difference. As long as I know he's doing well. And I feel excited about the opera. I'm on top of the music, and looking forward to getting on stage. And I'm in a different place, being looked after. Michael's a good cook and a wonderfully sympathetic accompanist. I've three recitals beginning next week, and two oratorios and then it's opera rehearsal full-time.'

'Do you listen to the other parts when you're off-stage?' Stella enquired.

'Yes. Toby, that's what we call him, Thomas Tyler, the producer insists on it. "Every note somebody else sings should colour your part for you," he says. In any case, I'd

112

do it.' She smiled, her teeth white and regular. 'And now this gorgeous afternoon. It's like spring.'

They walked on, so much at ease that they chanced a side turning on to a small unmarked path and after some floundering found their way back.

'I must turn aside,' Michael announced, 'into the bushes. The old man's complaint. Walk on. I'll catch you up.'

The women sauntered.

'He's an interesting man,' Stella said. 'I've only just got to know him recently. He taught my husband music at school.'

'Yes.'

'Is he happy, do you think?'

Lise laid a cautionary hand on Stella's arm.

'He's in love with you,' she said.

'How do you know that?'

'He said so.' Lise waited for a comment, received none, continued. 'He just told me this morning when he was talking about this walk. "I'm getting to an age when I can come out with such things," he said. "When I was in the junior school I used to take some third party into the corner of the playground and confess I was in love with one of the little girls. Now that time's come round again." '

'What did you say?' Stella asked.

' "Will you tell her?" That's what I said.' Lise giggled.

'I hardly know him. We can't have met more than half a dozen times. Neither does he know me.'

'He admitted that. "I'm in love with my idea of what she is, rather than the girl, herself," he said. We were running through some Brahms songs at the time. It seemed appropriate. Hush, now, he's coming.'

Stella looked over the approaching figure, noticing the high polish on Michael's brogues, a sharp crease in his cavalry-twill trousers, a British warm, scarlet scarf, the flashing ash stick.

'You two have your heads together,' he called out. 'Somebody's reputation will be suffering.' The girls laughed out loud.

'As long as it isn't mine.'

'We wouldn't dare,' Lise answered.

They marched on, Michael swinging shoulders and elbows in a military parody as he whistled a cheerful snatch.

'What's that?' Stella asked.

'Bach's "Little C Minor", Fantasy and Fugue, BWV 537.'

Stella, warm with exercise, considered Lise's revelation. It came as a surprise, and, worse, Lise appeared mischievous or naïve to report it. Stella wondered if he'd said more, over lunch, or waiting for her arrival. She could hardly make up her mind whether she was flattered, pleased, mildly annoyed. That last was wrong. She'd make sure that nothing came of it. Nothing would disturb her. She looked across at the sharp face, the aquiline nose, the now ruffled grey hair. He caught her eye.

'What is it?' he asked.

'You've stopped whistling.'

'I haven't the breath these days for walking and whistling.'

They walked on, suddenly heard voices. Two children, girls, burst out of the trees and stood perhaps a hundred yards ahead, looking about. A man in a knitted hat joined them, and when the three walkers had nearly reached them a woman stumbled from the other side. She seemed breathless and distressed.

The parents and children talked hard, pointed.

When Michael came up the man said, 'You haven't seen a little girl on her own, have you?'

'She's five, in a green coat.' The mother.

'No.'

'How long has she been gone?' Stella asked.

'Half an hour,' the father answered.

'More,' the mother said.

'No.'

'Where did she disappear?'

'Somewhere off this piece of road. She went into the woods.'

'We all did,' one of the children explained. 'We were running in and out.'

114

'Have you shouted?' Michael asked.

'We've done nothing else,' the mother snapped.

Michael frowned; he had heard nothing. The wind had perhaps been in the wrong direction.

'We'll keep our eyes open.' Michael sounded efficient.

'It'll soon be dark,' the mother said.

'What's her name?' Stella enquired.

'Patricia.'

'We'll look out.'

The father issued curt, breathless instructions to his party. The mother's face screwed desperately. She moved to the left, father to the right, the girls together.

'Keep on calling, and keep coming back to the road.'

The children dashed away. As Michael and his party moved off they could hear shouts now of 'Trish, Trisha'.

They had marched not more than a hundred yards and had surmounted the crest of the hill when a small child struggled out of the trees to stand by the newly dug ditch between wood and road.

'Patricia?' Stella asked. The girl wore a green coat. She did not seem distressed, more puzzled, as if it had all proved too much for her, as if the family-less road demonstrated yet another unfriendly, adult game.

'Hold on,' Michael said. 'I'll lift you over. Give 'em a shout, Lise.' He stood astride the ditch and hoisted the child, flying. Lise, back at the top of the rise, gave calls, a ferociously strong yodel, a coo-ee. Now she was gesturing.

'They're coming,' she reported.

'Let's go and find Mummy and Daddy,' Stella said. She and Michael took the child's hands. She wore gloves. 'Are you tired?'

They reached the brow of the hill, and they could see the father running ahead of his family.

'There's Daddy,' Stella said. 'He's coming.'

They stepped off again. Patricia had not said a single word. Now she spoke for the first time.

'One-two-three,' the child piped.

'What does she say?' Lise asked, though the words were clear.

115

'What was that?' Michael now.

'One-two-three.' Clear as a bell. Demanding.

'She wants a swing,' Michael said. 'Hold tight.' He and Stella took swift paces. 'One-two-three and awaaay.' They swung the child up at the full length of her arms.

'Again.' Up she flew. 'An' again.'

The father had reached them, stood panting like a dog, mouth wide.

'Where was she?' When he could talk. Michael gave an explanation. The father did not speak to nor touch the child who stood still holding on to Stella and Michael. The two girls arrived, less breathless than their father, and parked themselves at the side of the road, interested spectators of the next development. Michael's dry voice continued the exposition, the ditch, the difficulty for short legs. The father's eyes bulged. Now, at a sharp pace, the mother arrived.

She swooped on the child, picking her up from the hands of her saviours.

'Trisha, our Trisha.'

They hugged. The child hid her face in her mother's collar.

'Where did you go?'

'Mam.'

'We thought we'd lost you.'

The mother did not weep, but hung on to her child, squeezing her. The mother's face grew red and her eyes wider. She made no attempt to hide her relief, acted as if she and her child were alone.

'Trish. Our Trish.' Again the violence of arms. 'Where did you go to?'

The girl made no attempt to answer, but showed her content with closed eyes. She was probably worn out.

'Didn't you hear us shouting?'

This went unanswered. Father now walked about in a small, crooked square as if he could not contain himself.

'We called you,' one of the other children explained.

'Don't bother her now,' the mother snapped. 'There,

116

then.' Again the ecstatic bout of hugging. The child opened her eyes.

The rest had inadvertently formed a rough circle round the mother and daughter, and stood as if waiting for instructions. Faces lacked expression; no one knew the next move now that the brilliance of joy had begun to fade.

Michael spoke first.

'All's well,' he said. 'We shall have to be on our way.' He spoke to the father.

'We don't know how to thank you,' the mother said, rocking her child from side to side. 'I don't know what we should have done once it got dark.' She muttered endearments to the child, oblivious of the rest. 'There's a Trish; there's a big girl; who's the best baby?' She straightened the child up in her arms. 'Would 'oo like a duddoo?' She reverted to baby-talk. The child's face brightened. 'Dad, where's them toffees?'

Father grubbed in his pocket, came forward with a bag. Mother looked in with care, extracted a sweet.

'Red, look,' she said. 'Your favourite.' The child took the sweet in one hand and examined it with her eyes before pushing it into her mouth. The other girls came up to their father in expectation, were allowed a dip, exhibited their prizes to each other.

'I'll have one,' Mother said, 'while you're at it.'

Father returned; his wife took her pick as carefully as her daughters.

'Hand them round,' she ordered.

He obeyed. Lise, Stella and then Michael all politely helped themselves.

'Liquorice comfits,' Michael said, after thanks. 'I've not had one of these for years.'

'Torpedoes,' the eldest child corrected.

Father took his turn, folded the top of the bag, tucked it away.

'Well,' Michael said.

'Yes,' the mother answered. 'And thanks. Don't know what we should have done. I dread to think.' She switched attention to the child. 'We nearly lost our Treasure.'

117

'Goodbye,' Michael continued. 'We must be off.'

'Here, Dad. Take Trish. You carry her. Then we shan't get losing nobody no more.'

Father took the child easily, holding her high.

'Hup a daisy. Open them leggy-pegs.' He swung her up, parking her on his shoulders, her trouser-legs either side of his head. He trotted round. 'Gee up, Neddy, to the fair. What will yuh buy me when you get there?'

Patricia, bobbing, screamed delight, then, hardly differentiating, distress. Now the child pointed downwards. In the road, still faintly red, lay her liquorice torpedo.

'Oh, our Trish,' the mother said.

The father felt in his pocket, extracted a sweet, handed it over.

'It in't red.'

'Does it matter? They all taste the same. Oh, all right, then. Now you hang on.' He brought out the bag, found the wanted sweet which he handed to the child. 'Where's the other?' Patricia pointed to her mouth. 'Well, you crafty little sod.' He looked round the group. 'I'll give you the advice I give to all women. "Don't open your mouth so much." Now.' He glanced at Michael for support in this largely female gathering.

'Look who's talking,' his wife said.

The two parties separated, in silence. At the top of the hill, Michael looked back. The small child was still mounted on her father's shoulder, and they pretended to chase the larger girls who skipped and whooped along the verge. Mother walked on her own on the other side of the road, aloof from the gambollings.

'Look at them,' Michael advised.

'Poor old mother,' Stella said. 'She's the one who carried the responsibility and is still worrying about it.'

'If she worried most, she should be the most overjoyed.'

'Doesn't always happen like that. You can't turn anxiety off as and when you like.'

'I tell you what amazed me,' Lise said, 'and that's the stoical way the child put up with being lost. No crying, though she must have been frightened. And

118

yet when she dropped her sweet, she screamed the place down.'

'And what's the reason?' Michael asked them.

'Perhaps she lacks judgement,' Lise ventured.

'Or has it exactly. No immediate response in the trees. But parents or sisters to hand to carry out immediate replacement of sweet.' Michael spoke brusquely, almost as if reading out some often dictated note.

'I wondered if she was backward,' Stella said. 'She hardly spoke a word to us.'

'Frightened again,' Michael argued. 'Or had taken notice of warnings not to speak to strangers.'

'The sisters didn't seem to show much reaction, one way or the other.' Lise, now, striding, speaking straight down the road.

'They'd be pleased, I guess,' Stella answered. 'They might not like their sister all that much. Parents make allowances for the baby, and so on. But they'd see father and mother were upset.'

'Father was an odd bod,' Michael said. 'Did you see the way he stalked round and round in a confined space?'

'Excitement shows itself in different ways.'

'I thought the mother would squash all the breath out of the child,' Lise said. 'And yet the woman's face was set. Not crumpled.'

'She didn't cry at all.' Michael.

'Is that what you expected?' Stella probed.

'I don't expect anything.' He sounded angry, provoked. 'No, that's wrong. A woman weeping for joy would be the right sort of stereotype.'

'For whom? Men?' Lise, still ahead.

'Yes. I like a woman to show womanly traits,' Michael answered.

'Men must work and women weep. Is that it?'

'In some measure. Though nowadays women have a much greater scope, often to their disadvantage.' They were off, the two, on an argument about feminism. Clearly this subject had already been broached between them. They clashed in a friendly fashion, making allowances for

119

the other's point of view, almost as if they knew the limits of difference between them had been established, and would not be changed. But they enjoyed themselves, demonstrating their skill, she thought, for Stella's benefit. Now and then they socially tried to include her in the proceedings, but she offered little, encouraging them to continue on their own.

When the performance petered out, they walked in pleasurable silence, watching the low sunlight and keeping up a good pace. They were engaged, at Michael's insistence, on another round of comment on Patricia's family and the public expression of emotion as they walked the final half-mile of road to the noticeboard.

As they arrived, Stella consulted her watch.

'Sixty-two minutes,' she announced. 'Not too bad really. We had one biggish detour and five minutes with the lost child. And still eight minutes under.'

They decided it was too late to walk the path again and made their way back to the car. Outside Michael's house, Stella refused to go inside for a cup of tea. She claimed she was busy, the truth, and that she did not wish to upset their practice schedule. They did not press her, so that she felt slightly disappointed by the time she reached home. She read an act or two of *Measure for Measure* which she would teach when the term started. She sipped tea, kept warm, but in the early darkness regretted that she had not accepted their invitation.

She considered, not altogether seriously, Lise's confession that Michael Alexander looked on her with love, and pondered whether Lise would tell her father-in-law what she had let out to Stella. Lise seemed a serious, even solemn woman, not given to frivolity, and yet she had quite blithely admitted Stella into Michael's confidence. Perhaps the bit about the schoolyard encouraged her: you told your friend in the hope he'd pass the news on to the beloved. She had fulfilled the mission, and would make a report.

'What did she say?' the aged schoolboy would ask.

'You came back too soon,' Lise would answer. 'She was surprised, but you'd expect that.'

Stella decided that Lise had said nothing. The girl was happy with plenty on her plate, would be willing to discuss Michael's new-found love with him, to advise him even, but not to be serious about it. Stella forced herself to consider her own attitude. After all, she had not expected the revelation. Her husband admired Michael Alexander, said that given the opportunities he might well have been as famous as his son, but he described the man as short-tempered, sharp-tongued, lonely, embittered. She could not recall whether he was a widower, or whether Sebastian's mother had divorced him, or deserted him. All this added spice to the dull evening, but of a factitious sort. She read her Shakespeare carefully, but felt glad to be interrupted by the telephone. Her husband, also at a loose end.

John had been thinking about what she had told him, and he was sorry he had been so obtuse about her depression.

'You weren't to know,' she excused him.

'I feel I ought to have spotted it. As an illness. That could be cured or alleviated. By anti-depressants and so on. I was too selfish.'

He worked over this theme, as if trying to convince himself. She spoke non-committally, saying he need not feel guilty, that she had probably been unbearable to live with, but that they must now act circumspectly, not rush into unwise decisions.

'You don't want to come back, then?' he asked.

'I've put the question in front of both of us.'

'That doesn't sound very enthusiastic.' He blustered, not jovial, not reasonable.

'I'm older and wiser. More wary.' She would keep it light. She thanked him for ringing. His puzzlement was obvious, even over the phone. Feeling sorry for him, she described her walk with Michael and Lise.

'Did they sound satisfied with each other?' he asked.

'Oh, yes. More than satisfied. Delighted. They'd been rehearsing together.'

'He's a fine player. But he can be sarcastic. And impatient.'

'No signs of trouble. They invited me in.'

'To hear them perform?'

'No. At least, I thought it was for a cup of tea. I didn't go. I had too much to do.'

'Such as?' he asked.

She told him. He huffed and puffed, saying that she was far too conscientious for her own good. He gave his own impression of the teaching profession, not much of it favourable. Now he sounded out of humour. He would think again, he said he had already worked hard on it, about her proposal. He rang off, rather gruffly, at cross-purposes with himself.

She advised him to give Michael and Lise a ring.

Voice brightening, he said he would do just that.

12

John Taylor walked whistling into his office.

He had telephoned Michael and Lise, and they had invited him round this evening to hear Lise practise.

'What's she singing?' he had asked.

'Schubert, Schumann, Hugo Wolf, Mahler, Berkeley, Britten.'

'No Purcell?'

'She'll sing one or two on request.' Michael sounded confident. 'Why don't you bring Stella along?'

'I'll contact her in the morning.'

He had tried after breakfast, but his wife appeared to be out. At eight-thirty. Or still asleep.

Samantha brought in his letters. She spoke cheerfully enough, but did not look well; her face was puffy and she had a sore on her bottom lip.

'Are you all right?' he asked.

'I've got a bit of a cold.' She sniffed. 'Otherwise . . .'

He dictated his letters; she liked to use her excellent shorthand, and in the ordinary way looked smiling up to him, as if to tell him that he could increase his pace without losing her. This morning she stared glumly down at her pad, not raising her head.

'Are you sure you're all right?' he asked when they'd finished.

'Yes,' she said. Her voice snagged, broke in the course of the monosyllable, and she wept.

'Sit down.' He led her back to her chair. 'There. I'll get you a drink.' He walked outside, returned with a glass of water. She made a pretence of sipping. Her hand trembled. 'There, now, what is it?' He stood by her shoulder so that she need not talk right into his face.

'It isn't anything. Really.'

'Come on, Sam. This isn't like you. What is it?'

She gulped, drank again, but made no attempt to wipe the tears from her face.

'Now, what's troubling you?'

'It's my mother.'

'Is she ill?'

Samantha struggled in her chair, as if to establish mental equilibrium.

'No. Not really. It's since my dad died.' Her voice wailed. 'She's awful. Depressed. Can't do things properly. Or won't.' The girl steadied herself. 'She was fine at first. Brave, y'know. Kept on at work. Went out and met people. Talked about my dad and how he died, quite plainly. But now it's all different. She's not interested in anything. She has crying jags. She does prepare meals, but any old how. She was a good cook, but not now. And she seems to be blaming us, me and my sister.'

'Has she seen the doctor?'

'Yes. He gives her anti-depressant tablets and sleeping pills. But his line seems to be that her husband has died, suddenly her life has changed, and she ought to expect to feel sad. She'll get over it in due course.'

'Won't he send her to a psychiatrist?'

'She wouldn't go. She can be obstinate. But it's like living in prison at home. And if I go out, she says, "Not again?" I can't stand it. I shall leave, I think, take a flat, but I feel rotten about that. She won't be so well off. Doctors' receptionists are not well paid. But if I don't, I shall be as bad as she is.'

'And your sister?'

'She's harder. Perhaps it's what she sees in the hospital. It doesn't bother her so much. In any case she lives her own life.' Samantha did not explain this.

'Isn't it just possible that as all this came on her suddenly, it will disappear just as quickly?'

Samantha pulled a doubtful face.

'Could I just use your cloakroom?' she asked. 'To do my face. I don't want the girls to see I've been crying.'

Her voice sounded steady, and when she returned she had removed all trace of tears.

124

'Thank you,' she said.

'Let me know if there's anything I can do.'

'Thank you.'

She stared straight into his face, as if daring him to say more. The look was hostile. Perhaps she hated him to see her weakness.

Just before he went out to lunch he rang Stella to invite her to the Alexander house. She was at home, and agreed readily. Yes, she had been out at eight-thirty; she had driven to the supermarket before it became too crowded. He said he would pick her up at seven-thirty.

'I can drive you,' she said. 'Then you can drink.'

'We're going for music, not alcohol.'

'As long as you remember.'

She rang off, apparently busier on holiday than he was at work. That seemed unsatisfactory. He snatched his overcoat from the peg and broke the lace. He cursed, then laughed. Samantha's woebegone face spoilt his lunch. When he strolled back, she was at her desk; the other girls hadn't yet returned.

'Are we winning?' he asked her.

'I think so.' She smiled winsomely as she answered. Coyly she drew his attention to faxes and a phone message.

'Haven't you been out?' he asked.

'Not today. It's far too cold.'

She had resumed normality. He did not touch her.

That evening he was on time at Stella's flat, but she, already in outdoor clothes, did not invite him in. She talked neatly about her day during the ten-minute drive. At Michael's house, a 1930s detached, the four sat round a gas-fire in the sitting room which had no piano. Stella had formed the opinion that Lise did not much care for John; she had not kissed him on arrival and had made only curt answers to his plethora of questions. John, not noticing, seemed much pleased with himself so that his wife thought that he might at any minute break out in song or demonstrate dance steps. Michael, on the other hand, sat subdued, uncertain of his role as host. He pressed drinks on them, but hovered, not sitting, as if at any minute he'd be

125

called to serve them, to rush elsewhere. He had dressed smartly, but casually, in corduroy trousers, a sports shirt, a green cardigan and wore a yellow kerchief. He said little, leaving the floor to the garrulous John.

After a time Stella asked about *Oedipus*, the opera, and Lise talked freely, explaining how their rehearsals would start, in a church hall for the first fortnight, and then to a larger venue until the theatre was ready for them. Yes, one had to change tempo or volume to accommodate the vaster spaces and the orchestral accompaniment just as one had to alter movements to suit. She interested Stella, particularly with her account of how the musical performance, the actual singing of notes, would be altered by the drama. Her praise of Nicholas Webb, the composer, was unstinting. 'He can wring drama out of the simplest sentence, and yet be guided by order, shape. The fact that he uses a strict form, fugue or canon, say, does not dissipate the drama, acts exactly opposite, seems to strengthen it.'

'Shall we like the opera when we hear it?' John asked.

'Is one expected to *like Oedipus*?' Michael, before Lise had the chance to answer.

'What I mean,' John argued, 'is, will the music make sense as music, not be merely random sounds or noise?'

'It won't sound like Mozart, certainly,' Lise said. She did not speak friendlily to John.

Michael, after more discussion, suggested that Lise should sing to them.

'She's done a full day's practice,' he said, 'but for such distinguished guests . . .'

They went upstairs to the largest bedroom, now plainly furnished as a music studio. A grand piano, a harpsichord, four chairs and well-packed bookshelves, two modernistic drawings of Handel and Mozart made the total inside the stone-pale walls. The curtains were already drawn and the room suffused bright warmth. Michael pointed the visitors to their chairs and seated himself at the piano.

'We won't do too much.' He spoke like a schoolmaster. 'We've done a lot today.'

'Do you not like singing at night?' John asked.

'Most of my public performances take place then,' Lise said.

'Four or five songs at the outside,' Michael ordered. 'So choose carefully.'

'Could you start with Purcell?' John said, not waiting.

Michael smirked.

'I told you he'd want Purcell.'

'Your fault,' John said, unabashed. 'You were always telling us at school how good he was.'

Michael held up a copy to them: 'I attempt from love's sickness to fly'.

Now Stella was instantly amazed at the power of Lise's voice, though she clearly tempered its volume to the room. A kind of surprised simplicity invested the opening as though she was both startled and yet comforted by the foolishness of love. On the repetition both she and Michael decorated their parts delicately aptly.

'Superb,' John said, 'superb. Would you do it again, please?'

Lise bowed her head, and they repeated the song, both smiling this time.

'Your choice now,' Michael to Stella.

'What's on the programme?'

He listed composers. She chose Bach.

' "I follow with gladness",' he said. 'The *John Passion*.'

Lise with a magnificence of naïve ardour followed the Lord, and Michael followed her with the flute part. The listeners caught their breath at the singing, lifted, shining with treasure. Lise herself, dressed rather soberly, glittered with life.

'Your turn to choose,' she told Michael. He was already opening the copy.

' "*Meine Liebe ist grüne*",' he announced. 'Brahms.'

'He only chooses that to show how well he plays the accompaniment.'

'Is it difficult?' John asked.

'Fiendish.'

Now the room seemed to rock with sound, to whirl the listeners headlong round, dazed by the hugely brilliant power of golden voice and massive overwhelming piano. All sat, stood silent for a moment, after the last chord, overcome.

'More than somewhat,' Michael drily observed in the end.

John could barely believe what he had heard. He might well argue with himself that the effect was too great, that these were gigantesque performances shifting the song from the newness of love, the upthrust of human emotion to volcanic energy, the destructive shudder in the mountains. Neither performer had held back; each had encouraged the other from joy to upheaval. True, John argued with himself, in a packed concert hall this display of strength might be necessary to convey over vast distances the poet's delight. At a hundred metres one would smile with the dash and surge of love, but here, in this room, a listener was flattened, deafened, stupefied, Brobdingnagged.

'Your choice.' Michael to Lise.

Lise stood by the piano, a human being again. When John asked how and when she planned her recitals, she answered in a low voice, like a sensible woman, explaining that she had to please her audience, her accompanist, suit the programme to her total output, keeping herself interested and yet never taxing herself beyond her means with new or too demanding pieces. The giantess had disappeared, but nobody could forget the demonstration.

'Tell you what,' she whispered. ' "Death devours".'

Michael knew exactly into which pile of music to delve.

'This was written for me,' Lise said, 'by Nicholas Webb.'

'Is it dedicated to you?' Eager John.

'It happened that I was talking to Nick one day after rehearsals. Doesn't often happen; we're all too whacked and want to go home. But this time we were. And I asked him about his methods of composition.'

'Was he willing to tell you?' John again.

'Yes. I suppose so. He's a habit man, he says. Sits down every day he's at home to write. And thinks about it the rest of the time. He carries a little notebook about. It's in a hard

128

cover, but made up of printed staves, very narrowly ruled. He can jot ideas down at any time. He also has a "composing time" at the piano, playing things over, trying them out, if he's at home and on his own. I kept asking questions, and in the end he said, "I'll tell you what, Lise, you choose some words and I'll write a song for you." '

'How did you choose?' John asked.

'I wasn't sure. I asked Sebastian. He knows a great deal about literature, and though he was prepared to suggest things, he said I ought to make my own mind up. Nick had warned me not to have it too long. A song not an oratorio, he said.'

'And how did you finally . . .?'

'By chance, more or less. I had just read this. I liked the sound of it, though I wasn't quite sure what it meant. I asked Seb and he told me all about Catullus, and Lesbia and her sparrow. He did Latin at school. He thinks everybody should do Latin. Michael does.'

'Don't you blame me.' He stressed both pronouns.

'I had read the poem "Death devours all lovely things" in a magazine, and then by coincidence in an old book of my father's.'

'Who wrote it?' John.

'Edna St Vincent Millay.'

'An American,' Stella said.

'You've heard of her? Nobody else has.'

'She wrote that epigram about burning the candle at both ends.'

Lise blinked blankly. Clearly she had not looked up any more of Miss Millay's poems.

'People, serious people, used to make fun of her when I was young. Said her poems just vanished away if you examined them carefully. That was the *Scrutiny* line, anyhow.' Michael.

'Seb said it was sugar-pig poetry. A touch of the classics and an element of mystery, so you're not quite sure where you're sliding to, and then a dose of cynical sentimentality. But it appealed to me. And they always say that second-rate poems are the ones best set to music.'

129

'What did Webb say?' Michael asked.

'Nothing. He read it, put it in his pocket, and gave me a photocopy a fortnight later. He hasn't said anything about the poem.'

'But he set it?' Stella asked.

'Yes. Like a bit of jazz. Michael says I should sing it huskily, as if my voice was ruined by cigarettes and alcohol. It's odd. I've never heard anything else he's written in this idiom.'

'Do you like it?' Stella again.

'Oh, yes.'

Lise nodded to Michael who set off. She joined almost immediately in a catchy sweetness of grief. They could detect no attempt at mere popularity; discords clashed blue, but mutedly, and the voice aimed at poverty, even on 'libation'. The song, three verses with a snatch in between each, seemed over in no time, ephemeral, but making a virtue of transience. There was no heaviness about this, no glory. The words rose and fell smally over the syncopations of the thin nag of accompaniment.

> Need we say it was not love,
> Now that love is perished?

A final unrevealing, unrelated, eight-note chord but pianissimo, not left hanging, offered, withdrawn, and the song was done.

'Is it, the copy, in his handwriting?' Stella asked. They were all puzzled, Lise not least.

'It'll be a fair copy,' Michael said.

'Passer Mortuus Est' at the top in smallish capitals and, under, 'For Lise Martin'. The script was neat as the quavers and crochets. There was barely a dynamic mark. Nor an idea of pace. Nor of mood. The composer had signed the last page with a date, November 23–5, with a different pen.

'Have you done it in public yet?' Stella asked.

'End of next week.' Lise smiled mischievously as if the insertion of this little song in her programmes broke some important rule.

130

Michael had closed the piano lid.

'Would you sing it again?' Stella asked, diffidently. 'Please.'

Lise raised questioning hands towards Michael, who opened up the keyboard and lifted the song from its pile.

'For you, anything,' he said, and set off at once.

The song was again over in no time, the air scarcely disturbed, and yet Stella held her breath. Lise was watching her.

'Did you know the poem?' she asked.

'Yes.' Stella could place it. 'It was in an old anthology at my father's place. *The Week-End Book*.'

' "It is silly sooth",' Lise quoted, perhaps following her husband.

' "And dallies with the innocence of love, Like the old age".' Stella completed the quotation, but found it inapt. There was a sophistication about it, even in the Shakespearean sense of 'adulteration', she thought. She smiled. Lise took her hand. Michael ushered them downstairs, John three paces behind, still battered by Brahms.

They relaxed the rest of the evening. Michael made an attentive host, drinking little himself. He treated Stella with an over-elaborate courtesy, as if he realised she knew his secret. John, since the recital, sat quieter, barely touching his wine, but eating heartily.

'You were full of questions when you came,' Michael chaffed him. 'Now you're as silent as the grave.'

'Music has charms,' John said.

'To soothe a savage beast?' Michael, mocking.

At eleven o'clock Lise suddenly said that she was tired. 'We've worked rather hard today,' she excused herself. Stella immediately rose.

'Come on, John,' she ordered. 'Stir your stumps.'

As they put on outdoor clothes in the hallway, Lise said she had decided to spend two extra days in Beechnall. She needed to return for Monday for a run-through with her accompanist, and then she had recitals in Guildford on Thursday and Exeter on Saturday.

'Same programme?' John asked, livelier now.

'Not quite, no.'

131

'But Nicholas Webb on both?'

'Of course. If we get encores.'

'Will you all come round to see me?' John asked. 'Tomorrow evening?'

Lise looked at Michael who dropped his eyes before Stella's. They agreed one by one, but inhibitedly, like participants in some unfamiliar religious ritual.

John drove Stella rapidly home.

'It's living in a different world,' he said.

'You wish you had been trained as a musician, don't you?'

'Sometimes. But I wouldn't have been good enough.'

'Oh, dear.'

He did not kiss her when they stood together on the pavement, nor touch her, even to shake hands. He seemed like a man who had lost his bearings.

'You'll come? Tomorrow?' he asked.

'Yes. Would you like any help? I'll come round early.'

'Would you?'

They agreed a time. She nodded, unlocked her flat. When she peered through the curtains, her husband still stood in the street, holding the top of the car door, staring upwards. She waited until he drove off, when she shook her head.

13

The evening spent at John Taylor's was short, and to him disappointing. He enjoyed his time with Stella preparing the buffet, but when the guests arrived they seemed both tired and disgruntled, as if they had quarrelled or had discovered some other place they'd rather visit, so that conversation was broken, and John, broaching topics with élan, was left stranded in the end, wondering where his fault lay. Soon after ten o'clock Michael said they must go, and inside five minutes they were out of the house.

John shrugged his displeasure to his wife.

'What was eating them?' he asked.

'They'd perhaps had enough of one another.'

'What shall I do with all this food?'

'Some will keep. The birds will manage the rest.'

Stella helped him clear away. He groused at her the whole time so that when the final plate was dried and stacked she almost rushed for her coat.

'Won't you have a last drink?' he asked.

'No, thanks. It'll be a pleasure to be in bed before midnight.'

'Are we getting on any better or not?' he asked, foolishly. His face puckered.

'We did our best this evening. It wasn't your fault they were so offhand.'

'If we lived together we could tumble into bed and make it up to ourselves that way.'

'It's a thought.'

'Does it appeal?'

'I think not, John. If we failed there, that would put the top hat on it.'

'Oh, hell,' he said.

'No,' Stella said. 'Life.'

She kissed him warmly on the lips. He seemed barely conscious of it, so that as she drove home she puzzled herself why he so resented having failed to entertain his guests.

Next morning at the office he felt more cheerful. He greeted the girls by name so that Samantha, bringing in the letters, remarked on his high spirits.

'Have you won the pools?' she asked.

'No,' he said, 'no. Would you like to go out to dinner tonight?'

She knitted her brows. He recalled that small frown.

'I'm out all this afternoon, shan't be back home till seven. I shan't feel like providing for myself. A quick bath and change and we can be in that nice Italian place on Mansfield Road by eight o'clock. I'll book a table for us. How do you fancy that?'

'No, thank you, John. It's very . . .'

'Are you out elsewhere?'

'No. It's not that.'

'Oh. What is it, then?'

'I've been,' she hesitated, shorthand Biro and pad still in her hand, 'been going out with someone else these last weeks, and I don't think I should . . .' She left it there.

'Is it serious?' he asked, quasi-jocularly.

'It might be. The way he talks.' She shook her head. 'I've not known him all that long.'

'Do I know him?'

'No.'

'And he'd object if I took you out?'

'He might. I'm sorry. He works for the National Westminster. He might. I mean, you're married, aren't you?'

'In a half-hearted way.'

He issued her with instructions for the day and she tip-toed out glum-faced. He drummed fingers on his desk, unsure whether he wanted to take the girl to dinner, to bed, anywhere. He swore, walked round the room, washed his hands in the cloakroom and attempted to resume cheerfulness as he prepared for his afternoon's work.

For the rest of the week he watched Samantha, speaking

134

jovially to her, asking her to do a little more than her duty required. Oddly he admired the girl's refusal to go out with him. Whether it represented some puritanical principle, or merely demonstrated that he no longer attracted her, her polite rebuff added a moral dimension he had not expected. He asked, casually he thought, heavy-handedly in her view, if she was spending the evening with her young man, but she said that they wouldn't meet until Saturday afternoon.

'We lead busy lives, you know,' she chaffed.

'What do you do?'

'I'm learning Spanish, and I attend an aerobics class. I've also a video I study on Spanish. And we try to take our mother out once a week.'

'Where?'

'Cinema. Theatre. There are no end of things on in this place.'

'What did you see last week for instance?'

'*Tons of Money*. At the Arts Theatre.'

'I've never heard of it.'

'It's a farce. We don't like to take my mother to anything too serious. She's been very down. She doesn't want to go out with us, but we make her. Hilary, my sister's very good. She's a nurse. She knows her way round.'

'Is your mother no better?'

'No. I don't know what we shall do with her. Hil's going to whip her away for eight days to the Costa del Sol. She's never been there.'

As he observed Samantha moving efficiently about the office, mistress of her job, handing out advice, never short of a task, he wondered if the break between them had not been providential. Such secretaries as Sam were rare these days; he would have done badly to have spoilt that with sex. Of course, as soon as she married this young man she'd be starting a family. It was an imperfect world.

On Saturday he had spent the morning completing an audit, and after a frugal lunch of cheese and biscuits was considering going into the garden, though there was not a great deal he could do at this time of the year, when his doorbell rang.

'Mr Taylor?' A very tall young man in a green anorak. 'I've brought you a note. From Samantha Oldham.' He held out an envelope.

'Is there an answer?'

'I don't know.'

John invited the young man inside. He left him in the hall while he strolled into the kitchen, where he opened the envelope with a paper-knife.

'Sit down,' he said, returning, pushing the visitor into the sittingroom. The handwriting was not Samantha's.

Dear Mr Taylor,

Our mother is in hospital. Last night she attempted to take her life. She is in the City now and out of danger, but it is quite likely that Samantha will not be at work on Monday as she will be looking after her. I thought I'd let you know in good time so that you could make alternative arrangements.

H.R. Payne.

H.R. Payne was presumably the sister, Hilary.

John looked over at the messenger who perched on the edge of his armchair.

'I'm sorry, Mr . . . er, er? Who are you? Are you a neighbour?'

The young man lost his glazed expression.

'My name is Tim Thomas,' he said, his voice rather high-pitched.

'Are you a relative?' This sounded ruder than John intended.

'No. I go out with Samantha. Hilary, her sister called me this morning. Samantha and I were planning lunch and a ride round in the country. She'd had to go to the hospital with her mother, and so it had to be cancelled. When Hilary phoned to tell me, I asked if I could do anything, and she said it would help if I could deliver this note to you. I went round and collected it. Hilary was straightening things out, and then she was going back to the hospital.'

'Straightening . . .?'

136

'Making sure they had bread and so forth. They shop on Saturdays, it seems.'

'You know what's wrong with Mrs Oldham?' John asked.

The young man lowered his head.

'Attempted suicide. She had been suffering from depression. Since her husband died.'

'Would you like a cup of coffee?'

'If you're having one.'

'I can always join you.'

John was interrupted in his coffee-brewing by the telephone. Samantha, from the hospital, inquired if Tim Thomas had been yet. If not, she had a message. John called the young man over. Thomas hung about in the hall once the phone was back in its cradle. They returned to the sitting room.

'This coffee is very good,' Tim said.

'Would you like a biscuit?'

'I wouldn't mind. I've not had my lunch yet. I didn't bother about it when Hilary phoned. And I've had nothing since.'

'Pitch in, then. The more you eat, the fewer I touch. Bad for my waistline.'

'It doesn't seem to affect me.'

Certainly the young man, six foot-odd, was thin as a rake. His hair, light brown, hung straight and rather thin. He now appeared quite at home, explaining that the authorities weren't quite sure whether to keep Mrs Oldham in hospital overnight. In any case, he was to be at home by five-thirty awaiting another call from Samantha.

'Mrs Oldham was doing well?' John enquired.

'I think so. They'd swilled her out. It's an unpleasant business, apparently. Hilary explained all about a stomach pump. She took pleasure in it, I thought. Putting the worst side on it. But at her mother's age and state of mind, she said they'd probably keep her in, if they had a spare bed.'

'What had she taken?'

'Her tablets. She was unconscious when Hilary went in first thing with a cup of tea. She wasn't pleased. Especially with the psychiatrist, for giving her mother whole bottlesful of the things.'

137

'Presumably the doctor hadn't thought suicide a possibility.'

'Hilary had. She tried to keep them out of the way, and
when she was at home she issued the tablets herself. But
she couldn't altogether hide them.'

'What were they?'

'I don't know. She didn't say. Or if she did, I've forgotten.'

'It's a bad business.'

The young man, with encouragement, demolished the
biscuits, quite at home.

'You're Samantha's boss, aren't you?' he asked, collect-
ing crumbs, depositing them in his saucer.

'I am.'

'You're younger than I expected. From what bit she's said.'

'She's a very good girl. You're not thinking of marrying
her and taking her away from me, are you?'

'I work for a bank. And if I want to get on, I shall have to
move about the country.'

'So it's serious?' John asked, rather brutally.

'I'm twenty-nine now. It's time I thought of settling
down. You're married, I take it?'

'My wife and I have separated. But not finally. Not yet.'

'Do you think this business with her mother will make
any difference?' Tim now seemed to have lost his poise
again. 'She might feel an obligation to stay at home. Her
sister's divorced.'

'Have you talked to her about marriage?'

'Not seriously.'

'How long have you known her?'

'I met her first last September. At a party. She's friendly
with the sister of a colleague. I asked her to a disco. And a
show or two. Then she started putting me off. I thought at
the time she had someone else. I might have been wrong.
Then we met in the city just before Christmas.' He took out
a diary, consulted it. 'December the twelfth. We went out
together quite a bit after that.'

'She suits you?' It seemed an impertinent question, even
to John.

138

'Oh, yes. She's full of life and go.'

'And pretty.'

'Yes.' Tim seemed less than certain. 'She's not like her mother or father. I met him once. Before he died. Or her sister.'

'She's a first-rate secretary, and not only efficient. She chivvies the other girls along, keeps us all happy. And is invariably well dressed. Whatever the crisis, she looks as if she's just stepped out of the bath into new clothes. They don't come like her too often.'

John felt a hypocrite even when he spoke these trite truths. He remembered Samantha naked, intent on pleasure, a different being, powerfully dominating him with her bodily violence.

'She's had bad luck recently. First her father, and now her mother,' Tim said. 'Has it made much difference to her at work?'

'Not that I've noticed. She was upset over her father. It was sudden. But she seemed to have recovered.'

'The mother has been playing up recently.' Tim's verb seemed inappropriate. 'She's been acting very unreasonably. Samantha has even thought of leaving home and getting a flat.'

'Is that what you do?'

'Live in a flat? Yes, but on my next move I shall buy a house. The bank's very helpful about mortgages.'

'Is this your first place? Here in Beechnall?'

'No. Third. I started ten years ago, after A levels.'

'And you like it? You're doing well?'

'Yes. It suits me.'

They talked desultorily for a time before the young man took himself off. It hardly seemed worthwhile going out into the garden, so that John Taylor sat down to the newspaper and rugby league on television. Both interested and soothed him so that he fell asleep. Surprised, he muttered to himself when he woke, 'Working too hard again.'

Stella phoned while he prepared his tea.

'Are you free this evening? If you are, do you fancy a concert?'

'Yes, to both.' Pleased with himself.

'You should have asked what's being played.'

'What's being played?'

'Weber. Stanford. Malcolm Arnold. Brahms.'

'Who's playing?'

'Old friends. George Paxton and Michael Alexander.'

'Where is it?'

'Out in Pleasley. I only found out today. But I guessed you'd want to go if you could, so I bought tickets.'

'Great.'

They made their arrangements: his car at her flat, quarter to seven.

'I'll have to get a move on. I'm dirty. I must have a bath.'

'What have you been doing?'

'Dropping asleep in front of the telly.'

John's pleasure at the invitation grew larger. Stella had made a movement towards him, bought tickets on which she could have lost money if he had been otherwise engaged. She was now making considerable effort, and this delighted him. He liked women to go out of their way to catch his interest. His rejection by Samantha rankled slightly, but common sense told him that he was well rid of her. An affair with a good employee had too many snags. He remembered his father's boss who had begun a casual affair with his secretary which became an obsession and which had led the man, after a London conference where he had spoken in his usual forthright way, to throw himself into the path of an underground train. His behaviour on the platform had been so normal that eye witnesses thought it might well have been an accident, but he had written and posted letters, which arrived next day, to wife and mistress, to his son and daughter, explaining his behaviour. John remembered asking his father what the man was like. 'A martinet. As hard with himself as on us.'

John did not yet know his mind about asking Stella to return. Too many imponderables darkened the picture. Her period of depression went unexplained in his mind. To him still, she had seemed to dislike, to hate him, from near-choice not from physiological processes.

140

He arrived at her flat just in time. As usual, she opened the door dressed to emerge.

The concert took place in a sprawling, newish comprehensive school where they parked in the yard. The foyer was bright and led immediately into the hall of which the parquet floor had been extravagantly polished. Black curtains with stellar devices had been drawn over high windows, while the stage curtains, also closed, hung a resplendent red. The place looked unused; the wooden chairs, au naturel, with black seats, seemed brand-new, and were not uncomfortable. The grand piano and the clarinettist's stand were pitched below the stage on a level with the listeners.

'A decent audience,' John whispered.

The dozen double rows were fullish, but with strangers. None of the regulars at local concerts, that nucleus of well-to-do music-lovers appeared here. The people talked, not exorbitantly, turned round to widen the ambit of conversation, seemed much at home. John would have judged them as attenders at musical festivals, male-voice choir or brass-band concerts only. He listened to the strong female voice behind.

'I sent her some to rub on.'

'And it worked?'

'Like a charm. It might have been coincidence, but she's not bothered about that. So that's two of us it's set right. My shoulder had been giving me gyp for weeks.'

'And what did you say it's called?'

'Dog-oil.'

'Dog-oil? Where did you buy it? At the vet's?'

'From that herbalist on Bridge Street.'

That placed the audience. Stella had been all ears. She smiled at him, and he found the smile delicious. He felt pride in the appearance of his companion, wife.

Two minutes after the half-hour a man appeared, leaned on the piano, welcomed them, saying how delighted he was at the size of the turn-out. Even while he talked people continued to trickle in so that the door steward had to place an extra row of chairs. The noise of this did not deter the speaker, who informed them how privileged they were to entertain two such distinguished professional musicians. There was a treat in store they would remember all their lives.

This seemed to John naïve but essentially praiseworthy. Here a man could say what no one would dare in a more sophisticated venue.

'Who's that?' Stella asked, when he'd finished.

'No idea.'

'The headmaster.' The man on Stella's left had no compunction about giving them information. 'Name's Jenkins.' Their informant looked surprised to be thanked.

George Paxton and Michael Alexander entered in evening dress, which suited Michael's thin elegance but gave Paxton something of the air of a nightclub bouncer. They settled immediately to work on the Grand Duo Concertant of Weber, playing with gusto, Michael now and then almost overpowering his partner. They disappeared once the last movement was over, to considerable applause.

'What do you think of that, then?' Stella asked John.

'Clever. Diploma music. Showing how brilliant they are.'

'Oh, dear.'

The dog-oil lady behind asked the man with her, her husband perhaps, for his opinion.

'It looks a bit odd,' he ventured.

'What does?'

'A big chap like, blowing away at his little instrument. He's like a baby sucking a titty-bottle.'

The wife disapproved with a sniff of this criticism, but to John and Stella the comparison seemed not without validity.

Paxton, tailed by Alexander, returned, bowed perfunctorily. They played quietly their modest Stanford, three intermezzi, and then launched into Malcolm Arnold's Sonatina, both brilliantly, maddeningly on the chase for the other, whizzing.

'What do you make of that?' Stella asked again.

'Elves and fairies playing rugby football,' he said, mindful of the man behind, whose opinion was not this time can-

142

vassed. The audience applauded generously, and the head-master informed them that coffee and home-made cakes could be purchased at more than reasonable prices in the foyer.

They edged out and queued, sipped a boiling liquid, ate a sugared cake topped with cherry. Conversation spread widely but subdued, as if the audience knew better than to raise their voices at a classical concert. The headmaster moved amongst them, now gracious, now jovial. He bestowed a nod on Stella and John, befitting to welcome strangers. The school-bell rang to announce the second half before they were half-way down their scalding coffee. The headmaster vouchsafed a pleasant word to Stella as he held the door for her.

'What did he say?' John asked her.

'Something about "Music has charms except when it's Brahms", but he hoped not.'

'I thought as much.'

Michael Alexander appeared on his own and played, without announcement, two preludes and fugues from the '48'. These were not shown on the programme. Michael performed sitting upright, with clarity and careful strength. The audience lost its interval restlessness, listened to the full. When the applause had died, John said, 'By God, they're not tempering the wind to the shorn lamb here.'

'Why should they?' Stella returned.

'It's the back of beyond.'

She signalled him into silence, with wide eyes, listening hard.

'Didn't think over much of that.' Mrs Dog-oil from behind.

'What was it?' Another woman.

'Don't know. Wasn't Chopin, anyhow. I like Chopin.'

'Can you play the piano?'

'I had lessons.'

Paxton and Alexander sidled in and pitched into Debussy's first Rhapsody. Both appeared to advantage, clever and lively, engaged in music for the budding executant, a testing-out on their arrival at the Academy. Listeners frowned

143

slightly, as if puzzled, wondering what lay beneath the brilliant passage-work. Stella fidgeted, interest beginning to evaporate. The applause sounded loud. George Paxton had laid his instrument on the piano, and Michael stood wiping his hands on a clean, freshly ironed handkerchief before strolling across to exchange a word or two with his partner. The audience did not chatter while the soloists were in view, but watched, perhaps overcome by the sight of men of such accomplishments walking, using a handkerchief, talking like human beings. As the two stood together a scream of car brakes from outside brought sudden silence, then comment. Somebody had stopped a speeding car very close. Almost immediately the engine raucously revved; the car drove off, squealing again on accelerator and brake together. A burst of chat and interrogation spilt from the audience; Paxton and Alexander glanced towards the curtained windows. Paxton comically spread his arms, won a laugh. Michael returned to the keyboard. Stella glanced at her programme: Brahms, Clarinet Sonata in E flat major, Op. 120, No. 2. The audience settled down.

As the first movement began, and spread leisurely, John Taylor wagged an appreciative forefinger towards Stella, to assure her that this is what they had come to hear. He put his feet apart, lifted his face. His ease matched that of the players, and the mellow pleasure in their mastery seemed both instructive and perfect. The hall was full of rich sound, so that it was no longer part of a school, a utilitarian place, however new and tidy, but a fountain of late German romanticism. The music overlaid the plain walls with velvet, and the modernistic curtains were lost in a richness of plush embroidery, tassels of gorgeous sounds.

Outside, like blasphemy, they heard again the roar of an accelerator, the ferocity of brakes, a split-second silence, then right in amongst them an explosion of stunning intensity. The audience started to its feet, the players tailed off, clarinet first. All stared at the windows to the right of the auditorium. Ears throbbed with the violence. Stella shuddered.

One of the curtains had taken an uncouth shape, bulging

144

crudely into the small arcade. A car wheel spun a foot above the floor; slivers of glass shone dully flat on the parquet; they could smell petrol.

'Keep back,' a man in a suit shouted. 'Don't go near.'

Footsteps clapped outside, then a shriek answered a shout. The headmaster had joined the man in the suit. The soloists stood at the front, not together, faces shocked, snatched from the broad beauty of Brahms's maturity to this smash of noise. A young policeman ran in from the back of the hall.

'Keep back. Danger of fire.'

He lifted the curtain. They saw the wrecked bonnet, the blind-frosted windscreen, the twist of a wrecked mud-guard, the free-moving drunken wheel. Glass crunched under the constable's feet. Metal spars tenuously held together from the window drunkenly lolled across the car.

'We can get at him from this side,' a voice called from the darkness. 'Keep them well back.'

The man in the suit spoke to the policeman, and began to draw the other curtains to give light outside. The audience could see little but their own reflections in the polished black surfaces on either side of the grotesquely wrecked car, but already the chill of the night raked the hall. The head-master held a watching position; the caretaker arrived at the double with a fire-extinguisher which he handed over, and immediately trotted out.

'Move to the back of the hall, please, or just outside,' the constable ordered. 'And then don't wander about. Just stand still.'

The headmaster repeated the order and people reluctant-ly obeyed. The caretaker pushed against the flow with a second extinguisher, calling hoarsely. The opinions voiced by those about him suggested 'joy-riding', youths stealing and recklessly driving cars. They used the schoolyard, right on the main road, as a racetrack, a test ground for spectac-ular turns.

'Don't know why they don't lock the main gates,' one man muttered.

'They couldn't tonight. Had to let us in.'

'It's him.' A woman pointed at the headmaster. 'Can't tell him anything. Knows it all, and then some.'

'There's meetings and clubs every night of the week. That's why they can't.'

'They should have somebody on the gate.'

'Who'd pay for that? A watchman sitting out there this weather.'

A young policeman appeared and asked if any would volunteer as witnesses.

'Those near the windows. You won't have seen much. But it ties up. Could you file out this way?'

A good number stepped forward.

The headmaster spoke to the constable. The man seemed ubiquitous. He raised his hands standing on a chair.

'It's obvious that we can't continue with the concert. I apologise to you all for that, though I'm sure you'll agree we've had an evening of enjoyment and extraordinary quality, and a good cause, our orchestral fund, has been furthered. The thugs who are responsible for the curtailment, uh, of our pleasure have been arrested and taken off to the station. The car was stolen outside the campus, not from our car-park, so I can reassure you on those grounds.'

'Were they from this school?' A breathy voice.

'I believe not.' The head spoke with unctuous authority. 'Now, with the officer's permission, we can make our way home. My grateful thanks for your attendance. The end of the entertainment was not exactly what we envisaged, and for that my sincere apologies once again. Good night to you all.'

He stepped down, was immediately surrounded by questioners.

'Let's see if we can find Michael,' John said. Stella followed him into the chilling hall. One or two men stood round the gaping window, smashed bonnet. As the two entered, at the other end Michael emerged with Paxton and Rowena. John waited, touching Stella on the arm, halting her. The trio paused before the wreckage, speaking in low voices. Both men carried portmanteaux and Paxton his

146

instrument case. Rowena was the first to sight them. She slapped her companions and whooped.

'Well, well, well,' said Michael, turning. 'Look who's come.' They walked towards each other, slowly, almost formally. John held out his hand. 'What are you doing here?'

'Stella found out somehow.' John gabbled his explanation.

'I know Jack Jenkins. He asked us to use this as our first public appearance. He'd provide an audience, and we could make our début out of the way.'

'Was that necessary?'

'You can best judge that. Now you've heard us.'

Stella offered her congratulations.

'Pity we didn't finish the Brahms. But we rehearsed it thoroughly this afternoon. We were making a first-rate job of it.'

'When's the opening concert?'

'Next Thursday. In Newark. At the Music Society.'

The headmaster hurried across the hall towards them. Even at speed his movement appeared smooth, lubricated.

'Ah, gentlemen,' he began from ten yards away, 'I must apologise. Really. It hardly seems credible.'

'You were always ready with your bit of drama,' Michael ribbed him. 'You might have let us get through that first movement, though.'

They had not spoken for more than a few minutes when the caretaker arrived, asking permission to block the window once the car had been removed.

'Have the police done yet?'

'No. Nothing like. The CID people are coming. I shall be here all night. I've rung my wife to tell her.'

'Do you know the joy-riders?' the headmaster asked.

'No. Not from this end of the estate. The police knew 'em. Right rip-roarers, they said.'

The headmaster offered them coffee in his room. Alexander refused for them all. Jenkins thanked them effusively again, apologised, shook hands with all five. He made a little bow of his sleek head towards Stella, then ushered

147

them out into the yard. They parted without delay, finding the wind cold outside.

As John drove Stella away, she could see a small group of dark figures clustering near the accident. He hardly spoke, as though the evening's happenings had placed themselves beyond comment. Nearing Beechnall, he invited her in. They drank coffee.

'What did you think of that headmaster?' he asked.

'He made an unfavourable impression.'

'Too smooth by half?'

'Something like that.'

'And what about the players?'

'I was impressed,' she answered. 'Not that I'm any sort of expert.'

'Yes. It was an odd evening altogether.'

They talked, but not easily, as though the interruption of the Brahms had broken the social conventions between them. He did not mention her return, and she barely seemed awake.

'Not a good first week of term for them,' John struggled with the sentence.

'Not good for anybody.'

He muttered about terrorist explosions, and their effect. Both, young as they were, had lost their energy.

14

February demonstrated signs of spring.

'No snow this winter,' John informed Samantha, as he stood at the window. 'Look at the crocuses and snowdrops, and daffodils are nearly out.'

'It's nice, this little garden,' she said. 'Who looks after it?'

'The agents. I expect we all pay towards it in the rent.'

The girl sat down, crossed shapely legs, opened her pad, held Biro poised. She looked, he thought, quite radiant, healthy, cleanly attractive. He had enquired regularly after her mother, who, now back at home, was reported to be improving. Samantha talked freely to him, thanked him often for his help. He, for his part, even asked about Tim Thomas.

'I liked him,' he had said.

'Tell me why.'

'He seemed a thoughtful young man.'

'And you'd decided I'd choose a fly-by-night.'

'By no means. I pick him out as a bank-manager-to-be.'

'I don't see why not. He's clever.'

'I'm sure.'

This morning, in the pleasant weather, he felt cheerful, invited Samantha and her young man to his house to try the 'wine and cooking'. She accepted, said that Tim had liked him on their meeting. All smiles, he judged himself to have escaped any consequences of their affair. She, quite certain that Tim would do as she told him, fixed arrangements there and then.

On the day of their visit he left work early to prepare the meal. He had made sure they came on one of the two days his cleaners appeared so that the house would be spick and span.

He settled to his menus at four-thirty over a cup of tea when Michael Alexander rang. He sounded agitated.

'You're early,' John said. 'I thought your school didn't finish until about this time.'

'Four o'clock. I came straight home. It's Lise.' He did not continue.

'Is she ill?'

'No. But some bastard with the orchestra has written to say that Sebastian has been up to some . . . some foolery with a woman. Lise's very put out.'

'It came as a complete surprise, did it?'

'What do you mean by that?'

'There had been no hint before of anything untoward? As far as she knew?'

'Not as far as *I* knew. Though that's nothing. And when people are away from home for a month or more, well . . . But I'd heard nothing specific.' Michael coughed awkwardly. 'He had women enough when he was young. And these virtuosi get plenty of adulation. So.'

'And Lise?'

'She was badly upset. Torn apart. She had to ring somebody. And oddly she chose me. She'll have friends.'

'Has she started the opera?'

'Final rehearsals.'

'And when's Sebastian due back?'

'First week in March. They've been to Singapore, and are in Japan now, I think. Now what am I to do? For Lise?'

'Talk to her. Go down. Show a sympathetic face.'

'When? I'm working.'

'The weekend.'

'My Sundays are taken up with the bloody organ.'

'Give your assistant a break. If you were suddenly run over, he'd cope.'

'It's a clincher, John. I'm sorry to bother you about it. I'm like her, I had to say something to somebody. Not that you can cure anything any more than I can. You really think I should go down?'

'Make the offer.'

'You wouldn't go with me?'

'This weekend? Yes. If it's to her advantage or yours.' She wouldn't want him.

150

By the time Samantha and her Timothy had arrived he had been so busy that he had forgotten the Alexanders. He'd marked his diary for Saturday and Sunday with 'London?'.

The visitors made a nervous arrival, looking more like examination candidates than welcome friends. The girl held her cheek up to be kissed, and the young man thrust out a bony hand for shaking. They had come by bus so they accepted schooners of sherry which they held suspiciously, turning them in nervous fingers. He enquired after Mrs Oldham. Samantha described her mother's homecoming, her improvement.

'She's a thousand per cent better than she was. She's not normal, but she's back at work. Not so steady as she was when my father was alive. But it'd be too much to expect that, wouldn't it?'

'We decided,' Samantha continued, 'on the way here to get engaged. You're the first to know.'

'Congratulations.' Kisses and handshakings again. 'He didn't kneel down in the street to propose, did he?'

They would buy the ring, they had decided, this weekend and get married in the summer. Tim was already on the look-out for houses. 'It's a buyer's market,' she pronounced, 'and the bank gives really helpful terms for borrowing.'

'I don't think I shall be moved permanently this year, though May, June and July I shall be working in London.' Tim looked pleased with himself. 'So we'll need to get a move on if we're to marry in August.'

The young people ate heartily, especially the fiancé, who cleaned his plate, scoffed huge seconds.

'It has a long way to go down with him,' Samantha said. She slapped her own shapely, ample buttocks.

'You do the heart of this poor cook a power of good,' John told them. Three large courses had been demolished, and they were savaging the cheese dish and biscuit box. Champagne was being chilled outside. John, flushed with wine, saw himself *in loco parentis*. Neither of the two had a father. John, in fact, was only two years older than Tim.

151

They packed the dish-washer laughing, took the Moët et
Chandon and ice-bucket into the living room. Samantha
had embarked on a roundabout and hilarious account of
how she had made her fiancé sell his motorbike. He had
done so reluctantly. Even in the evening's euphoria he
still seemed to baulk at the idea, shaking his head mourn-
fully.

'Will you have a car?' John asked.

'Yes,' said Samantha.

'No. Not yet.' These delivered together reduced them to
hysterics.

By now Tim Thomas sat on the floor at the feet of his
fiancée. From time to time he put up a hand and unselfcon-
sciously stroked her legs. The already short frock was
rucked high; her tights gleamed, yet her face held a serious
air of happiness, like a mother watching her child win a
race. John could not decide whether she was pretty or plain;
her body, the breasts, the glistening thighs, the green high-
heeled shoes painted her true attraction. Tim pulled down
her right hand, covering it with kisses. She caressed his
neck with red nails. They did not seem to mind that Taylor
watched, and Samantha even encouraged his voyeurism, by
inviting him to look what Tim was up to now. She balanced
precariously on the edge of her chair, frock rucked almost
up to her waist, hair tousled blondly over his upturned face.
Propriety asserted itself as she pushed him out of the way,
sat straighter.

'Timothy Thomas,' she said, schoolmistress-stern.
'You're drunk.'

He drew himself straight, stood on his feet, holding on to
the table.

'Yes, I admit it. But, then, so are you.'

He staggered out to the lavatory. They could hear his
progress up the stairs.

'He's a marvellous man,' she said, suddenly sober. 'His
father died when he was only eight. He's been his mother's
boy all his life, and he's only just finding out how to live and
enjoy himself.'

'He's doing well at the bank?'

152

'Oh, yes. This three months in London is to introduce him to some new business schedules. He's a whiz with computer programmes already. They think highly of him.'

'Where does he come from? Is he local?'

'Not too far. Just outside Leicester.'

'And his mother still lives there?'

'She died last year.'

'How old was she?'

'I'm not sure. Sixty, perhaps. His father was forty-two when he died.'

'Both young. You never met them, I suppose?'

'No. He has a sister, but she's up in Scotland.'

'Is he in good health?'

'Yes. He's very tall, isn't he?'

They talked, freshly, friendlily until Tim returned humming. John gave a long-winded, broken account of the car smash at the clarinet recital. The listeners' eyes opened wide. At the end, Samantha asked, in a childish voice, 'What did your wife think?'

'She took it in her stride. As part of the evening's entertainment.'

'And is that typical of her?'

'I don't know. I can't guess how people will act in very unusual circumstances.'

Tim questioned him about Stella. Alcohol had blunted his diffidence. He congratulated John on his house, solemnly saying that he couldn't understand how a woman could desert such a comfortable, beautiful place.

'There speaks Mr Collateral,' Samantha mocked.

Tim pulled her from the chair so that they ended in a tangle on the hearth.

'Children, children,' John intoned.

They scrambled up, wondering if they had gone too far, and this spread a brief blight. They were cautious from now onwards, woodenly polite. John offered to put them up for the rest of the night, but at twelve-thirty Tim rang for a taxi. They seemed sober now, suspicious, babes in a darkling wood. John crept to bed in disappointment; he had hoped to please the young couple, but felt failure.

153

Next morning he found Samantha bright-eyed in the office, full of thanks, and began to be proud of himself again.

'I love that man,' she announced. 'He's a bit of a wimp, but pure gold. I've never met anybody like him before.'

John rang Stella to enquire how she was, and to explain that he'd be away over the weekend with Michael Alexander in London. He had, in fact, heard nothing more from Michael.

'I liked Lise,' Stella said.

'So did I. She could well do without this now they've started the opera.'

'It might do her good. Something else to think about. What's Sebastian like?'

'I don't really know him. He was a few years senior to me at school. Everybody admired him, even then.'

'But you stayed with them?'

'He was charming. Relaxed. Glad to see us.'

Michael Alexander rang John's office on Friday morning. He said he'd been undecided about their trip, but could they start early on Saturday morning and then, if it proved sensible, they could return the same day.

'What do you mean by early?'

'Seven a.m.'

'Have you arranged this with Lise? The last thing she'll want is two clod-hopping males suddenly thrusting themselves on her before dawn.'

'Speak for yourself.'

Lise seemed glad to see them, said that lunch was under way, settled them down to a pot of coffee in her sitting room. Michael sat disappointed, as if he'd expected a whirlwind of emotion. When Lise came back to them, excusing herself for the length of her absence, her father-in-law began to question her at once.

'Have you heard anything more from that bloody son of mine?'

'Two postcards, one from Singapore, one from Japan.' She had them ready, passed them over. Both were closely written in small writing, both interesting.

154

'Nothing more from our anonymous correspondent? I've told John here.'

Lise dropped her eyes. Her fingers intertwined.

'No. Nothing.'

'So we're no further forward?'

That went unanswered. Lise poured herself a half-cup, and stood, pot in one hand, cosy in the other, appealing to them.

'No, thank you,' John answered.

'So there's nothing more to be said?' Michael spoke provocatively.

'Probably not.'

When Lise went out to continue the preparation of lunch, Michael immediately turned on his companion.

'It looks as if we've wasted our time coming here.' He stamped a foot. 'I could have used the afternoon rehearsing with Paxton.'

'If she's coping, that's good. If not, it'll do her no harm to learn that you regard her highly enough to make the effort to see her. In your valuable spare time.'

'But if she's not going to say anything?'

'You're in your usual ruddy blush. Hang on. Give her time. If she wants to come out with something, she will.'

'I'm not so sure.'

Over lunch Lise talked freely about the opera. The company worked hard and had reached the stage where conductor, producer, singers had begun to lose faith.

'Is it good?' John asked.

'I'm as bad as the rest of them. We need an audience now to see whether we can affect them. Fortunately the producer's very level-headed. He reads us a lecture. Nobody knows, least of all Nick, whether this will be a success. But make sure that you're right on top of your part, so that you're capable of the small adjustments and switches we'll be pretty well forced into once we're in front of our audiences.'

'Does Nicholas Webb come in often?'

'Not much now. Once a week. Otherwise he's barred. Jules, the producer, told him that the work was public,

155

written down and revised, so it had to be taken out of his hands and put into those of people who could give it eighteen hours a day. They weren't friendly at all.'

'What did the conductor say? Whose side was he on?'

'Jules's, if anybody. We've got the notes right and now we're trying to fuse the action and the music. The music comes first with him, but he listens to the producer. Opera's difficult.'

'All compromise?' John asked.

'I suppose so. But compromise is the last word I'd apply to music like this.'

The men enjoyed the meal; and Lise their praise. She could laugh over her operatic difficulties, and once even demonstrated how she was expected to sing a tricky, very high line and stagger backwards.

'I'd prefer both feet on the ground and a solid grand piano to hang on to when I'm given stuff like that.'

'What do your experts advise?'

'Oh, Jules tells me to get into the habit. The trouble is I can't relax when I'm falling backwards.'

It did not seem a matter of life and death to her. Both men were convinced she'd manage. John helped Lise wash the dishes, while Michael upstairs played the piano. They could barely hear him through the closed doors.

'It's very good of you to drive Michael down,' she said.

'Not at all. He was worried, wanted to see if there was anything he could do for you.'

'Aren't you busy at this time of year?'

'Moderately. But it does me good to have a break, even when I'm up to the eyes in it. I guess Michael's more pushed than I am. He plays a church organ on Sundays, and he's doing these recitals with George Paxton.' He told her about the Brahms and the joy-riding.

When Michael appeared he seemed easier, as if the piano had eased his mind. Rubbing his hands together nervously, he sat down harder than was necessary. He made social conversation about London weather, state of garden flowers and his neighbours. He then forcibly criticised Paxton, who would not practise a piece towards perfection.

156

'He's very good, better than I am on the first half-dozen times through, but he won't take the last mile.'

'Perfectionist, you,' John said.

'No. Nothing of the kind.'

'Have you told him?' Lise asked.

'Yes, I have. Yes.' Michael rubbed his chin. 'I praise when I can, but sometimes . . .'

They all sat chatting without difficulty. John described how bad times in industry both provided him with, and deprived him of, work. Michael set out what he thought music-teachers in schools could do for pupils with no great talent or interest. Lise described how she spent her spare hours.

Michael Alexander, in a pause, grabbed the bottom of his sleeves, dragged on them, perched straighter and said in an unusually soft voice, 'Lise.' She smiled at him encouragingly. 'I don't want to raise matters out of turn, but what brought us up here was this Sebastian business. If you don't want to talk about it, just say so and that'll be that. But I don't want the chance to help you to go by default.'

He spoke quietly, but clearly. He had the look of a broadcaster making a moral point against hectoring opponents.

'Just say the word, and that will be it.'

'Thank you for coming,' Lise said. 'It's good for me to know that there are people who will go out of their way to support me.'

'If you like,' John interrupted, 'I'll trot outside while you chat. I'm . . .'

'No,' Lise answered. 'There's no need. You know about it.'

'But I don't want to be in your way.'

'You heard what the lady said,' Michael warned oddly, with a grin, like a wicked pantomime uncle.

They were silent for a few moments.

'It's like this,' Lise started, nodding at her father-in-law. 'When I rang you – when was it? last Wednesday? – I felt absolutely desperate. I was tired. I'd given a recital and had to come home late, and spent the next day slaving at rehearsal, so I was shattered. I'd had the letter on Monday,

I think, but with all the work I'd somehow kept it at bay. I'm not saying I put it entirely out of my mind because I didn't. I didn't sleep well that first night. But I came home that evening, Wednesday, about five. I dropped down on the settee,' she waved towards the place where John was sitting, 'with a drink, oh, it would be nearly six o'clock, and then it was that it hit me.'

She paused, pointed again towards the settee, kept the men waiting.

'When I sat down, I was fagged out, and miserable, with this letter at the back of my mind, but coping. I'd poured myself a weakish drink. I'd turned the immersion heater on for a bath. I'd decided what to eat, had taken it out of the fridge. A minute later I was, oh, out, incapacitated.'

They did not speak.

'It was a kind of pain in my chest and shoulders, but I knew it wasn't a heart-attack or anything like that. That would have been more violent, I think. This was as if I'd collapsed. I was overcome with a sense of everything running down and with no chance of recovery. I knew for certain that for the rest of my life I'd be good for nothing. I wouldn't be able to sing again, or teach. But worse, I wouldn't be able to be a wife again, or a friend, even a person able to go down to the shops. My will was broken. I was nothing but pain and uselessness with no opportunity to escape.'

'Have you ever felt like this before?' Michael asked.

'I've been depressed many times. Ours is a very up-and-down business. You get panned by the critics, or you don't perform as well as you know you can, and you feel bad. But this was much worse. I suppose the letter, the recital, the rehearsals all came together and took their toll.'

'And what happened?'

'I just sat there.' Again the finger pointed at John's settee as if the exact location held crucial importance. 'I don't know for how long. Perhaps for twenty minutes, half-an-hour, though it seemed much longer. I had a bath. I don't know how. And I started to cry. The whole world had turned against me. When I finished weeping I mixed myself a drink and rang you. It does good sometimes to tell people.'

'Did you feel better?'

'Not immediately, no. I kept having crying jags. I didn't eat much or drink much. I went to bed earlyish. And in the end I slept.'

'Did you contact anyone else?'

'I tried to get hold of Francesca Bayles. She was at college with me, and we've kept in touch. She's a motherly soul, but she was on holiday. I felt awful the next day. We rehearsed but I was dead as a doornail. I just dragged myself through. Nobody noticed much. I said I was off-colour, time of the month. By the following day, Thursday, I began to see I could just about manage, at least for the present. When he comes back,' she broke off, pursed her lips, 'if he comes back, then it may be a different story. I don't know. But for the present I can put up with it.'

'That's good,' John said.

'Well, yes. Especially as the first reaction was so violent. It seemed then as if nothing could ever be right again.'

'That might have been your salvation,' Michael murmured, judicially.

'Yes. I've thought about that. Perhaps I'm shallow. Nothing very deep, lasting. A little storm and back to normality.' Lise laughed nervously. 'I don't feel on top of the world, but . . .'

'Would you like us to stay overnight?' Michael asked.

'Not unless it's inconvenient otherwise. There's no real necessity. But if you wish . . .'

'No. It's you we're considering. We've come prepared for either contingency. We'll stay if it helps you. Otherwise, we'll leave you to it.'

Lise did not answer but stared again at the offending settee. John left the decision to Michael who himself seemed distant, half-listening only.

'You think you'll manage? Then we'll go back tonight. About six, if that's all right for you, John. As long as you're sure?'

'Thank you. Yes.'

159

At least five times in the next two hours Lise expressed gratitude. She also enquired after Stella, saying how much she had liked her.

'There's something about her. I don't know what it is but I really enjoyed her company.'

'I think that's right.'

'Is there any chance of the pair of you getting together again?' Michael asked.

'We keep meeting. That's the most obvious strategy. We'll gradually come to see what we want.'

'You don't know for certain?' Michael pressed.

'No. I can't forget what it was like in those last weeks before she went. It was hell.'

'For you both?' Lise.

'Yes. Probably worse for her. She suffered from depression, and I guess could do little about it. I didn't know what was going on. I thought I'd blotted my copybook with her some way, but I wasn't sure how.'

'She doesn't seem a moody sort of girl,' Michael glossed.

'No. And it made it worse that I tried to be civilised about it. We didn't have blazing rows. Perhaps it would have been better if we had. I was miserable as sin, but what she felt, God alone knows.'

'Is she better?'

'She claims so. I think she now tends to put it all down to chemistry, and that's righted itself. I'm not so sure that I'm not in some way to blame.'

'In what way?' Lise.

'Other women?' Michael, expansively.

'No, not that. Not at that time. When she left me, yes. It hurt my pride. My wife is mine. She's no right to clear off. So I had to prove to myself that I wasn't utterly repulsive to the female sex. But when she was at home, no. I'm not making out it was a penance.'

'She's offered to come back, hasn't she?' Lise asked. 'She made the first move?' He did not answer. 'Why didn't you respond?'

'It was awkward. I was caught up in another relationship that I was greatly enjoying.'

'Thoroughly selfish, in other words?' Lise's voice cut sharply.

'Yes. That's so.'

'And that relationship now?'

'It's over, done with.'

'So you're now considering Stella again?'

Lise's questions probed rudely. John wondered why he bothered to answer, what business it was of hers, but ascribed her tartness to her own harried feelings. She looked calm enough, hands in lap.

Michael paid little attention to them. He sang to himself, quietly, purely, in a high tenor, near-falsetto, every word crystal-clear. With his right hand he slowly conducted himself. John recognised the song: Tom Moore's 'Oft in the Stilly Night', not music he'd easily connect with this singer. Michael's eyes, half-shut, smiled. The mouth moved cunningly, careful of each syllable:

> The words of love once spoken.
> The eyes that shone
> Now dimmed and gone
> The cheerful hearts now broken.

John and Lise looked at each other in a conspiracy not to interrupt the song. Michael barely noticed them. They allowed him to complete the song, to appear like one tiptoeing through an empty banquet hall alone. When he had finished he let out a sigh, and smiled at them wanly.

'What was that in aid of?' John asked.

'I'm beginning to appreciate sentimentality. For the first time in my life.'

'Don't believe it,' Lise said.

'Which bit, the first or second?'

Michael delivered a lecture on popular song. They were not sure he had convinced himself. After this, though they tried hard enough, they had less to say for themselves. Slightly earlier than they had arranged, having refused food, they set out for Beechnall. En route they discussed the visit.

161

'Did that do any good?' Michael asked.

'Yes. She was glad to see you. She doesn't like me much.'

'That's not so.'

'Well . . .' A comical demurring.

'Why do you say that, John?'

'The way she talks to me. But I'm a change. And it meant you could get there in goodish time. I'm pretty sure she was pleased that you'd given up your time to visit her.'

'But the way she said she could cope? It sounded cold-blooded.'

'She may be trying to convince herself. I don't know her well enough to say.'

They repeated this conversation, slightly altered, at least four times on the journey. Each version grew more unreal, as if they discussed a fictional character from a novel in a language they could read only moderately well.

John dropped his passenger, drove home and, stiff from the journey, walked down to his local pub, the Lord Nelson. Tonight it glittered, rocked noisier than the night when he and Michael had met Paxton. Roars of cheering and laughter tore the other bar.

'Some sort of prize draw,' a sad-faced man explained.

'Haven't you bought tickets?'

'No. I've something better to do with my money.'

The beer tasted sour; John dispelled his hunger with crisps and a hot pie. The sad fellow seemed disposed to talk. He came in, he confessed, every Saturday and Sunday. His wife – they had been married thirty-two years – had died on Christmas Day in hospital. Yes, it had been expected, was a happy release. He talked on of the scattered family. No, he came from Birmingham originally, and worked in electronics. His wife had been eight years older than he. He'd been twenty-one when they married. It was a biggish difference, but it had worked out well enough. Hobbies? Yes, he made and mended furniture. He called it 'repro stuff', and had a workshop with lathes, built on to his house. No, his wife hadn't begrudged the many hours he'd spent there. She had her own concerns. They came to the Nelson occasionally, once every month or six weeks. He missed her. No, he had a hot meal at midday at work, but the house was quiet when he got back. They had never said anything very interesting, as far as he could remember, bits of neighbourhood tittle-tattle, but it felt like a morgue now. His children, three married daughters, were very good, but they all lived away, the nearest in Hull. They'd invited him up to stay, but he wasn't going to be a burden to anybody.

In spite of his facial expression the man's voice rang cheerfully enough. He allowed John Taylor to buy him a drink.

'You're still at work?' John asked.

'Thankfully. But even in a big concern like ours they're standing people off. And not in ones and twos either. My turn might come. I shall get redundancy pay. I shall be able to live. I hope so because I shan't have much chance of another job at fifty-three.'

'You won't be pleased to retire?'

'I shan't. It gets me up in the morning. The job's quite interesting. I've good friends there, though I never meet them outside the factory. Perhaps that's a comment on me. But what shall I do? The chairs. My garden. My weekend evenings here. I think if I'm not careful it'll be bloody telly all day and night.'

'Foreign holidays?'

'Never appealed much. Neither to Eileen or me. We usually had a fortnight somewhere. Scarborough, More-cambe, Scotland. Yes, we had one holiday in Newquay. But it was a long way. Eileen wasn't keen on car travel. When I was a boy we went to North Wales.'

'You go to work by car?'

'Yes. It's a bit silly, because there is a bus service. Doesn't take ever so much longer, with these hold-ups. I'll have a rethink. When I know one way or the other about my work. And when I've come to terms with Eileen's death. I'm in limbo now.' The man smiled, then frowned, at his word.

John watched him nod, breathe regularly as if preparing for a test. 'I've just been to visit a lady,' he said slowly, 'who thinks her husband's committing adultery.'

'I often wonder about that,' the man said.

'Go on.' Nothing. 'What do you think?'

'Some make a life-and-death affair of it. And others pass it off as if it's nothing.'

'Why's that?'

'Well,' the man frowned again, writhed slightly, 'it's only putting a part of a man's body into a woman's. It gives you pleasure. I'm not saying it doesn't. I've had a good deal of enjoyment out of it. We kept it up until Eileen's last illness. But it's the ideas and feelings we attach to it. We don't like other people trespassing on what's ours. We've bought it, or earned it, in one way or the other, and we resent other people making free with it. Depends on how you look at it. At one time, if a man kissed a woman out of turn or held hands with her it caused a scandal.'

'Sex is a very powerful instinct,' John said solemnly. 'Perhaps because of the procreating of children.'

'Yes. It varies. And there are always those who hanker after forbidden fruit.'

'What would you have felt if your wife had gone off the rails?' The feeble metaphor excused the incivility of the question. John hoped so.

'It never arose.' The man had no objection to the query. 'She wasn't that sort of woman. She had plenty to occupy her. We enjoyed it when we had it. I don't suppose it crossed her mind.'

'Some man might have been attracted to her?'

'Possible. But she would soon have told him where to get off. That's what I think. I don't know. We can't know. Every man or woman has his or her secrets. We didn't live the sort of life where sex was flung in our faces every minute. I mean, if a woman came flaunting herself to me, and I'd had one or two and thought I could get away with it, I'd be as bad as the next man. Opportunity wasn't there, the way we lived.' The man looking up, leering. 'I suppose you're not married.'

'Separated.'

'Why was that, then?' Sharp. Rudeness answered by rudeness.

'We just couldn't get on. Everything we said and did seemed to jar.'

'Possible,' the man admitted, chewing on the word. 'How long had you been married?'

'Three, four years.' He wondered why he answered so vaguely. He knew to the minute.

'And you were scrapping all the while?'

'No. The last few months.'

At this the man lost interest, or retired with his own thoughts. He lifted his glass, barely wetted his lips, and returned it to the table. He did this twice more, not using the handle. Finally, sluggishly he returned himself to the conversation.

'It's habit,' he said. 'I knew a man, decent chap in many ways, who couldn't keep his hands off women. Always chasing them. Didn't seem to be able to help himself. He'd a very nice wife. Good-looking girl and pleasant. And it cost him no end of money. I think, with me the money had more pull than sex. I suppose it's as if I'd taken up, say, snooker, and found I was good at it, I'd have spent more and more time with it. But as it is I've barely played the game, so it's no skin off my nose to say, "No." '

The man now began a series of anecdotes about acquaintances. Sexual predators, cuckolds, games-players, gamblers. He took pleasure in his stories, like a teacher amusing his class, but drew no moral from them. One followed another in a steady succession. This surprised John who'd judged the man rather taciturn at first, but now found him a dedicated tattler. The voice seemed all, like that of a man repeating obvious instructions or ordering a dull commodity in a shop, but he showed determination, moving from one story to the unconnected next.

He bought John a half-pint and ended with his father's sister, a woman who 'enjoyed bad health'. His listener had no idea whether the word play was intentional. Years later, it appeared, the man had learnt that his uncle had a fancy woman, about whom he and his father used to argue during the old man's last illness. Was she the cause of the aunt's ailments, or the result? The voice with its faint West Midlands

165

twang, had little expression, but the speed and vocabulary somehow conveyed interest, enjoyment. He gave an account of a friend, a footballer, who never seemed to do anything on the field, but then, like a ghost, would appear with the ball the other side of a blocking opponent, or slip a perfect pass as if it had bounced by chance off his boot.

'What do you do for a living?' the man asked. 'If you don't mind my asking.'

'I'm an accountant.'

'There's money to be made there.' He then lugubriously quoted reports on the radio which claimed young qualified accountants could not find work. John gave such explanation as he could.

'Would you advise it as a career? Nowadays?'

John talked about his work. The man listened, said a few words about his grammar school, which he'd left at sixteen. In the middle of a sentence of self-condemnation – he hadn't known which side his bread was buttered, and his parents had been no help – he looked at his watch, drained the last inch of beer, stood, said he must go.

'I haven't enjoyed a conversation like this for long enough. It's a real exchange. All they're on about is darts and dominoes and football. I hope to see you again.' He marched, without haste, out of the room, speaking to no one.

The place reverted to noisy chaos next door, with a few coarse groups in the lounge. John amazed himself. A nameless man with his flat voice had captured his interest for three-quarters of an hour. The man, John wished he had named himself, was clever, careful, had a kind of rough skill in talking, artless mastery with his bits of tales, his unexpected banalities, and these had caused his listener to put himself aside. He would tell Stella about the evening. But would he come in at the same time tomorrow or next Friday, make a point of reunion? John could not answer himself. This boon, this slight stroke of good fortune (the man would have expressed it thus), had served a perfect purpose, concluded the inconclusive day in London, rounded a flat weekend.

John finished his drink, said goodnight to the people on the next table, to their surprise, and walked home in cold drizzle, dark streets, humming.

15

John Taylor walked to his front gate. The weather shone spick and span as his house. March had come in like a lamb, and continued in mildness. Yesterday a cleaning firm had rid his rooms of dust, hoovered the carpets, squirted the furniture with environmentally friendly polish. The sun glinted through fast clouds, as his next-door neighbour's mobile clashed faintly, like agitated milk-bottle tops. Uncertain how to spend his afternoon, he pushed indoors and settled to the arts pages of the *Financial Times*. He had lunched out frugally, and had made no plans for the rest of the day.

To his surprise he did not altogether welcome this period of leisure, because he was unsure how to occupy himself. He read a book review, plainly written, praising the novel in question, but making it clear to him that he did not want to read that or anything like it. Feeling rather pleased with this decision, accounting it intellectual, rational and not philistine, he went out to the kitchen to make a cup of coffee. Once he had filled and switched on his kettle, he considered why he needed a drink to complete his pleasure. It demonstrated, he concluded, his mental state. He found it difficult to spend leisure to his satisfaction. One of the secretaries, not Samantha, had told him that she could not just sit to watch television; she needed to use her hands, to knit. 'I don't feel I'm wasting my time, then,' the girl had said. John had nodded at her, but enigmatically. She showed none of this dedication at work.

He telephoned Stella, found her at home. Yes, she was busy. Yes, she would spare him an hour this evening. He talked about the man in the Lord Nelson, and she said she'd accompany him there. She had a whole lot of marking to do, and hadn't touched the flat with a duster for weeks. They'd meet at eight. He'd excuse her now.

Pleased, a man of decisive action, he made his coffee and stood stirring it.

He looked up his garden. Crocuses bloomed, earlier than usual. The trees stood leafless. No blossom as yet on pear or cherry, but his camellia sported its first exotic red flowers. He started in surprise, put his coffee on the draining board.

On the cross-path at the top of the garden an eastern dancing-girl performed, gently moving from side to side, but remaining on the spot. Occasionally she extended an arm, but always kept with small hand-movements the shawl, which covered her head, in place. He could hear no sound of music, so clearly she did not carry a radio. She undulated from the hips, gracefully, with little thought of show, merely for her own satisfaction.

The county council, he cynically told himself, has decided to delight selected tax-payers with oriental dancers, ladies from the zenana, as a gesture in these days before spring decorated the gardens, made them beautiful of themselves.

John watched the graceful movements of the girl, the swaying, her hands stretched with a peculiar horizontal beauty. He wondered where she'd come from; perhaps she had clambered over the garden wall from the next street, but that seemed an uncouth, awkward manner of entry to one dressed with such care, and who danced with such elegance. She must have walked in from the road, through the back gate, past the kitchen window, but he'd heard and seen nothing. He looked along the garden, wondering if the dancer could see him, but she continued with her slight, delicate oscillation, quite preoccupied.

In the end, curiosity got the better of him, and he let himself out of the kitchen door without too much noise. Then he walked slowly along the path towards the girl. She lifted her head, making sure with her left hand that her hair was covered. She wore trousers caught in at the ankle. She must be a Muslim.

As he approached, she moved away along the cross-path and edged down the second on the far side of the garden.

169

She did not seem to be trying to escape, only to keep a seemly distance between them. He stopped. She did likewise, holding on to her headgear.

'Can I help you?' he asked.

'Do you live here?' she replied.

'Yes.'

'That is your house?'

'Yes.'

She spoke quietly, the accent chi-chi, but not markedly so. She did not smile, and kept her face half-turned from him.

'Is there anything you want?' he asked.

'Is this your house?' On his second affirmative she spoke slightly more confidently. 'Will you give me a drink of water?'

'Yes. Surely.'

He turned, walked normally towards the house, stepped in but left the kitchen door open. She followed him inside. He lifted a glass from the cupboard, filled it, handed it to her. She looked modestly about her as she sipped.

'Thank you.'

She placed the glass, still two-thirds full, on the draining board. Her sandals were gold, and she wore no stockings. Her eyes stretched large, and her face was slightly pitted with smallpox scars.

'You will show me your house?' she asked.

He gestured her towards the passage to the main rooms. She crossed in front of him, looked about her in the hall, moved, danced without haste into his sitting room, where she walked slowly around, pausing, touching nothing, but lifting her hands.

'It is heaven,' she said. She looked to the ceiling. She made another leisurely circuit of the room, nodding at the plants, the flowers by the windows.

'This is heaven. I have been here before.'

'I don't think so,' he contradicted her without force.

'How long have you lived here?' she asked.

'Four years.'

'I have been here. In these rooms.'

170

'It's possible.'

She walked out in front of him, and into the dining room. She seemed certain of herself now, almost like one dispensing hospitality to a visitor.

'Where do you live?' he asked.

'I have lived here, but now . . .' She named quite clearly a street not far away. 'Carborn Close.'

He wondered how old she was. In her teens. Her clothes were too voluminous for him to judge the development of her body. She paused in front of the piano.

'Can you play it?' she asked.

'Yes. After a fashion. Can you?'

'When I lived in London I had lessons.'

'But not now? Sit down and play.'

'No. You play to me,' she begged, backing away towards the hearth.

John sat and tinkled two lines of a Bach invention.

'Ah,' she said. 'Ah.'

'You play now.'

She took the seat, and jangled the keys. The noise made no sense. She had forgotten if ever she had learnt anything. She continued with the uneven discords; he stood by the door pretending not to notice.

'It is heaven,' she said, rising. 'I have been here before.' She came towards him without fear. 'Show me the rest of the house,' she ordered. He motioned her forward, then followed her upstairs.

'Why did you come to live here?' he asked. 'Why did you leave London?'

She stopped on the stairs, turned, adjusted her headgear.

'To live with my father and my stepmother.'

'Have you any brothers or sisters?'

'Six. Brothers. They do not like me.'

'How old are you?'

She drew herself up with dignity before she answered.

'I am thirteen,' she said, 'but I am not yet born.'

She turned, leading him upwards to the landing where she stood in front of a picture. John felt bafflement, unable to account for her appearance. Perhaps she spied out

171

houses for her burglar brothers; usually one blamed casual window-cleaners, but . . . The girl was staring still at the picture, a seascape by moonlight.

'What's your name?' he asked.

She murmured something he did not catch. Again he asked and the second time he still did not grasp. It began with 's'.

'This is the moon,' she said, quite clearly. She was pointing at the picture. 'My friend, when I was in hospital, used to show me the moon.'

'What hospital was that?' John asked. 'One in London?'

'Saxondale,' she answered. The local mental asylum.

'Are you still there?' he asked.

She laughed, a small uncertain cackle, slightly foreign, alien.

'No. I am here in your beautiful house.'

Again she led the way, opening doors into the bedrooms, once walking over to the windows to look down through net curtains into the street. She stood by the mirror in his room, removed her headshawl and, picking up his comb, began to straighten her hair. He remembered a friend whose father, a professor of morbid pathology, had created a scandal in one of the Arab Emirates by arriving early for his lecture to find his women medical students combing their loosened hair. This girl showed no embarrassment, but soon tired of her occupation. In the last upstairs room she sat down on the end of the bed as if weary, and then lay back. There was nothing voluptuous about the pose, nothing inviting. A childish experiment to satisfy curiosity.

'It is heavenly,' she said; then more strongly, 'I am confused.'

'Come along,' he spoke cheerfully, 'some of us have things to do.'

She got up from the bed, at once but without speed, and walked back with steady confidence to his bedroom where she peered again at length into the mirror.

'That is not me,' she told him.

'It is,' he said and stood behind her so that she could see

172

both faces, hers brown and puzzled, his smiling, brick-red. She drew her shawl tighter.

'Downstairs,' he ordered.

She complied with the command but walked aside into the bathroom.

'It is heaven.'

'Strictly utilitarian,' he answered. He wondered if she understood. Her grammar and syntax had been correct.

Once they were back in the kitchen, she said, 'I would like something to eat.'

'Such as?' he asked.

'Something sweet.'

He sought out the biscuit tin, pulled off the lid.

'Not much of a selection,' he said. She helped herself to two, nibbled uncertainly. 'I'm afraid I shall have to get on now, so you'll have to go.'

'Can I walk again in the park?' He smiled at her word; certainly his garden had a tree or two in it. He opened the door for her, and she stepped outside. John returned to his abandoned *Financial Times*, which he read desultorily. He tried to make sense of the girl's visit, but could not. Presumably she was not right in the head, but her sentences held together and made grammatical sense. He returned to the kitchen, and looked out of the window. She stood in the yard. He waved; she beckoned him. As he opened the door, she walked in, as of right.

'Can I use the toilet?'

He pointed it out, but a moment later she called out to him.

'Where is the tissue paper?'

He showed her the toilet roll. She closed the door. Her headshawl lay on the floor. John returned to his newspaper. When she called out again after a few minutes he found her in the hall standing in front of the mirror.

'Do you go to school?' he asked.

'No. I do not.'

'What do you do all day, then?'

'I do nothing.' She giggled tentatively, and pulled the shawl forward to shade her face. 'I must go home.'

'You know the way?'

'I do.'

He led her to the front door.

'Goodbye,' he said. 'Come again if you want to.'

'Thank you.'

At the front gate she turned and made again for his garden.

'That's the wrong way,' he warned. 'You can't get out that way.' He pointed in the direction of Carborn Close. Obediently she let herself out of the front gate, leaving it slightly ajar. 'Be careful on the roads,' he said, as to a small child.

She walked away.

Puzzled, he looked round the hall, and then made his way into the garden. She had thrown the biscuits, one whole, one quarter-eaten, on to a lawn. He retrieved them, carried them to his compost heap, dropped them there. The air struck cold. That quarter of an hour, twenty minutes, with the strange girl, puzzled him. There had been no obvious madness about her, merely a childish belief in her right to move about his house, to ask for what she wanted, to speak as an equal. Muslim girls of her age did not usually thrust themselves into male company of a different race or religion. Perhaps she had escaped from her father's, her stepmother's custody. She was one of the inmates of a mental institution forced back into the community? To walk about the quiet rooms of his house, out of the way of boisterous, uncomprehending, shouting brothers, baffled parents, explained her restrained delight. Ought he to have turned her loose in the streets? He did not know. She had not appeared vulnerable. The adjective he would have chosen would have been 'distant'. She moved around his possessions with quiet pleasure, in some world of her own devising.

John told the story to Stella as they walked from his house to the Lord Nelson later that evening.

'And what did you make of it?' she asked.

'I think she must have been mentally deranged in some way.'

'Go on.'

'But she was so gentle. She made her demands: Show me round, give me a drink. Politely. Like a well-brought-up child. They were not the sort of things one adult would say to a stranger in our society.'

'Suppose she had been English and dressed in ordinary clothes?'

'I asked myself that while she was walking round. The clothes seemed beautiful, perhaps because they were unusual. They were gold and patterned, but not new. And her headscarf was white.'

'Silk?'

'I don't think so. The fact that she came from a background different from mine led me to misjudge perhaps. As far as I understand it Muslims keep their daughters under control. They are keen on single-sex education. They believe in arranged marriages. So that puzzled me. In any case it's not safe for girls of any age to go wandering in and out of houses with strange men. There are odd enough people about on the streets.'

'She made no sexual advances towards you? Even innocent ones?'

'No. Nor could I say she treated me as a father-figure. I was there. I owned the place. I could give her a guided tour. Once she was used to me, she acted as if she had bought a ticket at the door.'

'Was she attractive?'

'Not really. Her face wasn't beautiful, and the rest of her was bundled up in clothes.'

'What if she comes back?'

'I'd give her ten minutes. Talk to her. I didn't understand sentences like "I haven't been born yet". It may be a normal, perfectly acceptable metaphor in her language.'

Stella spoke without warmth, as if he'd made up a story to enhance the interest of his own life. They sat quietly at the table he'd occupied on his last visit. The stranger was not in, this evening. John recognised none of the people in the room.

'We don't seem to be getting any forwarder on this

175

reconciliation business,' he ventured. His language sounded suitably indecisive, at least to himself.

'No.' Stella did not look at him.

'We must make our minds up,' he said.

'Must we?' She did not hide the hostility.

'Have you changed your mind, then?'

'I made the offer months ago. And you've vacillated. Ever since. I think we've run out of time. You can't be altogether keen.'

'That's not very friendly.'

'I'm willing to be friends,' Stella answered, sharply. 'But not to treat the subject of our reconciliation as a topic like the cup final or the election result or conservation or the ozone layer. To be aired from time to time.'

'You've given me up?' John asked.

'You've given yourself up. You don't want me back.'

'When you talk like this,' he said, 'it reminds me how I felt just before you left.'

'I'm sure.'

'I must say,' he began, 'I must say I'm disappointed.'

She smiled, weakly, refused another drink so that they left the pub almost at once. They walked back to her car in silence. Outside his house he invited her in for coffee. She refused, offered a hand and a word of thanks, and drove off.

He stood perplexed.

16

In the brightness of an April Saturday morning Stella received a phone call from Lise Martin-Alexander.

'May I come to see you?' Lise asked in due course. 'If you're sure it won't interrupt anything?'

Stella, in fact, had been writing out applications for the headship of her department. The present senior man, a bachelor, was making what he called a parallel move, one with neither promotion nor advantage, and he had surprised her by taking her to one side and advising her to apply for his position. She did not trust him entirely, thought he was efficient, if idle, and felt certain that he had resented her infrequent criticisms of him. She asked him at once why he made the suggestion.

'You know the school and the department better than anyone else here. Your teaching is good. You know what's wanted. You've introduced several novelties.' He paused on the word, looking on her expression with suspicion. 'You're due for promotion somewhere. But if you don't believe me, go and ask the head.'

'There are three people senior to me.'

'And just look at them. Ask Martin' – he usually referred to the headmaster by a rude sobriquet rather than by his first name – 'and put an application in. He'll have to advertise it, I guess, but I'm not even sure about that.'

Stella felt both pleased and uncertain. Peter Booth was a devious creature, restless, fond of stirring the waters. He would enjoy troubling her life, or putting the headmaster, whom he disliked, into an awkward position. She wondered how many of her colleagues he had advised to apply.

She made an appointment with the headmaster.

Martin Wakefield ruffled his thin hair. Yes, he had already sent off an advertisement though it had not yet appeared.

Yes, Mr Booth had suggested that she was a strong candidate, and he agreed. He would certainly consider seriously her application if she cared to put it in. She would understand that he could promise nothing, of course. Posts, especially senior posts, in well established sixth-form colleges were highly regarded and eagerly sought after so that the competition would be keen, stiff. But, but they were all pleased with the work she had accomplished (Wakefield relished such words) for them, and he advised her to set about her application this weekend. He thanked her courteously, though for what she could not make out.

Stella wrote off at once to two of her referees, Booth would be the third, but she shivered at her own uncertainty. She did not consider her chances very great, but it was experience. What worried her most she recognised as feelings akin to those of the blackest stage of depression: the world turned against her; nobody appreciated the efforts she made; nemesis waited. In the veiled morning sunshine, her weekend shopping done on Friday, she worked out her CV, and tangled with the letter of application.

The rough draft was half-corrected when the doorbell rang. She tucked her papers into a neat folder and went to greet Lise.

Two figures through the glass.

'Stella, this is my husband, Sebastian.'

She took them through to her dining room, switched on the percolator.

'It's not quite warm enough to sit outside,' she instructed them. They observed the garden through her french windows. Blossom bunched, sud-thick, pure white on the cherry trees. The arrival of an unexpected visitor in no way threw Stella, to her surprise. She looked the pair over; Lise seemed radiant.

'Sebastian can't stop,' Lise instructed Stella. 'But I insisted that he came in. He has to run his father out to East Bridgford to visit an old friend.'

'Lise was full of you,' Sebastian said, 'when she came back last time. All about the lost child. And your husband had a squint at my financial affairs. So I feel I know you.'

He spoke without force, a tall, slim, impressive man who brushed at his hair with a flat palm. He smiled at his wife, held her hand without embarrassment. 'And I'm paying no attention to what Lise says my sainted father thinks of you.' Stella blushed; it sounded awkward on his part.

'What are you doing here? Shouldn't you be singing tonight?'

'No.' Lise grinned. 'We have a five-day holiday. We've done two and a half weeks, and now they're going to reorganise the stage. Not just for our scenery. I think it's mainly electrical. But they've had it under way, under arrangement for long enough.'

'I've never heard the like,' Sebastian said.

'I guess,' Lise said, 'that there was a strong possibility that the whole thing might come to grief at the end of two and a bit weeks. They warned us it might be so. And then some wholesale alterations would start at the theatre. The electrical business was the prologue. But we had marvellous reviews . . . .'

'I read them,' Stella said.

'Yes. You sent me a lovely card. D.H. Lawrence as a young man. It cheered me when I was on top of the world. And people kept buying seats.'

'That's not always the case even after rave reviews,' Sebastian glossed.

'We're subsidised, of course. I don't understand it at all. We lose money on every performance. But we shall now do another month. That apparently is unimaginable. We and the building contractors have to be out of the theatre by the beginning of September, but there is plenty of time for the alterations. And sponsors have taken us up. We're doing a week or two in Germany.'

'Where is it?' Stella asked. 'I've forgotten.'

'The Queen's. Not a usual venue for opera.'

Husband and wife talked of the opera as if they did not quite understand financial implications. Opera stars of the first and second magnitude were booked years ahead, so the authorities had descended – her own word – to the likes of Lise, but all this over eighteen months ago. She had

179

cleared her decks, and now had to do so again for the next month or more on account of the success of the venture.

'Is it a marvellous opera?' Stella asked.

'In a way.'

'Yes, it is. Nick Webb has a great deal going for him. They love old hands and young men in our culture, neglect people in their prime. He's lucky. He's talented. There's a first-rate libretto, and he's made the most of it.'

At the end of half an hour Sebastian said he must leave to chauffeur his father.

'He ought to have come round,' Sebastian said, almost waggishly, 'but he daren't because he was afraid Lise and I would be watching him. And you, of course.'

He and Lise kissed. He left jauntily, lightly bussing Stella.

'All's well with the Alexanders, I can see.' Stella laughed. The two women went into the kitchen, made coffee.

'Yes, it sorted itself out.' Lise pirouetted. 'I don't know how much you knew. About this anonymous letter. By the time Sebastian arrived home his father had warned him of what I had heard.'

They made their gingerly way back to the armchairs in the next room. Stella, trying to piece things together, preferred not to ask questions. Lise apparently took it for granted that her friend knew more than she did. It seemed wiser to allow her to spend her happiness as she wished.

'Have you brought your reviews with you?' Stella asked.

'No. I'm not quite so far gone in self-love.'

'My newspaper described your performance as "the finest piece of operatic singing in England in the past twenty years".'

'That can't be true.'

'Why can't it? Do you know the man? Is he a friend?'

'He is now. No, I hadn't met him before.'

'It's doing your career a power of good, I should think.'

'So my agent says. Enquiries galore. He wasn't keen on my leaving this big hole in the year just to perform an opera that might well pack up after a few nights.' Lise slapped her knees. 'Now, of course, he knew all along what a success I'd

180

be.' She laughed outright. 'And this little holiday has come just right. Sebby has a day or two off.'

'Are you singing? Practising?'

'No. Not yesterday. Not today. I'll start a few exercises tomorrow.' She burst through a complicated roulade, waving her hands around, caricaturing a diva, smiling and all teeth, but completing the tricky sequence of notes with power and formidable skill. 'How's that?' She laid a hand on Stella's arm. 'But best of all was sorting my husband out.'

'Go on, then.'

'I didn't know whether to raise the matter of this anonymous letter or not. I had thought I'd come to terms with it, could put it to one side, wait for Sebastian to do or say something first. But it didn't work out like that.'

'Why not?' Lise seemed to expect a question at this point. Stella supplied it.

'Father. Michael. He stirred the waters. He waited until he knew I'd be out at the opera house, and then rang.'

'Was that wise of him?'

'Wise, I don't know. Typical is more like it. He had to interfere. Partly to put Sebastian in his place. Partly because he probably thinks it best to be open, honest. Mostly because he likes to court trouble. There was no need for him to do anything.'

'You mean he should have left you to confront Sebastian or keep your mouth shut, as you chose.'

'Exactly. But that's not our Michael.'

Nor our Lise, either, Stella thought, remembering how she had blurted out that her father-in-law had confessed love for her friend.

'I see.'

'Sebastian waited up for me that night. I don't get home till eleven-thirty or later. Offered me cocoa, Horlicks, Ovaltine and good quiet questions about the evening's performance.'

'And was that unusual?'

'Yes. Well, yes and no. We're often not at home together. But I thought he'd just come back from this tour, and was pleased with himself, and showed it this way. He never said a word about the letter. He was really nice.' Lise poked a finger out. 'No, we didn't make love. I was too exhausted. He knew that. But he put his arms round me in bed. All very sedate and domestic. He was down before me next morning, brought me breakfast in bed about ten – I wasn't intending to get up very early – and the newspapers. He cleared the dishes. I had a bath, came down at leisure. He'd already told me he was taking me out to lunch. I didn't think anything of it at the time, but his exact sentence was "Other things being equal, I'll take you down to Dino's." I didn't notice anything out of the ordinary. When I finally arrived downstairs, he'd been practising, but not in his studio, in the living part of the house, as if he'd been waiting for me. He asked me if I wanted anything to drink, and then said, "My father rang last night." He looked serious, but that could have been because he was still wrapped up in his Bach suites. But I did notice this time. "About the letter you had. About me. Have you still got it?" I told him I had. "Could I see it?" he asked. By this time I was shaking, shivering, along my spine.'

Lise paused to hold her coffee cup to her lips. She'd learnt the value of the dramatic pause.

'I had to go upstairs for it. I felt awful when I made my way out. My legs were trembling. I handed it over, and he read it. "I can guess who wrote that," he said. I just sat there mum, not even looking at him. He rustled the paper, and read it again, folded it and handed it me back. "What do you think?" he asked. "Is it true?" I asked. "Yes," he said. "Does it matter?" "Not to you, perhaps," I answered, without thinking. It fell out of my mouth. "It wasn't serious," he said. "Then why do it?" I asked him. "I can't answer that," he said. "There's a bit of a challenge, and I'm chasing after it. I realise it might hurt you, that it might be the cause of a break-up of our marriage. But I take the risk. I think you won't find out. As you wouldn't without that busybody." I was calmer now, not trembling. "Somebody must dislike you to bother to write to me," I said. "I make enemies." He looked grim.'

182

Again Lise paused as if bracing herself to tell all, or perhaps to comprehend implications.

'You know, Stella, I wasn't shocked, once he'd come out with it. I even thought how polite he'd been not to mention it the night before when I was so tired. I could still feel this shivering down my back from time to time, but I think now because I didn't know exactly what I was going to do. I'd guessed all along that the letter spoke the truth. I've been married to him long enough to know what he's like.'

'Is this the first time?' Stella broke in.

'No, it isn't.'

'What would he say or do,' Stella put her query slowly, 'if you were the one at fault?'

'How do you know that I'm not.' Lise's rather solemn face was alight with indecorous mischief.

The two women stared at each other.

'I'm not, as a matter of fact. Perhaps sex is not so import-ant to me as to him. I've been very busy while he was away. And when he is here, it's very good in bed together.'

'You've made love to him since he came back?'

'Yes.' Again the improper grin. 'With relish.'

'That makes a difference,' Stella asked, 'in law, doesn't it? It means you've condoned his adultery.'

'Very likely.' Lise did not sound much concerned. She now seemed intent on what she said next. 'Once he'd told me straight out, I let him stew a bit. Oddly he wasn't sure what I'd say or do. "Who is she?" I asked. He told me. The name meant nothing. She was one of the orchestral violins.'

'Married?'

'I don't think so. Unattached. Ingrid Lake.'

'English?'

'I think so.' What did it matter? 'I asked him, "What are you thinking of doing about it?" "That depends to a large extent on you." That seemed a careless answer, as if he wasn't much concerned either way. "You must have been pretty open about it if other people knew." "It wasn't so," he said. "We were extremely circumspect. The woman who wrote was Ingrid's room-mate. She was a nutter. And jeal-ous. She found out by mischance." "And didn't she spread the word?" "No. The rest of the orchestra didn't know, as far as I could make out." When he told me all this it was in a dull dead sort of voice. He was extremely nervous, though it took some time for me to realise it. But in the end I took the battle to him. "What do you intend to do?" I asked him again. "Come back to you, if you'll have me." "As if nothing had happened?" "Yes. It seems heartless on my part," he said, "and I see I have no rights in the matter, but if you'll have me, yes, I want to ask your forgiveness and come back." That sounded terrible to me. A cliché. As if he'd sorted it out beforehand, or learnt it from a fifth-rate play.'

'He didn't say anything about loving you?'

'Well, yes. In due course. He can talk freely enough when he wants to. He said how much he loved me, and respected me, and that I was the only woman he'd met he had ever wanted to live with.'

'Do you believe that?' Stella asked.

'Yes and no. He's a fair idea of what I'd want to hear. But I hung about, and when he tried to touch me, I shooed him away. And he backed off, though he's miles stronger than I am, physically. I asked him, what about Ingrid. He seemed to think he owed her nothing. Her reward was to have caught the passing attention of this godlike figure. I didn't much care for that.'

'Is that how he thinks of himself?' Stella pressed.

'He likes adulation as well as the next man, and gets a great deal more of it than most. It's easy to have your head turned when you do as well as Sebastian has. But, no, he's fairly level-headed. It took him long enough to arrive where he is. He's had to work at it. And he's getting on for middle age. And he knows he's up against some powerful opposition. He's not like a young pop-star with very small talent, hurried into the limelight by hype and luck. No, he's a serious musician. And I guess this girl threw herself at him. I guess so.'

'But what starts off as a little spree might develop into . . .'

'The real thing?' Lise laughed, quite loudly. 'I know that. There doesn't seem to be much danger in this case.'

184

'He's not seen her since they came back?'

'Apparently not.'

Lise looked quizzical, shrewd. It seemed to Stella that her friend was now much at ease with herself, savouring her role.

'What do you think?' Lise suddenly asked.

'You're enjoying yourself telling me this.' Stella did not know if she was wise to speak the truth. 'Isn't that so?'

'I suppose it is. Yes. That's about right.'

'And that will mean,' Stella pursued her earnest line of enquiry, 'that you don't mind overmuch what he's done? It's not a matter of life or death, is it?'

'Yes.'

Lise giggled. Stella was not yet prepared to let her go.

'But did you know that at the time? When he confessed?'

'It's hard to say. Exactly, you know.' The adverb hung loose from its verb. 'I was on a high from *Oedipus*. It seemed unimportant compared with my success. Especially as he sounded so hangdog. I wondered if this Ingrid hadn't been the one to break it off.'

'Were you not jealous at all?' Stella asked.

'No. It surprised me. I'm usually not one to have my toys pinched without squalls. I suppose it was the time. But I brood. And it may be possible that in six months or a year when everybody has forgotten about *Oedipus*, and the engagements are sluggish, I might rake the question up again. I can't guarantee him immunity from trouble. I don't know. But we made it up, and he's been very nearly perfect. It's been heaven since he came back. But I don't suppose it'll last. Why should it?' She sighed, laughingly, and yawned. 'Anyhow, is your reconciliation any closer?'

'I seem quite satisfied just to let things drag on as they are,' Stella said.

'And your husband?'

'He's another such. Perhaps he's keener than I am to try again. Now. I'm not sure. Now he thinks he understands the cause of our trouble.'

'Which was?' sharply.

'My depression. I think he blamed himself, but he

185

couldn't see why. Now he knows it was an illness, he wonders if it won't work out right if we get together again.'

'And you?'

'I'm unsure. At first he took up with his secretary, and while that was going on he felt right as ninepence. That's what my grandpa used to say. Then that went awry. I don't know the reason. After that he seemed a bit keener to accept my offer. But now I'm the one who's more hesitant.'

'Go back to him. And if it's hopeless you can always leave again.'

'No. If I went back, I should mean to stay.'

Lise shrugged, as if this made no sense to her.

'What about Michael? Has he made any approaches?'

'No. I've heard nothing. Not that I expected to.'

'I'm sure he was serious when he said he'd taken a shine to you.'

'For the minute,' Stella answered.

'What do you mean?'

'He's a romantic. And lonely. But I'm only guessing. It seemed to him an interesting line to raise with you.'

'I oughtn't to have told you,' Lise said slowly, rubbing an eye with an index finger. 'I've thought so since. It was not fair either to you or him.'

'It made no difference.'

'I don't suppose it did.'

They settled down to talk about their work. Lise promised to send two tickets for *Oedipus*.

'They're not easily come by. Especially at the weekend. But I'd specially like to think you were there.'

'Why?'

'Don't know. Whim. But I would. And you can bring John with you. Perhaps that'll make your minds up about marriage.'

'Has Michael seen it?'

'Yes. Twice. He's impressed. He's a bit anti-modernist, but he praises this.'

186

17

Three weeks later, John Taylor made his way to the Lord
Nelson. He felt pleased with himself; a dozen or more of his
firms, including Steelbright, were embarked on the new
financial year with some hope, partly on his account. He
had plenty of work, and both time and inclination to do it.
On Saturday he was to drive Stella, on her invitation, to
London to hear *Oedipus*, and they had decided to return the
same night. The expedition excited him; he did not know
why. Caution reigned, but he whistled as he walked.

The pub was not well patronised. As he was ordering his
beer, a man sidled up to him. He recognised his acquaint-
ance, the widower. He had not seen him since that first
meeting.

'What's yours?' John asked, euphoric. The sight of the
sad cheeks sobered him.

'Well, no. No thanks. I've a friend here with me. A lady
friend.'

'Then let me buy her a drink as well.'

The further orders were placed: a half of lager and a
tomato juice.

'Just come and join us,' the man said. John followed, not
unwillingly, to the tables where they had sat at their previous
meeting. A middle-aged lady, wearing a two-coloured, hard
hat with a feather, sat very straight there. She wore glasses
on a plump face, and the bosom in a white blouse hung very
large. 'May I introduce you,' the man began. 'This is
Mrs Little.' John held out a hand. 'I'm afraid I don't know
your name.'

'Taylor.'

'Mr Taylor.' The handshaking completed, the man raised
his glass to John. 'Good health.'

The three drank.

'This is the first time I've been in here since I saw you last. You don't come in often, if I remember rightly what you said. But Mrs Little, Cathy, and I have come to an arrangement.' He lifted her left hand, straightened her fingers. She wore a wedding and two engagement rings. 'And so I thought . . .'

'You'd have a celebration?'

'No. Not really. No. We've been engaged now for a fortnight. We're getting quite used to it, aren't we, love? No, it's by way of showing Cath some of my bad habits. Bringing her down to my level. In my local.' The woman beamed.

'I shall find out soon enough, I expect.' Her voice sounded louder, less ladylike than John expected.

'Well, congratulations to you both,' John said, lifting his glass. 'My very best wishes.' They raised glasses again. 'Have you known each other very long?'

'It depends what you mean,' the man answered. The woman, for all her brassy voice, showed no eagerness to speak. 'We've known each other by sight for years. When her husband was alive. And Eileen. We might say "How d'you do?" We didn't live too far away from each other. But we met, properly, if that's the word, well, much the same time that you and I first came across each other here.'

'Two or three months?'

'That's about it. But I can't say which came first. You or Cathy.' The man bit his lip. 'But it's made a difference. I'll tell you that for nothing.'

'I could tell you the exact date,' the woman said.

'Go on, then.'

'The twentieth of February.' She sat back proudly.

The two men laughed.

'It was one of these retirement clubs. I said I'd never go, that I'd plenty to do. And I wasn't retired. But they had a social and dance . . .'

'St Valentine's,' the woman said, 'but they couldn't get the rooms at all that week. Everybody was at it. All celebrating.'

'I bought a ticket. From our butcher. Best move I ever

made. He said it was for charity. I didn't think of turning up, but then, something made me change my mind.'

'Fate,' Cathy said.

'I went. Cathy had been giving 'em a hand there running the place since Charlie, her husband, died. And they had a "Ladies' Excuse Me", and she butted in.'

'Are you a good dancer?'

'I can shuffle round. Eileen and I used to go when we first went out together. And we'd also have a turn or two on the floor at the firm's parties. Dancing, ballroom, that is, died out in our day. It was all disco and noise and strobe lights. But it's coming back, they say. Just in time for me, and my advantage.' He laughed, though the dull face did not much alter its expression, as he swooped on his fiancée's left hand, lifting it on to the table, where it lay like a pig's trotter. 'We talked a bit, and had a drink, and before the night was out we'd arranged to meet again.'

Cathy lifted the handled hand, placed it on his shoulder.

'Les,' she said. 'Les.'

'I'm surprised at myself,' the man said. 'Just look at me,' he invited. 'Fifty-three years of age. Three married daughters. Four grandchildren. Responsible job. Just ask the men under me at James Limpenny's what I'm like. They'll tell you Les Straw's a man who wants a job done properly, and won't be fobbed off with any old bodge. There's no green in his eye.' John could easily imagine that sad face hardening, the West Midlands voice freezing into a drawl of sarcasm or rank abuse. 'And yet. And yet.'

He made them wait. Cathy looked modestly away.

'It's something I didn't understand. I don't think many people do. When I fell for Cath here, I was like a schoolboy. I couldn't eat properly; I couldn't sleep. You talk about a dog with two tails. Me, fifty-four next week, and I was in a turmoil. Caught up with it. Head in air one minute, down the next. I thought all that was damn near forty years behind me. I thought life had knocked it out of me.' He paused. 'It hadn't. And that's what people don't understand, especially young people, that inside weazened old drop-deads, stumble-bums like me, lives the lad I was at

189

eighteen, as excitable, as impressionable, as delicate,' he looked up for approbation of his word, 'as ever I was then. And it's not until something like this happens that you find out. Why, I saw two old pensioners, nearer eighty than seventy, standing hand in hand at the bus-stop. A year ago, I'd have thought, 'You silly old boggers', but I know better now. They look wrinkled and ridiculous, but they feel like kids again. And in their case, they were so ancient, it must have been without benefit of sex.' He laid a hand in the crook of Cathy's elbow and she blushed darkly.

'Have you a family, Mrs Little?' John asked sociably.

'Two sons,' she answered. 'Both married. One in Portsmouth, one in Leicester.' She gave an account of their careers, wives, children. Her voice was still too loud, as if she had been trained to pierce muzak or television. She smiled, exophthalmically; her bosom swung; the small rounded hands tapped the table-top.

'Let me buy you a celebratory drink,' John said. He felt elation.

'No,' Les Straw objected. 'It's my shout.'

'No. This is my pleasure. Mrs Little?'

'Cath,' she said.

'Cath. What will you have?'

'I'll have a Babycham for the special occasion.' She looked down at the barely touched, dull tomato juice, moved it an inch. 'If that's all right.'

'And you, sir?'

'Same again. I'll not go mad. Lager's good enough to drown my sorrows, so let it be good enough to toast my happiness.'

John fetched the drinks, and they raised the full glasses. Les shook John's hand. Then the three fell silent, even mournful, not quite believing their claims.

'When's the happy day?' John asked, to rouse them.

'Not fixed yet. Sometime in the summer. We've got to make up our minds where we're going to live. We both own houses.' Les cheered up. 'We're both members of the property-owning democracy. We spend a day or two in one, then a break, then try number two. We're not hanging about. In the one sense.' Again Cathy blushed. Her skin was extraordinarily smooth, but powdered unevenly. 'If these young people can, we're not going to lag behind. There's not that much time to waste.'

They drank healths again.

'I think we shall live in Les's house, when it comes to the push,' Cathy confided. 'It's got a bigger garden, and a place for his lathes and machines. You should see the furniture he makes. I don't exactly know about selling my house. The market's not too good, so I might hang on to it.'

'In case she changes her mind,' Les intoned.

'No,' she said. 'No. It isn't that.' She seemed distressed. 'You know it isn't.'

'I'm only pulling your leg.'

'There are some things not to be joked about.' She laid that law down, but in a softer voice, a mutter away from the men. Les Straw put his arm through hers, so that she lifted a compliant face to his. For a short time they forgot Taylor.

The conversation turned to house prices, letting furnished accommodation, removal firms, solicitors. All provided anecdotes, with Les easily in the lead. They drank little. After half an hour John left them. A few minutes earlier Les had gone out to the urinal, and John had said, 'He's a changed man. Last time I saw him he seemed very subdued, depressed. As if he couldn't come to terms with his bereavement.'

'He's up and down,' Mrs Little said.

'And you're very happy?'

'It's nice to be made a fuss of. He's a good, hard-working man. Very thoughtful. Like my first husband. Leslie's decent. He talks too much for me, I wish he'd shut up sometimes, but I see it's him. The way we are now is ideal. We aren't under each other's feet. We have some days when we don't see each other at all. And nights.' She fixed him with her eyes, though she blushed. 'To all intents and purposes we're married.' She meant, John interpreted, that they had sexual intercourse. 'This is perfect. We're close enough in case there's illness or something.'

191

'Are you saying that if it was left to you, you wouldn't get married legally?'

'No. And yes in a way.'

'What will happen, then?'

'We shall get married.'

'Easy as that?' John laughed friendlily, in equality.

'He's not a wife-beater. He'll be fair. But neither was Charlie. I don't like to be lonely. But there's worse things. My friend has just had a breast removed. I didn't think they did it so much now, but they did in her case, and she was a woman who took great pride in her appearance. It's cruel.' Her own breasts heaved. Les Straw returned. 'I was just talking about Marilyn Guest.'

'Ah. Bad job.' The thin frown reigned. 'But it's better than being dead.'

As John walked back along the main street where the newly burst lime-leaves hung magically in the lights, John pondered the compromise. Neither Les nor Cath had beauty. They were middle-aged and both had been pushed about by life. Both were intelligent, could argue a case for themselves. Their accents marked a provinciality they would not themselves notice. They spoke normally though quite differently, and both would condemn or feel suspicious of cut-glass voices. John knew they would marry, and wondered how they'd fare as they grew older. He had been shocked by Mrs Little's frankness. She recognised reality, but put it to the side. Her Les, flat-faced, dully talkative, felt love like a boy or a poet or a drunk, and she was prepared to accommodate him by appearing at the altar or the registrar's desk.

John talked of these contradictions as he drove Stella to London to see *Oedipus*. He had arranged a parking place not ten minutes' walk from the theatre, and now on a burning afternoon, more suitable to a Mediterranean August than May on the M1, he drove at speed. His car was comfortable; he had provided cool drinks; they knew where they'd eat; the weather reflected their own ease. Traffic was heavy, but without jams. They made good time, talked without restraint, each pleased. Both were comfortable.

192

'And what conclusion did you reach?' Stella.

'They'll do well, married to each other.'

'Yes?' Her interrogative tempted him further.

'They're different. But they'll do well enough. If something like redundancy happens to him, that might alter the situation.'

'Why do they bother about marriage if they're satisfied as they are?'

'I don't know. Perhaps the neighbours would talk.'

'These days?' She laughed timorously.

They parked with permission in the locked yard of a firm he dealt with, made their way to a restaurant where they ate at leisure. John questioned her closely now about her application for headship of department, which she had mentioned on the way up. Wakefield, the principal, had told her she was on the short list.

'Are you nervous?' John asked.

'No. Not yet.'

'Who'll interview you?'

'The principal will draw the panel list up. It'll consist of himself, the chairman of the governors . . .'

'Does he know anything about it?'

'He has a boy in the place, and a daughter who did English at A level and is at the university now. He's a consultant. A cancer specialist. Rather quiet. And then one of the deputies and the English inspector.'

'Do you know him?'

'Just about. He gives the impression of a meetings man. Must have training courses, public exchanges of ideas, that sort of thing. I suppose that's what he's there for. I don't think he knows much.'

'But he won't be against you?'

'No. Why should he?'

'And the rest? Will they be on your side?'

'Not particularly. There are two PhDs on the short list. And in education it's an advantage if you've been round a bit, in different schools. It won't be much in my favour that I know the local conditions better than the rest of them.'

Stella did not appear unhappy, chatted about what

193

matters she thought they would raise, and ideas she'd like to broach herself.

'Are you hopeful?' he asked at length.

'No. I shan't get it.'

'And will that disappoint you?'

Stella thought that over, breathing deeply through her nostrils.

'Yes. I suppose it will. But it will be good for me. And it might well encourage me to apply elsewhere.'

'You'd leave this part of the world?'

'That would be highly likely.'

'And that would be the end of our marriage?'

Again Stella considered it.

'Yes. It would. But this isn't the time to go into that.'

'No,' he said humbly enough. 'You're right.'

They finished their excellent meal, made their way on foot to the theatre, spent half an hour sitting in the bar, drinking iced lemonade, the best of friends, listening to conversation, admiring or mocking dress, looking at photographs or reading posters.

'We ought to do this more often,' John said, 'never mind what's going on in there.' He poked a satirical finger towards the auditorium. As they chatted, Stella was surprised that he did not seem to know about the Oedipus legend. She had read, in preparation, the old Everyman translation of Sophocles by Sir George Young. She briefly outlined the story.

'Incest?' he said at the finish. 'She must have kept her youthful appearance. That would be unusual.'

'How do you know that?'

'I don't. But in sunny countries like Greece, faces soon wrinkle.'

He sounded so confident that she glanced at him with annoyance. He seemed to diminish Sophocles and his art. He noticed her quietness, understood it and said, 'Let's go in for the goings-on, then, shall we?'

The stalls, fewer to accommodate the largish orchestra, filled up. They took their seats under the gallery, studied the glossy programmes, standing to let late-comers pass.

The opera had no overture. After five brass chords, violent and discordant, the curtain rose on Tiresias and the Thebans. The libretto had been printed in full in the programme, but minutely, so that it was useless in the half-dark. Stella found it difficult to follow the words on stage. The music itself was strident, acid, set teeth on edge, plague music. When Lise appeared she was unrecognisable. She seemed larger than life, able to still the quarrel between Creon and her son-husband by her formidable beauty as well as the egregious strength of her voice.

The sounds went quite against Stella's expectation. The music flattened the listener, rough-hewn, aiming at the gut rather than the brain. Lise had said that there were tunes, melodies once one became used to the idiom, but nothing of these could be detected by a first-time listener. It was, even before the interval, as if the composer slapped hearers across the face, harshly and with jagged rhythms.

As they came out for the one, over-long interval, John Taylor wiped sweat from his brow.

'Christ,' he said. 'That takes the tartar off your teeth.'

'I imagine the composer meant to make us feel uncomfortable.'

'Well, he succeeded with me.'

'Do you think it's any good?' she asked.

'It's dramatic. It attacks the audience, and we haven't come to the climax yet. It screams. And I wonder if Nicholas Webb could write an opera about happiness, let's say, or pleasure or contentment. Not that they're very likely to be the subjects of opera, but we do get drinking songs and so on. This is all blistering horror.'

The second act spoke, screeched, as powerfully.

Jocasta's death was not reported as in Sophocles, but seen in a small, black, back-space. There she hanged herself, singing with the same regal potency her grief, her sin, her determination to blot herself out from the knowledge of Thebes. Oedipus's blinding took place off-stage, but he walked about, bloody bandages falling roughly from bloody troughs of eye sockets. He seemed greater than the ruler of the city they had seen at first, one huge enough to pay out

195

malicious gods. When Creon, near the end, brought on the children, Ismene and Antigone, to see their father, Webb reduced his orchestra to quickly varying solo instruments, acidly scored, and used his chorus as accompaniment to Creon's pompous, almost monotonous pronouncements, while Oedipus raved, his voice strong with sobbing, gluttonously so, loving his daughter-sisters, recognising the unjust justice of gods, asking but once for the company of his beloved children in his exile, and on Creon's inhumane and schoolmasterly refusal, set his face with blood-streaked stoicism. As he stumbled his way through last embraces and then out of sight, the final comment was left not to chorus but to the full orchestra, never more than *mf*, as discordant as ever, but with a parched and subdued ferocity of acceptance. Creon, the children, the chorus turned staring at the retreating figure, and for some seconds, minutes, it seemed, stood frozen, eyes towards the unseen blind king as the orchestra writhed through its muted lamentation, then stopped in mid-phrase, without cadence, the curtain still up as the Thebans gazed after their king in the pitiless light.

The curtain fell in silence.

Applause, delayed and hesitant at first, grew strong; perhaps Nicholas Webb had scored that. The principals, the chorus, the conductor appeared, each bowing stiffly as if the evening's performance had thrashed all fluency out of them. Oedipus, eyes open but still bloodied, held hands with Jocasta who had regained her serenity as in the next world.

Stella and John hurried out.

'Would you like a last drink?' he asked.

'I don't think so. What time is it?' She carried her own watch.

'Only quarter-past ten.'

'Only.'

They rushed out into the streets, walked fast to the car, hardly speaking a word. They arrived back in Beechnall before two o'clock.

'I'll put you up for the night,' John said. Too tired to

argue, she agreed, and slept in one of the spare bedrooms. He provided her with morning tea, a new toothbrush and paste. They ate breakfast together at eleven.

'Quite like old times,' he said.

Stella looked round the dining room. When she had lived here, they had eaten breakfast in the kitchen. This place was tidy, and the meal laid on a starched, white cloth. Windows shone clean, furniture polished.

'Do you use this room much?' she asked.

'No. If I have to give people a meal, it's easier to do it out.'

Neither said a word about her return, but she walked the whole house with him. She wondered if he interpreted this as an admission on her part that she seriously considered coming back. They inspected the garden.

'Lacks your touch,' he admitted. A gardener came in twice a week.

'This is the best time of year,' she said. 'This is when I miss the garden most.'

He did not take her up on this, and when he invited her to stay to lunch she refused, saying she had a great deal of work to do.

'Such as?'

'Marking. And writing down the things I'm going to say to this interviewing panel.'

'Let me know how it goes.'

'I will.'

18

In the last week of May, Stella was interviewed for the headship of the English department at her college.

She had prepared herself carefully, asked questions of others, used her experience, such as writing a letter of thanks to Lise Martin-Alexander about *Oedipus*. She determined not to flannel; if someone asked her whether Earle's *Microcosmographie* or *Love's Labour's Lost* or *As If By Magic* were suitable for A-level study by her pupils, she would immediately admit she had read none of them. She'd offer equivalent works she had studied and give them an opinion on their suitability, but that would be all. If this admission of ignorance told against her, so be it.

On the day concerned, she met the other candidates. Originally four, one had withdrawn at the last minute. The other three were men, well qualified, not unpleasant, all quite different, all roughly of her age, all three higher in status in their own schools. She had lunch in the college dining room with them, the headmaster and the chairman of the governors, a consultant physician. Interviews began, alphabetical order, at one-thirty; she, Taylor, came last so that it was three forty-five before she was called in. She occupied herself, she had been freed from teaching, by looking over her notes, walking behind the trees at the far end of the grounds, twice cleaning her teeth, three times washing her hands so that when Terry Stacey, the senior deputy, called her in, it came as a relief.

'It's warm work,' he said as they walked the corridor. 'Still, we know you, so it shouldn't take quite so long.'

He meant well.

He ushered her in; the chairman invited her to sit, apologised for keeping her so long, told her to make herself at ease, and quickly worked through her CV. She only twice corrected him. The rest of the panel, Martin Wakefield neat and business-like, Stacey, a woman from the parent-governors, Mrs Bridge, smiling encouragement amongst all this masculinity and Nicholas 'Toby' Todd, the English adviser.

The chairman handed her over to the lady member, who read her question, duly prepared, from a slip of paper; what did she think she could offer the college? Stella, expecting this, outlined her virtues and her suitability to this place. The lady smiled, said that sounded admirable, but asked nothing further. Stacey came next. 'What are the advantages of a sixth-form college?' She was ready. Wider range of subjects; a change at sixteen which many wanted. Adult atmosphere. She spoke without heat; any tremor in her voice had gone. 'Are there any disadvantages?' Stacey came back out of his remit, drawing a surprised glance from the head. Again she had a quiet fluency. No chance of looking after younger children; not everybody wanted a change; different sort of responsibilities from a sixth-former in a comprehensive or grammar school. Stacey nodded as if he'd heard none of this before.

So far, so good. She had not made a fool of herself.

Now the chairman called on 'Toby' Todd, the inspector. He lounged, had his hands in his pockets, asked what she thought the duties of the head of department were. She told him. 'You know this school, college,' Todd drawled, once she had finished. 'Would that apply to the present régime?' Stella said that in generalities it would. 'But you would make changes?' She admitted that she might well. 'A suggestion or two, please,' Todd begged. She confessed herself not altogether satisfied with the less able A-level students, and described how she would alter the course and the books to suit these students. 'Would that not work to the disadvantage of the more academic students?' Stella explained how she would see to it that it would not. 'Would you encourage the study of Shakespeare?' Now she came into her own. Here was the world's greatest poet, dramatist, and she felt she did nothing to prepare her students properly if she did not give them the opportunity to study this towering figure. 'But he presents great difficulties,' murmured the urbane Todd. 'So do physics and mathematics,' Stella answered, 'but we don't cut them out of the syllabus for that reason.' The panel, the doctor and the lady at least, raised a smile. 'What do we do, then?' Todd consulted the nails of his left hand, raised parallel to the floor, eighteen inches in front of his face. 'Try to teach them better.' 'But how?' The inspector delivered his knockout into the far corner of the room. Stella began to explore, emphasising that one should not underestimate the abilities of the pupils, even less able children. 'I don't think I do,' Todd interrupted, stupidly. 'I don't think, Mr Todd,' the chairman said, 'that Mrs Taylor is personally accusing you . . .' The inspector smiled pityingly. Stella now knew that the chairman sided with her. Wakefield, the principal, to restore order asked what were the advantages of written examinations at the end of the year over continuous assessment.

He courteously handed Stella back to Todd who questioned her closely on the teaching of pupils who were repeating GCSE. As she answered, Stella noticed how hot and bored the rest of the panel appeared. She therefore answered briefly, once threw in an anecdote, without much effect. The headmaster then asked her opinion of games as education, and when she had answered, stressing that placings at charitable shops and institutions suited many pupils, especially girls, better than hacking and throwing balls about courts, the headmaster sat upright.

'Why did I ask you that question?' Wakefield asked sweetly.

'Presumably you regard the Head of English as a senior member of the staff who would be consulted on general policy outside her departmental duties.'

She could barely contain a smile of contempt at her answer. If Wakefield ever condescended to ask her opinion, it would be to canvas support for his own ideas.

'Exactly,' he was saying, and suddenly switching to show his catholicity he gabbled, 'Do you agree that there has been no great poet writing in English since Yeats?'

Stella dredged up some names: Auden, Hughes, Larkin, Wallace Stevens, Eliot, she reminded him, had all written after Yeats's death. Nothing controversial, she thought.

The committee sat stunned.

'Thank you, Mrs Taylor,' the chairman said. 'I wish I had your knowledge. Now, are there any more questions?' His face forbade them. 'Thank you very much indeed. Thank you.'

Stacey jumped up from the end of the judicial row, rounded her and held the door politely open. In the corridor she glanced at her watch. Twenty-five minutes. Short measure compared to the rest. She swilled her hands and face. Her hair, she noted with satisfaction, seemed as tidy as at the beginning of the interview. On her trek back to the common room to await the decision, she met Peter Booth, the present head of department, on his way home.

'Have you been in yet?'

'Yes. I was last.'

'How did it go?'

'I couldn't grumble.'

'Who asked the questions?'

'They all had their share. Todd was inquisitor-in-chief.'

'Really? You surprise me. Still, he's never backward in coming forward.' Booth rocked on his heels. 'Toby Todd, an ignorant sod, whose wisdom equals that of God.'

He wished her well, waved a limp hand, and strolled on.

Back in the common room she made coffee, offering cups to her rivals, one of whom refused. They lounged gloomily, stirring themselves with a question or a polite observation now and then.

At ten minutes past five Terry Stacey burst in.

'Dr Denton, please,' he said. One of the young men stood. 'If you'd be kind enough to go into the principal's study.'

Stacey waited until the door closed.

'Sorry,' he said. 'That's how it is. They're offering it to him.' He fiddled with the papers in his hands. 'I wonder if you'd be good enough to fill these in before you leave. I'll collect them. It'll only take a minute. It's the usual claim form for expenses. Save us and you time and postage.' He handed Stella hers with the other two. She stood, wearily, wished the remaining candidates goodbye and walked out. Stacey immediately followed her.

'By God,' he said, outside the door, 'that was close. You did very well.'

'Thank you.' Politely cool, she nodded thanks. Beaten.

She did not wait for further information, but turned her back on him.

In the women's cloakroom she wept two or three small tears, washed her face and marched smartly out to the car-park. She admitted her disappointment to herself, surprised that she wanted the job so keenly. Back home, she kicked off her shoes, put her legs up on the settee, found no comfortable position. She felt sick. Arms and shoulders pained her. The room was tidy except for an envelope jaggedly ripped open with a finger, from a college friend who had decided at last to marry. Stella had read the letter before she set out for the college that morning. She would write her congratulations to poor Sarah in due time. Poor Sarah? Her husband-to-be was their university tutor, clever and unworldly. It all sounded as unreal as a magazine story, as lifelike as sci-fi.

She forced herself up, changed out of her interview clothes, fished out track suit, took a hot bath. Her mind rushed, thrashed madly about the interview, tippling among the questions. She made and ate a sandwich, but could not remember what was in it. She walked violently from room to room; speed anaesthetised her pain. Trying this chair, that stance, she drank her last cup of tea.

Stella could not admit that she had not done well at the interview. *Pensées d'escalier* occurred, but they involved only small alterations. The egregious Todd, in spite of his manner, had fed her the right questions, and she had not fluffed her answers. True, she could now polish her offerings, but she had made the right points clearly and forcefully enough. Wakefield had given her the chance to air her knowledge of contemporary literature, and the chairman had congratulated her on her answer. She had done as well

202

as ever she would, and they had rejected her. Denton's PhD had turned the scale. What would it be about? Some mixture, she guessed: 'Wordsworth and Thackeray, a study of moral crises'. 'Ben Jonson and Englishness'. 'Pope's Homer, the art of translation'.

The telephone rang.

Peter Booth asked how she had fared. Carefully paring her language, she gave a brief account of the interview. He asked a few questions, distantly.

'I'm sorry you didn't get it,' he said. 'I'd have felt safe with you. You'd have changed things, but you're interested in books.'

She thanked him for his help. He rang off, again muttering regret.

Surprised that she had answered so rationally, she wept again, briefly, against her will. She went to her bedroom to put away her glad-rags which she had dropped, she suddenly remembered, across a chair. Straightening the clothes on a hanger, she considered she had demeaned herself, putting on this show only to be rejected. She thought of Terry Stacey doing his best to comfort in his rough and ready way. Again the small tears forced their way out. She dabbed her face.

A pile of exercise books awaited marking. She ought to have marked them last night, but had been too immersed in her preparation. Sluggishly she dragged them towards her, read a paragraph on 'commodity' in *King John* and found she retained nothing. Almost savagely she made herself mark the essay, then the next, the next.

The phone interrupted.

Lise Martin, ringing from her dressing room. She had suddenly, for no reason, thought of Stella. They had only a minute or two, but she had to check up; she didn't know why. She knew nothing, obviously, of the interview and Stella deliberately did not mention it. How was that husband of hers? Would she go back to him? Lise said she often puzzled over that problem. 'And if you were in my place?' Stella calmly enquired. 'I'd give him another chance.' Stella breathed a non-committal answer, and asked how Sebastian was making out. 'He's in Edinburgh tonight, Glasgow tomorrow, then Germany for a five-recital week from Monday. But he's wonderfully attentive when he's at home. It's perhaps because he's so successful just now. What do you think?' Stella agreed tactfully. Lise said she must ring off. The producer did not like outside calls once the curtain had gone up. She must put the instrument down, and begin to live in ancient Thebes. They wished each other goodbye.

Stella stared at the phone in disbelief.

She had not mentioned *Oedipus* in the interview. What difference would that have made? That would have impressed them? Would it? Todd perhaps had heard of Webb's opera, or Sophocles. Not the rest. Well, Wakefield?

Lise had asked after John, her husband. Seated at the table, red pen in hand, next exercise book open, she considered the question. If she had been successful today, she might well in her new self-confidence have offered to go back to him. That seemed now academic, irrelevant, like the difference of squares or the meaning of oxymoron, something worth knowing for itself, but inapplicable at present. She would have rung John up with the good news, she thought, even invited him round. Instead she sat with third-hand, third-rate husks of scholarship and a cold cup of tea.

John telephoned twenty minutes later.

'How did you fare today?' Straight off.

'I didn't get it.'

'I'm sorry.'

He questioned her about the interview, the other candidates, her own estimate of her performance. She spoke with great speed at his encouragement. Wakefield, Stacey, the great-I-am Todd, Dr Hanson, Mrs Briggs, Terry Stacey again, Dr Denton. John seemed not only interested but knowledgeable so that she assessed her answers for him almost brightly, became nearly jovial as she suggested how she could have improved herself. At the end of a quarter of an hour she felt cheered.

'And what's the next move?'

'Give me time, give me time. I have to get over this.'

'You'll start to apply elsewhere?'

'It would be sensible.'

'Just sixth-form colleges, or any sort of school?'

'I'll need to look hard at the market.'

'Yes. I'm sorry you didn't get today's little promotion.' She wondered at his use of the word 'little'. 'It would have been a good step in your career, I daren't say "careerwise" to you, and you would have stayed here.'

'Yes.' She felt grateful. 'But it can't be helped.'

'You must be disappointed, especially if you know you did well.'

'I'm only human. Yes.'

'Do you feel like stepping out for a drink? I'll bring the car round,' he asked.

'No, thank you. I'll drown my sorrows in Shakespeare essays.'

'They're not dry, then?'

Stella did not answer his 'little' jest.

John began again. 'I don't know if it's the time or place to mention this, but if you'd have got the job I would have asked you seriously to think about coming back here.'

'I see.' Coldly.

'In the general euphoria.' He coughed, realising perhaps he had been tactless. 'I don't suppose,' he spoke slowly, 'it's any use repeating the offer.'

She waited, collected the voice in her throat. 'No. But thank you.' She owed him further explanation. 'I don't know exactly where I am just at present.'

'I'm not surprised. But if a bit later in the evening you fancy a half-pint or a bit of sympathetic male company, I shall be in.'

'Thank you, John.'

'It's not very often you call me by my name.'

'From today I'm changed,' she said.

'Don't sit there grieving. Come on out for a drink. You need to wash the taste of those prats out of your mouth.'

Again she refused, instancing her marking. John did not give up at once, but had no success. After he had rung off, she realised she'd chosen wrongly. She would not make a hash of marking her essays, that was next to impossible, but she'd not do them justice. That a failure elsewhere should mar her performance as a teacher came as a surprise to her, though she warned herself that such was always the case.

The evening passed both dully and painfully. She completed her marking, listened to the ten o'clock news, decided on a glass of whisky but found herself too listless to fetch the bottle. In bed by eleven she did not sleep well, constantly waking with the adversarial give-and-take of the interview racing through her head. She ate breakfast, read the post, even opened the paper without paying attention.

The common room seemed much as ever. One person only asked how she'd got on. They were all at their usual early-morning routines, opening cases, retrieving books, patting hair into place. She saw nothing of the principal, nor of Stacey. At break Booth, her head of department, asked what this Denton was like.

'Quiet. Rather posh.'

'Any good?'

'I'd no chance to judge. He said something interesting about the use of pastiche in the contemporary novel.'

'For or against?'

'Didn't say. It was a method that had caught on, he thought.'

'Why?'

'Don't ask me. There it was, and he'd noticed it. Not the highest form of art.'

Booth spat out a sound of exasperation.

'Wakefield's not said anything to me. Not that I expected it. He made no enquiry about what sort of teacher we needed here.'

'I thought he asked if I was suitable?'

'He asked that. But you'd think he'd trawl for my ideas, even if he rejected them out of hand.'

Stella half-enjoyed her lessons, found she had the energy to make something of them. The principal was not in the dining room. Her colleagues were full of their own concerns. They were decent, hard-working people, capable now and then of laughing at themselves, not without ideas. Stella walked twice round the playing fields.

Her last period of the afternoon was with a small lower-sixth-form group in one of the rooms in the science block. They had just begun to read Marlowe's *Faustus*, and she was horrified to discover that the class had no idea what she meant by an 'iambic pentameter'. She took to chalk and blackboard, and was immersed in her explanation, and determined that they should know something before she left the room, when a knock on the door interrupted her.

A young man with fair wavy hair and a white doctor's coat came in.

'Mrs Taylor?' he asked.

She stiffened and sighed agreement.

'Mr Pinkett sent me.' Head of chemistry. So this young man would be one of the lab assistants. She had never seen him before. 'There's been a telephone message from the principal. Would you go and see him at the end of afternoon lessons?'

One of her pupils rounded his lips to make a subdued noise of mock apprehension. The youth with the message grinned. He wore a small gold earring in his left lobe. Stella thanked him, and returned to 'tetrameter'.

At the end of the lesson she walked without hurry to the cloakroom, tidied herself, put away her books and knocked at the door of the principal's study. The secretary answered, holding the door three-quarters closed, gently anouncing the caller over the shoulder, and then asking if she'd mind waiting just a minute.

Stella turned on her heel. Typical. Wakefield had summoned her to congratulate her on her interview, to keep her sweet so she wouldn't spread discontent, and to make promises for a bright future for her, either here or elsewhere. He'd do it well; he was no fool. He would make sure that she attached no blame to him.

She would be duly pleased, she knew; we all crave praise. But she would be no more than polite, thank him, and take his compliments as her due. She might even ask his advice about career moves, but distantly, as if he were an examinee to be tested. She stared out into the car-park, now twenty minutes after the last bell still three-quarters full. Her colleagues were in no hurry to rush home. The sun shone. Two students passed, swinging tennis racquets. A caretaker rattled with mop and bucket. The secretary crept behind her, but Stella knew immediately that she was there.

'Mr Wakefield will see you now.'

'Thank you.'

She knocked, waited, was invited in. The principal stood behind his desk, a man of affairs, a middle-aged young fogey tugging at the points of his waistcoat.

'Ah, Mrs Taylor.' He did not use first names on formal occasions. He'd get them wrong. 'Please sit down.'

A chair had been placed. Each now sat, face to face at seven feet.

'You did very well yesterday. Outstandingly so. The short list was strong, but in the end it was between two of you. You made a very favourable impression, so much so that the committee was divided.'

'Thank you.' She modestly lowered her eyes, not helping him out.

Now he tapped his desk-top with the nail of the middle finger of his right hand, rhythmically, alla breve.

'There has been a further development.'

Stella made no answer.

'This morning, Dr Denton withdrew.' She offered no comment. Wakefield rubbed the surface of his desk with his ring finger, and as if fascinated watched himself. 'I have been in touch with the rest of the panel, and we are now unanimous in offering you the position.'

'Thank you.' She contained her surprise.

'I feel no disappointment in the loss of Denton, though he was a strong candidate. But I think he wanted to stay in the South. When he arrived home there was this other offer waiting for him. He slept on it, talked to his wife, and rang me first thing. I telephoned Dr Hanson immediately and he made me a ten-minute interval in his very busy schedule. He did not need ten minutes. As soon as I'd arrived and said my piece he immediately told me, "Appoint that young woman. There'll be no loss there. She was the better of the two of 'em in my opinion." "I shall have to consult Mr Todd and Mrs Bridge," I told him. "Consult whoever you like," he said, "but appoint that Mrs Taylor. We should have done it last night." I have done the rounds now, Todd, Emma Bridge, Terry Stacey, and they are all agreed. So, may I congratulate you? All's well that ends well, as the poet said.'

'Thank you.'

'I'll talk to you again, when you've become a little more used to the idea.' He laughed, throatily curt. 'We'll make the offer to you in writing, of course. Have you anything you want to ask me?'

'Did you consult Peter Booth?' she asked, mulishly.

'No. Should I have done so?'

'He would have appreciated it.'

'Booth,' the principal said, 'was one of your referees. When he handed in his written statement, he made a point of talking about you. That is typical. If you asked him why, he'd say, "Oh, Wakefield's incapable of reading and under-standing anything in print more complicated than a match-box joke." So I knew pretty well what his views were. Very favourable, I must add.'

'Oh, I see.'

'I haven't had time to contact him today. What with rushing out to the hospital to Hanson, and to call in on the director. I need to keep him up to date. Yes. There. Yes. Well, allow me to congratulate you once again. I think we've got round to the right person in the end.'

He stood, held out his hand. They two shook, slightly awkwardly.

'Thank you.'

'Well done, Stella,' Wakefield said solemnly. 'Well done.'

Terry Stacey hovered, unusually, in the common room. As soon as she entered, he beamed and stuck out his big hand.

'You should have been offered it last night, never mind waiting for Denton to withdraw. You were by some miles the best. In my opinion. And Emma Bridge's.' He picked up his sheaf of papers and marched out. He'd obviously been waiting for her return. He talked on, confidentially congratulatory, then left exuberantly.

A colleague, a woman sociologist, came in, called across.

'Sorry you didn't get the job,' she said, gathering books. 'It's a rough world for women.'

'I did.'

'Did what?'

'Get the job. The favoured candidate withdrew.'

'Jesus.' The woman laughed. 'Sorry. Congratulations. What's it feel like to be one of the establishment?'

'I haven't been there long enough to know.'

'Well, nobody could be worse than Pretty Peter Booth. Bye. Keep off the booze tonight.' She rushed out.

Stella grinned. Three out of five were on her side last night, and they offered the job to Denton. Wakefield and Todd, the experts, came down against her. Or one couldn't believe Stacey. She ought to be jubilant, not suspicious. She tiptoed out to her car and met no one. She sat there in the park, fondling the wheel, staring no further than the windscreen.

As soon as she reached home she telephoned her husband's office. No one there, at five-past five. She rang his home. A blank again, though she left this time a message on the answering machine asking him to ring her. With spirits rising she made herself a curry, mixing ingredients, enjoying her experiments. When she had eaten, had cleared and washed the dishes, she sat down. As she was both excited and restless, immobility did not suit her. She walked into each of the three rooms of the flat. In the bedroom she leapt with a whoop on to the bed, fell headlong there and lay prostrate, legs bent, arms out, face deep into the coolness of the duvet. After a few minutes she scrambled to the ground ruefully, straightened the cover and her clothes. The bizarre physical action had done her good, but was more suitable to some rugby-playing, fifth-form oaf than the respected head of a large department. She grimaced at the passing figure in the wardrobe mirror and moved sedately into her sitting room, then to the front door and out into the fresh air.

She scribbled a note to her parents announcing her promotion. They had been cagey since she had informed them of the rift between her husband and herself. They and she wrote or rang only occasionally; this might please them, or convince them that she could look after herself.

Stella received not a word from her husband until Saturday. Later she learnt that he had been away dealing with a large new account in Birmingham. He did not sound too cheerful when he caught her on the phone at her lunch. He explained why he had not rung before, and set off on a long melancholy account of how he had wasted three days in Birmingham, not returning at night.

'You didn't lose money, I hope,' she mocked.

'No. But I had to work hard chasing them up. I was amazed that so large a concern had been so careless.'

'How did you come by the job?'

'They asked Stephen Williams for the name of an efficient, but tactful accountant for one of their smaller concerns. They'd run into trouble, and thought that unless somebody came up with something like adequate figures, they might even fall foul of the law. They'd already sacked the MD and two other people.'

'So you're a kind of cosmetic surgeon, are you? A make-up artist?'

'Yes and no. Williams, of Gower and Black, you know, had apparently been talking to the Nicholson brothers at Steelbright. And they'd praised me up to the skies. So when the chief of West Midlands Enterprises was lunching with Williams, Steve mentioned me for his "Comet" affair.'

'Surely they had their own accountants?'

'Exactly. But West Midlands weren't mad keen to put them in. They didn't want a cover-up, but they didn't want to look silly, or slap-happy, or careless to their own men. So they were willing to spend good money on me.'

'I see. And is all well now?'

'As ever it can be. They'll have to shell out. But nobody

211

will end up in jail. We've straightened the paperwork. We can see our way through. But how are you?'

'Fine,' she said.

'You rang me up.'

'The candidate they chose for head of English withdrew. They offered me the job.'

'And you took it?' John's voice sounded anxious.

'Of course. What do you think?' She could not, to be truthful, exactly remember formally accepting the offer.

'I'm never quite sure with you, Stella. You might have turned it down on some principle or pretext. But it's great news. You're pleased, aren't you?'

'Yes.' His disclaimer had not pleased her. She knew that.

'We must celebrate. I'll take you out to dinner. Tuesday if you're free. I'm in Brum again the whole of Monday, so Tuesday's the first . . .'

'Can you make it Wednesday?' she asked.

'Surely. In fact that's rather better for me. We can have a drink together tomorrow evening just as a preliminary. I'm over at my parents' tonight. For a concert. So Sunday is the day. I'll be back at, oh, eight. How's that suit?'

They arranged the time he'd pick her up.

She now enjoyed the exchange. He could have taken her out to dinner Sunday, but he liked a period of anticipation, perhaps even consultation about the most favoured restaurant. A careful man, her husband. An accountant.

So they'd spend an hour in the George or the Bell or the Lord Nelson to prepare themselves for high dining on Wednesday. He asked her plans, her 'reforms', his word, of the system.

'Nothing, as yet.'

'You surprise me.'

On Sunday evening he arrived at eight, the hour she had nominated, and she chose the Lord Nelson. They walked there, a twenty minutes' stroll.

'We might meet your friend,' she said.

'Nothing very interesting about him. You wouldn't think much of him.'

They had barely settled over their drinks when Les Straw

212

and his Cathy made an undistinguished entrance. The lady waddled her way over towards them, inspected chairs, loosened her coat, tried her handbag in three different places on the table in front of her. John wished her good-evening. She eyed him with surprise, as if she didn't quite recognise him, and answered the greeting diffidently. When Straw brought their tray across, John introduced Stella. The man immediately looked bothered; he clearly remembered that Taylor had told him he had separated from his wife. He recovered, shook hands, took as much time as his lady-friend in easing himself and his raincoat into a chair, and then ventured, to Stella, 'I thought he was a bachelor gay.' He coughed. 'Though that's not a word I should use these days.'

Straw touched on the weather, its effect on his garden and on Cathy's, the beauty of the time of year, the sudden and unexpected rush of work his department of the factory had thrust on it, some contract for Middle Eastern telephone systems.

'I'm not saying I'm not pleased,' he told Stella. He had stared, fascinated, since his arrival, and had addressed all his remarks to her. Cathy did not appear to mind as she beamed into the adverts for sparkling wines on the far wall. Her face seemed unusually healthy, smooth and ruddy. 'We were feeling the pinch, and then suddenly out of the blue this little lot.'

'Will it last?' Stella asked.

'Six months at least. And if we pull our finger out, longer. It's put my redundancy back.'

Straw, much at ease, explained the nature of the contract, and though Stella could understand what the man was saying, she soon lost interest, turned her mind elsewhere. Straw had no idea that he had failed her, continuing to chatter, to wave his hands about; Cathy followed his every word with nods and smiles. John enquired whether or not the firm had had any idea that this contract was on the way.

'Must have,' Straw said, 'must have. They'll have been negotiating for months. But they never say a word to us. That's their trouble.'

'No rumours flying about?'

'Rumours, yes.'

'Where did they come from?'

'God knows. Under-manager level. There'd been talk. But the bulk of the work might well have landed in the Liverpool or the Essex factories. Trouble with a big concern like ours is that they've always got new irons in the fire. They don't make official announcements to us, because if a contract falls through, we'd blame them. So they leave the future vague. They've stood a good number off in the last two years, slimming down. That's what they call it.'

'And the unions?'

'They do their best. But there's a recession. They'll arrange the best redundancy settlement they can, but their hands are tied. There's not that number of jobs going. Even for highly skilled men. If the firm pushed somebody like me out, I might, if I was the right age, which I'm not, find work elsewhere, but it would be different, and paid less.'

Straw was in full mutter. He admired the top administrators, who were in touch with reality. They searched business out, deserved their fancy salaries, made sure that shareholders earned a decent return. If Sir Graham Pike didn't organise new contracts, the factories would close and that was that.

'You sound satisfied.' John suggested.

'I like my work. I give value for money. But unless this lot on the board in London didn't do their thing, I'd be on the labour market.'

He'd once exchanged a few words with Sir Graham. 'Very quietly spoken. Younger than me. He knew exactly the process we were on that morning, and the why and wherefore. Before he went, he turned to me and said, "I want you to think of ways of improving efficiency. We used to get quite a few suggestions from the foreman, under-manager level, but not now. If you aren't careful, you'll all be replaced by bloody cassettes." Just what he said.'

'A threat?' John asked.

'I'll say it was.'

'Have you put in any suggestions?'

'I have. We have a box. Not that you get much response from the floor, except about tea-breaks. One chap did . . .'

Cathy Little suddenly interrupted with a question thrust at Stella. Her face was wooden, but the strength of voice momentarily stopped Straw.

'Do you work, Mrs . . . Mrs . . . ?'

'Taylor,' said Stella. 'Yes, I teach.'

'Where, then?'

'Birkin Sixth Form College.'

'One of our Peggy's boys went there. Brian Makepeace. Did you know him?'

'Don't be daft, Cath,' Les chided. 'He'll be older than Mrs Taylor.'

'I suppose he will.' Mrs Little blushed, and opened her mouth wide.

Les Straw lectured them on the value of education. John interrupted to fetch a fresh round of drinks. Straw held back, did not advance his thesis until the new tray appeared. If one worked hard at school, college, whatever, and obtained professional qualifications, one would spend the rest of life in comparative ease.

'I guess,' John said quietly aggressive, 'that I work longer hours than you.'

'I'm there at eight-thirty in the morning and I'm not out until five.'

'I'm at my desk at eight-thirty and it's often seven or eight before I leave. And then I have to take work home.'

'Yes, but you have long dinner hours, and women to wait on you and run your messages and type your memos, and in comfortable chambers.' He leaned on his last word.

'A sandwich is often all I have until I get home.'

'But you're working for yourself. You'll be the one to profit by it.'

Mrs Little intervened again.

'It's Les's belief that nobody works harder than he does.'

'But is it true?' John enquired, grinning at both.

'He's like all men,' she said in her loud voice. 'What they do is best.'

'Somebody's due for a thick ear,' Straw growled, unhurt.

'Have you fixed the great day yet?' John asked.

'No.' Straw seemed still immersed in Cathy's strictures. 'There's no hurry.'

'Since the prospects at work looked up,' Cath spoke strongly, 'there's not been quite so much urgency about the ceremony. We're very happy with our present arrangements. We shall get round to marriage, don't you fret. But now Les knows his job's safe for the next few months, he doesn't seem so, I'll not say "keen", that's wrong, but "concerned".'

'Why is that?' Stella, all bright eyes.

'He thought he'd be at a loose end, out of a job, no chance of employment, so he needed buoying up. And marrying me was the solution.'

Straw, silenced, stared in awe.

'It gave him something to do?' John joked. 'To think about?'

'It set him up. It restored his confidence.'

'His self-esteem,' Stella added, shyly.

'The words I'm searching for. Somebody loved him, appreciated him. Now he's Les Straw, the big chief foreman at James Limpenny's, METE, again, he doesn't need me quite so much.'

'She's got it all sorted out,' Les said. He seemed not displeased.

'Is it anywhere near the truth?' John, chaffing again.

'She's got her wits about her,' Straw answered.

'It doesn't seem quite right that love should depend on economics.' Stella.

'But I should guess, it always will.' Straw, seriously.

'I wasn't talking about love, exactly,' Cathy's voice rang loud, but slow, as if each word had been hand-picked, 'but about getting married. It's different. I love him whether we're married or not. And I expect he feels the same about me, except he'll be too embarrassed to say so.'

'I do.' Straw, parsonically.

They laughed. The young people refused a further drink and made their way back, walking quickly in the warm dark of the streets.

'I think Mrs Cath is intelligent,' John said.
'They both are.'
'But will they profit from it?'

19

John and Stella met promptly at eight on Wednesday at his house.

'Let's not go out,' she had suggested on the Sunday. 'A light collation chez toi, cooked and served with your own fair hands.'

'It won't be much.'

'I don't want much.'

'We're supposed to be celebrating your headship of department.'

When she arrived, John looked unusually well dressed, but preoccupied. She asked what was wrong.

'I was just starting to prepare the salad when bloody Alexander rang.'

'Father? Son?'

'Father. Michael.' John turned away, sighing. He stood scratching with his right hand the left arm of his alpaca jacket. 'Bad news. Sebastian and Lise are splitting up. He's very seriously upset.'

'When did this happen?' Stella asked.

'Happen? I don't know. He rang about an hour ago, and I think he'd only just heard. He asked me what he should do.'

'I'm surprised. Lise recently rang me, and she sounded perfectly all right.'

'When?'

'The evening of my interview. Sebastian was in Germany. She sounded very happy. They were getting on well. In fact, she tempted providence, I thought, by saying that he was perfect.'

'He isn't now.' John clenched his fists. 'I don't know whether Sebastian has taken up with some woman in Germany as he did in Australia. He can only have come back on Sunday or Monday, so it must have blown up suddenly.'

'Who rang Michael?'

'He didn't say. I took it to be Lise, but I didn't ask. He was in a terrible state, kept repeating, "What shall I do?" '

'And what did you tell him?'

'What could I? I said I was engaged this evening. To tell *you* the truth, Stella, I was going to ask you if you'd come back to live here. Since Sunday, when we decided to eat at home, I'd decided to walk you all over the house, and then pop my question. So I couldn't do anything for him today, even if there was anything that could be done. I just said he was to keep ringing her. Or writing. The poor sod was in such a mess that I couldn't make out whether Lise had left home, or had decided to, or if it was Sebastian who hadn't come back.'

'Is she still singing in *Oedipus*?'

'I did ask that. Yes. She is.'

'I'm sorry.'

'He was talking about driving down. And he hates his car. And he was worried about taking time off from his school. He sounded like a really old man, Stella, with a croaking voice. He was angry, and frustrated, but weak with it. I think some of these old-fashioned teachers think they ought to be able to sort out pretty well any problem. I suppose he'd judged all was well with them, as you did, once the Australia hoo-ha had settled itself.'

'And what did you decide in the end?'

'I'm no good at giving advice. I told him to keep in touch with Lise, and he asked me if I'd drive him down Friday night or Saturday morning. I said I would.'

'That's good,' Stella said.

Though he had taken great care over it, and probably an afternoon off, he dismissed the meal he'd prepared as 'café grub'. He served melon, leek soup, gammon with pine-apple, all deliciously cooked; Stella realised how hungry she was and ate with rare pleasure. They ended with fresh fruit salad, drinking no alcohol, only iced or mineral water. John explained.

219

'I knew you would come by car, so it's not sensible to drink. Secondly I wanted to ask you my famous question, and you needed to be sober for that.' He sounded both facetious and guarded. 'But I let that out of the bag too early. I must have been really disturbed by what Michael said.'

They sat staring at empty plates.

'I'll give you your answer,' Stella said, gently. He gripped his chin. He could tell that her tone was kindly, but could not guess what she would say. He did not speak. 'I'll come back.'

John stood; so did she. He edged round the table, clasped her in his arms. They kissed, deeply. Then she shook herself free, and sat.

'We'll clear the dishes, and then we'll have this famous walk round the house, this inspection, and I'll give you my proper answer.'

'The same one, I hope.'

'Of course.' She sounded pert.

They washed the dishes, and he resumed his jacket.

'Are you ready for the trip?'

'I am.' Stella felt not altogether comfortable now. The element of farce was strong.

'The kitchen,' he announced, waving his arms, ridiculously. 'Under-used but in good order.'

'Let me look in the freezer,' she ordered. He obeyed and she expressed satisfaction at what she saw. Next she stared about her, at the shelves, the utensils.

'It's all very clean.'

'I'm out most of the day. I have a firm in to do the housework. That could continue.'

'We'll see.'

'Pantry, larder, cellars?'

'Show me all.'

They did the rounds, rather subdued; it seemed unnecessary. Back on the ground floor, they stood at the door of the small study.

'Do you use this?' she asked.

'No, never. Upstairs if I have work or in the dining room.'

The dining room she looked briefly over again. It was pleasant with a large table, solid furniture matching the oak mantelpiece and fender. The corner where the cat, shut in, had scratched the carpet, was no worse. She found the design and colour of the carpet surprisingly attractive.

He switched on all the lights in the sitting room. Ornaments, aligned books, fresh-cut flowers, the glass in pictures were gleaming. Curtains had already been drawn.

'You've decorated this,' she said.

'I haven't. I had old Hobbs in. And the downstairs loo, and two of the bedrooms.'

'But things are still in the same places. You haven't moved the pictures round.'

'No. I was satisfied.'

This she took to be a compliment. She had charge of the buying and hanging of pictures. He'd not complain about the bare walls of a prison cell, provided the furniture was strong, and would consider it a life of luxury if one put a vase of artificial flowers on a table. He looked smart as he stood there. Stella was glad this room had been cleaned up; she had hated it when she was ill, found its formality overwhelming, without comfort. She remembered cowering in an armchair, locked in a paralysis of misery, noticing nothing, receiving nothing but echoes of her inner anxieties. Now it was bright. She stepped across the room, sat down in the same chair. It supported her; the plush arms responded gracefully to her touch. The oil painting she had bought from the art-mistress, a green pond in a copse, hung to her right in a broad gold frame. Comfort, cheer, beauty, care, solidity, money surrounded her, and she could appreciate it.

'This feels like home,' she said, slapping the chair arms with flat hands. She had despaired of herself in this room, lost in her tunnel of depression. Now she could take it as an adjunct of her personality, new-made, old-founded. John was explaining that he'd fetched his home-help firm in on Tuesday to hoover, clean the windows, dust the surfaces.

Stella sprang to her feet laughing, clapping her hands. She thrust her arm through his.

221

'Ten out of ten,' she called.

'Yes, miss.'

They made their way upstairs. Though the two main bedrooms had been decorated, furniture stood unchanged. The third bedroom shone fair as the other two. In the study her desk stood in the spot she had chosen, leather top polished, but with only a calendar on the surface. He had not cluttered it with any of his papers. His desk, though tidy, was crowded, his chair pushed back as if he'd only just risen from it.

'You've really looked after the place.'

They examined both bathrooms, upstairs lavatory, box-room, all extravagantly neat, in T-square order.

'Will it do?' he asked.

'Oh, yes.'

He followed her downstairs, careful not to touch her. They stood in the hall, she looking at the stained glass of the front door, dull now in electric light.

'Will you give me your answer, please?' He spoke slowly and formally. She could imagine him thus addressing a client who could not make up his mind. He did not press or badger, but one did not mistake his seriousness.

'Yes. I'll come back.'

Stella spoke lightly, but stretched out her hands to him. He took them, thanked her, then drew her to him. They kissed; she felt the hardness of his sex.

'When?' In a moment of respite.

'We'll start tonight. We may as well.'

He kissed her again, almost furiously, then jigged her round.

'Then that means we can celebrate properly. With alcohol. What do you suggest?'

'Oh, I don't know.'

'Champagne.'

'I tell you what I would like.' He put on a mock-judicial face. 'A Scotch and water.' He looked pleased.

'I didn't know you drank spirits.'

'I've learnt some bad habits on my own. Now, I'd also like to take the weight off my feet, if you don't mind.'

He apologised, led her back to the drawing room where she chose the chair of shame, stepping boldly across.

'I feel like singing,' he said.

'Don't let me stop you.'

Standing back like a waiter he named the varieties of whisky he could offer. She chose a well-known brand.

'How will you have it?' he asked.

'In a glass.' Relenting, 'With water. Half and half.'

They drank, not excessively, went to bed to make naked love. He used a condom, but would not have minded wearing a stovepipe hat. Next morning, downstairs, they felt slightly awkward but each clumsily happy to get into the other's way. Stella felt subdued, glad but sober, as she drove in good time to collect books from her flat. She had expected more, but was glad that the reunion had been achieved without histrionics. She would return to the house that night to sleep, having worked at her flat. John would not show up until seven at the earliest, he thought, but neither would need feeding. After a day's toil, they'd be at each other's beck and call for love and intimacy and pleasure.

It was nearer eight when Stella arrived, and John was already at home. Not until they had kissed and rolled like lovers did they speak seriously.

'I've been in touch with Michael,' he announced.

She sat, knees together, whisky in hand.

'He's contacted Lise. She wants us all three to go down on Sunday. Is that possible?'

Stella acquiesced, and he went to telephone Mr Alexander. She could hear the urgent voices outside, but not make out what was said. John returned, drew his chair alongside hers, held her hand.

'He didn't know much more. Sebastian's away in Brighton, at the university, and she's singing. They're both living in the house; they can keep out of the other's way if they wish; she'll knock up something to eat for lunch, and we can talk.'

'Has Sebastian agreed to this?'

'That I couldn't make out. I quizzed Michael hard, but I don't think he knows. Sebastian realises that we're coming

223

down, but whether he's agreed to be there, or take any part, I couldn't say. Probably Michael's not clear. He's still unlike himself, gabbling. He has always been sharp-tongued. Never said much, but able to do damage. But now he just spewed words.'

'Why do you think that is?'

John bit thoughtfully on his right thumbnail.

'I guess . . .' John broke off. 'This is all fantasy, but I guess his life seemed somehow completed, made perfect in that marriage. They are not only man and wife, but very successful in their competitive world, the musical métier where Michael is a very inferior practitioner.'

Stella, slightly put out, commented on his use of words. She saw him as one putting formality on to hide insecurity.

On Sunday morning they set off sharp on eight o'clock.

They had spent their evenings together and their nights, had even brought work home. It all seemed easy, not passionless but not spiky, never awkward. Stella turned up with a new picture, a Corot print, to fill a dark space in the dining room. She felt successful, flicking a duster about the house. Her husband seemed diffident about making comment on her return, but he touched her often, kissed her, as though they were new lovers.

The early start on a Sunday morning of bright sunshine presented them with no difficulty; they rose, ate breakfast, cleared and washed the dishes and still had ten minutes to spare.

'I said I'd start exactly at eight,' John informed her, 'so I won't jump the gun.'

They took a turn round the garden, at its best, scented with buddleia alternifolia, though John regretted he had not spent much time on it. The wodge of Sunday newspapers had not yet arrived.

'I've cancelled mine,' Stella said.

'Already?'

'Why not?'

'Isn't it what you call tempting providence? It may not work out here for you.'

'It will if I have any say in it. Next week I shall give my three months' notice on the flat.'

She walked back into the house, shoulders stiff, a determined little madam, so that John both admired and feared.

Michael Alexander locked his front door gloomily, refused to sit by the driver, said he'd perhaps snatch a few minutes of the sleep he'd missed this last week. He was tidily dressed, with open shirt collar, but flounced like a scolded child, slammed the car door brutally, sighed. Yes, he was perfectly all right, quite comfortable, didn't want for anything. He seemed determined to be uncooperative.

Once they skimmed down the near-deserted motorway, Michael became more sociable. He had spoken every evening to Lise before she set off for the theatre. She had sounded calm, expressed pleasure that all of them were coming. 'It will give me something to do, to have to prepare lunch.' He had not spoken to Sebastian, who was apparently still in the house, but Lise had said he knew the three were coming. She and her husband were presumably talking.

'I asked her,' Michael huffed, red-eyed, 'if he'd raised any objections, and she said he hadn't. But I wouldn't put it past him to slip out of our way this morning.'

'You're not optimistic?' John asked.

'Never. Especially about this. But we shall see Lise, and she'll be certain she has our support. The opera finishes next month, and she'll need to know that the people she likes are prepared to do a bit for her.'

'You think they'll part?' John pressed.

'It sounds like it, doesn't it? Might be the best thing. I was pleased, I can tell you, when Joyce upped sticks and left me. My pride smarted, but I began to realise I was better off.'

Michael slept during part of the journey; they could hear the stertorous breathing. They stopped twice at service stations to allow him to visit the urinals.

The London street where the Alexanders lived stretched sunny and deserted as if the inhabitants were still in bed. Many curtains, upstairs and down, were indeed still closed.

225

'That was a respectable journey,' Michael told Stella as they walked the lane at the back of the house. 'The car makes a difference. That's fast and comfortable. Makes the world of a difference on a long journey.' He had recovered, and had assumed, with his usual dissatisfied, sharp persona, a jaunty walk.

Lise let them in, immediately served coffee.

Curtains were drawn against the sun, so that light in the room swam pleasantly dim. Sebastian came down ten minutes later, shook hands stiffly with the visitors. Lise poured and passed him coffee in silence. He thanked her curtly.

They talked, not without inhibitions. John asked about *Oedipus* and the German tour. Sebastian described how little he and his accompanist had practised together, as the pianist had suffered from a feverish cold and spent most of the time outside the concert-hall or car in bed. Had it made any difference, John wanted to know.

'Yes and no. And if anything, to the good. We didn't play works that we hadn't done together before, and I suppose that made a difference. And Stephen's the sort of man who'd get up from his death-bed to give a good performance. I was a bit on edge, I can tell you, and perhaps that's what I need.'

John raised the matter of Stella's promotion, and Sebastian cross-examined her politely about what differences this would make to her job. The others listened. Lise reported briefly on the end of *Oedipus* and said that the opera might be mounted in Chicago in two years' time. 'Would she be in the production?' 'They're talking about it.'

Stella helped Lise to clear the coffee cups before their hostess dismissed the men to the pub. It sounded planned.

'Lunch at one-fifteen. So it's one drink. Back on time,' she ordered.

'One is the operative word,' John agreed.

The men left almost jovially. In the kitchen, Stella helped prepare the salad, two quiches, scrub the new potatoes. She wondered how she should introduce the subject of the

226

broken marriage, but there was no need. Lise raised it bluntly.

'I suppose you've heard about our quarrel?'

'Michael said one or two things. He seemed very upset.'

'It was immediately after Seb came back from Germany. Stephen Steinberg's illness had put him out, because it meant much more work. Steve usually sees to their end of arrangements. As far as I understand it, the actual recitals went very well. But the authorities squeezed another performance in, at a handsome profit and good publicity for them all, be it said. But it half-creased Steve, who felt so ill that he didn't want to do it, and so what with the arguments and extra travelling they were just about bushed when they got back.'

'How's Stephen now?'

'He's much better. They had a rehearsal yesterday.'

Lise bustled about, deliberately saying nothing, clashing colanders, saucepans, plates.

'And?'

'He slept in one of the spare rooms. He was whacked and told me to let him have his sleep out.'

'Is that usual?' Stella said.

'No. He's usually pretty spry. But this was Sunday evening. I'd no opera to go out to. He went up to bed about ten. He'd said very little. To tell you the truth I put it down to making a hash of one of the recitals, or pieces. He sets himself such incredibly high standards, and is inconsolable if he doesn't do something well. So he was grumpy, and I kept out of his way as far as I could while I looked after him.'

Here Lise replaced talking with a rush of kitchen duties. For five minutes she seemed utterly occupied, speaking only to issue orders and once to swear. When culinary preparation became placid once more, she turned almost dramatically on Stella, wiping hands on apron, face stained.

'I heard nothing of him Monday morning. I didn't get up very early myself. I lunched from the fridge. There was plenty for him when he rolled out. He came down at a quarter to two. He hadn't shaved or dressed. And he looked thoroughly disagreeable. "Look at the bloody time," he said. "Why the hell didn't you roust me out?" I said something cheerful about his beauty sleep, and that didn't please him. He stamped off upstairs.'

'Were you surprised at his ill-temper?'

'No, not really. He's hard on himself. I've told you. And he'd just wasted some study time. He often grumbles at me when he's displeased with himself. So, no, this was nothing out of the ordinary. I shouted up to the bathroom to ask what he would like for lunch, but he told me not to bother. I saw him next about four when he went out to post some letters.

' "What about your lunch?" I asked him when he returned.

' "I'll get a snack when I'm hungry."

' "Are you all right?" I said.

' "As ever I shall be."

' "What's wrong with you?"

'He slapped himself down into the nearest chair as if he wanted to break it, and sat there with his face in his hands.

' "There's something wrong. What is it?"

' "Doesn't matter."

' "I don't like to see you like this." I went and perched on the arm of his chair. He just held himself there, stiff.

' "It's our marriage," he said in the end. He spoke so slowly and quietly that I thought he was trying the idea out on himself, without letting me overhear.

' "What's wrong with it?"

' "It's not any good to either of us. It clamps us to each other without any advantage that I can see."

' "And when did you come to this conclusion?" I asked.

' "I've known it for some time now."

' "That's not how it seemed before you set off for Germany."

' "No. I did my best to make it work." Sebastian jerked his head upwards. "But it's useless. We're just hopelessly incompatible."

' "And what do you suggest we do?"

' "Just keep out of each other's way until we see things a bit straighter."

' "Until you do, you mean." He didn't answer. "And who is it this time? Some little German beauty?"

' "It's not like that at all." '

Lise retold the story dramatically, but without overstatement. She continued with her preparations for lunch, but these in no way interfered with her recital. She had sat on his chair arm; they were like two statues she said, until it was clear that he was not going into further explanation, and then she rose and stood looking straight down at him. He didn't turn towards her, or speak. She walked out, and upstairs to her room.

'Were you angry?' Stella asked.

'Angry? Furious. And shivering with cold, though the weather was warm. And surprised. I mean, he just sprang it on me. As if he was testing me. I'd no idea. I thought we were getting along well. Once I was clear of the room I began to cry. That surprised me, too. It was so violent. I ran to my bedroom and sat on the bed and howled. And I kept dashing my head down on to the pillows to knock sense into the situation.'

'How long did this last?'

'Half an hour. A shorter time perhaps. I knew that I should have to leave soon after six for the theatre. That was the last thing I wanted to do, but I couldn't cry off at this late hour. I dragged myself to the bathroom, raked my things together. I even walked downstairs to see if he was still there, but he'd gone.'

'You didn't say any more to him before you went out?'

'No. He'd hidden himself away.' Lise was counting out forks and knives for the table. 'The most horrible thing about it was that he spoke so softly. He wasn't angry with me. He can rave and rant and bawl. He's even used his fists on me once. But this was so calm and flat and deliberate and calculated. As if he'd worked it all out, and convinced himself. And I hadn't even noticed. Oh, I gave him all sorts of excuses and benefits of the doubt. He was exhausted after this German tour, and it had changed his personality. Temporarily, I hoped.'

'Did you sing that night?'

'Yes.'

'It went well?'

'As far as I know. It's killing work, battling with Nick's orchestra, but I forget everything else, and by the time it's done, and I've cleaned up, I'm ready for the taxi home. Sometimes we stay for a drink and a chat, but not that night.'

'When did you see Sebastian again?'

'Next morning. I was up moderately early for me, not long after nine. I ate my breakfast, but there was no sign or sound of him. I read the newspaper and wrote a letter or two and then went up to my room to look at some new songs I shall need next season. And I met him on the first-floor landing. It's rather narrow, so he drew himself back into the wall.' Lise glanced up, harassed even now. 'I swear he wasn't going to speak. He just stood there cowering back, holding himself off so that we shouldn't touch. It made me wild. I wasn't having that. I stood straight in front of him, and I said, "You're mad." He didn't answer. "You're not sane." I think I was shouting by this time. He didn't alter his position or his expression or anything. "You ought to be locked up." I couldn't get through to him. He drew himself in further, and sidled off along the wall. It made me wild, because it looked cowardly and dignified, and silly. When he was just past me I called out, "What have you got to say for yourself?" '

(Perhaps the fact that he was now a yard or two past her allowed him the use of his voice.) 'I don't think this is a good time,' he said, pacifically.

'For what?'

'For discussion of our problems.'

'There's been no bloody discussion. Just a pronunciamento from you that it's all over and done with, that we're incompatible.'

'Isn't it so?' He spoke very softly. 'Isn't it obvious?'

'No, it's not. Not to me it isn't. It's some bloody lunatic change of mind on your part. For what reason I don't know. For no reason, I guess.'

He tightened the belt of his dressing gown.

230

'This is not a good time,' he said.

'When is, then?'

'Later in the day perhaps. That is, if you've the inclination.'

'Oh, fuck off.'

Sebastian bowed his head, turned about and went to his room, or elsewhere. A few minutes later Lise heard the sound of his electric razor.

'And what did you make of all this?' Stella asked.

'I was frightened. He sounded so calm and collected, so rational.'

'And did you see him?'

'Yes, I did. After he'd washed and dressed, and presumably had breakfast or coffee, he came up to my practice room. I'd done a few exercises, and was casually looking through a couple of Mahler songs I hadn't sung since my college days.'

'Were you singing well?'

Again the angry toss of head and hair, the fierce grimace, but when she spoke again, Lise's voice was low, flat.

'I can't remember. I think I was pleased enough. Though I churned this business over and over in my mind.' She now made no pretence of cooking. 'He knocked on the door.'

She had invited him in, but had not moved from her piano stool, so that she had three-quarters of her back towards him.

'I think I owe you some explanation,' he had said, gently closing the door. Seb's clothes were informal but neat, his thick hair newly washed. She smelt his perfume, aftershave, temperately used. Very carefully he had picked up a chair and had placed it so that he could at least catch a glimpse of his wife's face. She made no attempt to turn full features to him. He cleared his throat.

'While we were in Germany, we had trouble. Bad arrangements and Stephen's illness made the whole trip something of a nightmare. It also made spare time for me. After the first day we didn't practise together. I practised, but on my own. The weather was also bad, so that I couldn't go out a great deal. We had hassle, about the extra concert, and some changes in travel arrangements. It was rotten, and unusual, and not really anybody's fault. But it left me with time on my hands, in hotel bedrooms. We didn't go out after concerts. Steve made straight back to bed. And it was one afternoon, pissing it down outside, I suddenly realised I did not want to come back home. To this house, I mean.'

Lise now swivelled to face him though that meant she sat awkwardly on the stool.

'Do you understand that?' he had asked gently.

'No.'

'Why not?'

She thought hard, clutching at her clothes.

'Was it, did it come as a surprise to you?' she had asked, icily now.

He smiled momentarily, the slightest alteration of his lips, almost as if in approbation of her intelligence or sarcasm.

'Yes, I see what you mean.' He nodded, as if he had not considered this. 'It did in a way, in that I had not formulated it precisely before. I'd known, known vaguely, if that's the word, that there was something amiss. But I hadn't tracked it down.'

'Because it didn't exist,' Lise said. He nodded to acknowledge the point, but ignored it.

'Our marriage is a waste of time. We live together, share a convenient house, seem friendly, have sex sometimes when we're not too tired, but . . .'

'But what?'

'We're not the same people we were when we were married.'

'It's not to be expected. We're both more successful. That means we're away much more.'

'It drags me down, Lise. Clearly you're satisfied with this convenience.'

'What more do *you* want?' she had said.

'It's not what I want. It's what I don't want. Our life here inhibits me, stops me working properly.'

They had argued like this, unsatisfactorily, for perhaps a quarter of an hour according to Lise. Always they returned

232

to the same obstacle: the marriage not only meant nothing to him, but in some way prevented his full development as a virtuoso. When she pressed him about the sort of woman who would suit his demands, he seemed not to know, claiming that until he had sorted out what was wrong with this marriage it would be foolish to set up, or even try to describe, the next. Always, very quietly, without anger or a raised voice, he returned to his point: their marriage was dead to him, hung round him like a corpse tied to a murderer. He was prepared to blame himself, but could not be moved. He saw no point in their continuing. He seemed unable to name her faults, only to state and restate his conviction.

'I told him he was unreasonable, insane. He agreed, saying the strength of his feelings seemed outlandish, but he saw no prospect of change. He couldn't be moved.'

'Was he sorry? For what he was saying?'

'He expressed regret a time or two. But it meant nothing. He was convinced.'

'Is this irrational conviction usual with him?'

'I'd say no. He's very articulate, can argue a cogent case. That's one of the things I first admired about him, outside his musical ability.'

Lise stared hopelessly at the floor about her. Their preparations for lunch were now complete. The men had ten minutes' grace.

'And what was the outcome?' Stella asked.

'I asked him what he intended to do.'

'And?'

' "Move out," he said.'

Lise had argued with him, demanding again if the bad week in Germany was the cause of his dissatisfaction, but he had denied this. It had brought it to the forefront of his mind perhaps, but that was all. Sebastian had spoken all of this dully, a dumb ox unlike his bright self, and when she had said that the trouble between them lay in him, and not in something she had said or done, he had agreed.

At this point they heard the men come in through the front door.

They entered quietly, not bringing the easy companion-
ship of the pub back with them.

'Get your hands washed,' Stella told them, on instruction. 'We're serving now.'

The meal proved not as gloomy as Stella expected. Michael pressed his son about the German trip, about the size
of the audience, the hospitality, the venues, the ambience,
the reception. Sebastian answered reasonably enough,
while Michael interspersed comments about his own recitals with George Paxton. Sebastian seemed genuinely
interested, pressed his father hard about rehearsals.

'I'll tell you why I ask,' he said. 'I'm sometimes short of
a pianist.'

'I'm too busy.'

'But you've been talking about retirement.'

'I thought you were very settled with Stephen Steinberg.'

'This last little effort has shaken him up. He thinks I was
unsympathetic.'

'And were you?' John, interrupting.

'You could say so. But he would have been bloody annoyed if they'd provided me with a good German sub-
stitute. He wasn't having that, ill as he was supposed to be.'

'But he hasn't forgiven you?'

'We're contracted for concerts until October. And he
needs the money. But he's disgruntled.'

Michael now seemed thoroughly lively, as if what he had
found here in the house this morning had somehow
cheered him. He quizzed Lise about *Oedipus* and about her
recitals. No one spoke a word about the rift in the marriage.
At the end of the meal, when they were arguing about
clearing the dishes, Sebastian suddenly moved, pounced,
she thought, on Stella, took her by the elbow.

'Could I have a word with you? If you please?'

'Yes.'

'In private.'

He led her off to a small room on the ground floor,
formerly a pantry or storeroom, but now carpeted, with one
Parker Knoll rocker, and two small Windsor chairs and a
table. The sash-window was curtained but barred on the

234

outside, showing the green sun of the garden through a darkening frame of Virginia creeper. The walls of clearish grey held one picture, a small oil-painting in a wide, tarnished gold frame. It seemed to depict a naked woman, kneeling, vulnerable, unerotic. Sebastian indicated the rocking-chair to Stella, who sat, very comfortably. He parked himself by the table, but realising at once that he presented a mere silhouette to his guest, drew back to the wall.

'I hope you don't mind my dragging you off like this,' he began.

'No.'

'Both John and Michael suggested that I had a word with you.' She nodded, murmured. 'You know about the trouble between Lise and me?' He waited for confirmation. 'Has she spoken to you about it? This morning while we were out?' Again the pause. 'She has. Then you'll know something of it from her point of view. I'll lean towards my side, I expect. But John said you had left home, as I intend to do, and that the reason was depression. And now quite recently you had returned. Is that roughly it?'

' "Roughly" is just about the word.'

'What do you mean?'

'I had a bout of depression beginning some time towards the end of last year. I was under pressure at school, chiefly because I felt I wasn't making any progress. I knew I ought to be applying for promotion, but though one or two openings inside the college came up, the principal wouldn't look at me. His view was, he's told me since he's made me head of department, why should he shift me from doing a very good job, and pay me more to do something I mightn't enjoy so much or do so well. I didn't see it like that. I was down, unappreciated, unloved.'

'And your husband?'

'It happened he was particularly busy at that time, and so he was away a great deal, and uncertain about timing. He might be out until all hours of the night. He seemed not to notice what was happening to me. I dreaded school, and I dreaded home.'

235

'Did you consult your doctor?'

'In due course. But I blamed John for my predicament. With depression one can't think straight. I felt ill, all aches and pains, nauseated, feeble. I also couldn't easily manage normal things like meals, or students' reports or even anything straightforward at home, such as paying bills without heart-searching and trouble. I slept badly. This loss of everyday confidence, I believe now, was due to my depression. And at the time I laid the blame on my relationship with John. That I considered was the basic cause of my unhappiness.'

'And it wasn't?' Sebastian asked.

'I guess it was a contributory cause, though I think now my dissatisfaction with my progress at college was probably more important. It is even possible that the main cause was chemical. But at the time I blamed John for my predicament.'

'Wrongly?'

'Wrongly. But that was what it felt like. There was no support or understanding from him. He didn't seem to know how I felt, or care. I needed looking after, fussing over, and I found none of that at home. He was too busy.'

'Did he not see how you'd changed?'

'Yes. But he couldn't think why. We were settled in a place we liked. We went out together to meals and concerts. He was making more and more money in spite of the recession. But I, and this is how it must have seemed to him, had for some reason taken against him. He could do nothing right for me.'

'Why did he think this was so?'

'I don't suppose he could account for it. I'd fallen out of love with him. Some such expression. It happens.'

'Does it?' Sebastian snapped.

'It appears to. There must be good reasons. But they're not always obvious. It just looks as if a person has changed his or her mind. Arbitrarily. Wilfully.'

'And you left home?'

'Yes. I'm amazed that in the state I was in I managed to

236

pack my traps and go. By that time my doctor had sent me on to a psychiatrist, and perhaps that, and the drugs, gave me sufficient energy or incentive to clear off.'

'And it proved successful?'

'Well, I had removed myself from the main cause of my condition: an unsympathetic husband. That's how I would have put it at the time.'

'And you began to be . . . better?'

'I suppose so. I began to be able to cope. I had to. My period of depression, which seemed shattering at the time, was, I'm coming to see now, not as serious, well, as some. People commit suicide, become useless, incapable, withdrawn, content to be tucked away into mental hospitals, utterly dependent on drugs . . . Oh, God. They're nothing like human beings.'

'Are you still on drugs?'

'No. Not now. And I'm also able to make judgements about myself. That's why I say it wasn't very serious as these things go.'

'What triggered it off? Can you put it down to any one event?'

'No. Every little happening seemed to batter my confidence. I've told you it was, in my opinion now, for what that's worth, my lack of success in my career.'

'Are you very ambitious?'

'As the next woman. And there is stress on women.'

'And yet at the time you would have blamed your husband?'

'That's what it felt like. He was at home. At nights, sometimes, and weekends. He's an unimaginative man. Kind, generous, all the rest, but with no understanding of mental illness.'

'Why is that, do you think?'

'He's perhaps near it, himself. Tends to be very down if anything goes wrong. Needs a nanny or a mummy to fuss him. Or he had never met it in other people.'

'You don't think very highly of men?'

'I don't accept their own valuation of themselves, if that's what you mean.'

'I see. Now what about my dissatisfaction with Lise?' he asked.

'I'm in no position to judge. I'd have to hear why it is that you can go off to Germany apparently much in love, very satisfied with your marriage, and not much more than a week later come back with the story that you're going to leave her.' Stella could not keep the scorn out of her voice.

'I don't know that I'd accept your scenario, that I was in love with Lise, satisfied with our marriage.'

'Wasn't it so?'

'Do you always believe what you're told?'

'In a case like this it's all I can do. What other evidence is there?'

'And, therefore, if both Lise and I are liars, or self-deceivers, you'll never get it straight. And you'll never solve it.'

'I am not promising solutions. I'm listening, in so far as you give it to me, to your side of the story. If you now confess you're lying, then there's not much hope. You certainly seem on the defensive.'

'That's true,' Sebastian answered. 'I don't think talking it over with you will make much difference. But I promised my father and John that that's what I'd do, and here I am doing it.'

She did not answer, buttoned her lips. He sat swinging a leg, rather shamefaced.

'Do you think it's depression in my case?' he began.

'How can I decide that? You'd know if it was, I can tell you.'

'I think you're angry with me,' Sebastian said, mildly enough.

'It's the "little woman" attitude you take. You've told your wife that you're leaving her, and this has had a dreadful effect both on her and on your father. But you take a superior attitude when you talk to me, as if to question the usefulness of the exercise. You make no attempt to explain why you've acted as you have.'

'Would it do any good?'

'There you go again. It might clear your mind for you if you tried to explain your unreasonable behaviour to someone who doesn't think like you.'

238

'I'm unreasonable, am I?' Sebastian asked affably.

'If the account which Lise gives is anywhere near the truth, you are, and make no mistake about it.'

'You're a very fierce young woman, aren't you? It's no wonder my father fancies you. He likes people who stand up to him.' He tapped his fingertips together. Stella could have kicked out at him. 'When I'm away on a recital tour, I practise hard, on my own and with my pianist. I'm careful, on the look-out for error or passages to improve. Then there are recitals which are exhausting.'

'Not exhilarating?'

'To some extent, yes. But the concentration drains me. The time between, the meals, social contacts, sightseeing I try to make as restful as I can. That's not always in my hands. This last time in Germany, everything went to pieces. Steve's illness, bad weather, one unsuitable hall, changes of itinerary meant that I was constantly on edge, dreading the next bad turn. And during this time I became convinced that my marriage was useless to my career.'

'On what grounds?' Stella pressed.

'It had not prepared me for times like this when everything went awry.'

'Should it have done? And how, exactly?'

'Well, it ought to be a stay, a foundation. Otherwise, what's the use of marriage?'

'There are financial advantages, for instance. Social. Legal, perhaps.'

'Yes. Probably. But . . .' Sebastian broke off, let his hands dangle.

'But what?'

'It hardly seems worth the trouble. Worth cultivating.'

'Just because,' Stella's voice hardened, 'it doesn't from a distance magically solve the problems of an unfortunate tour in Germany?'

'When I thought about marriage, and I did, quite hard,' Sebastian spoke without anger, 'it seemed to be a millstone.'

'Why? You go off round the world exactly as your agent asks. You don't consult Lise, do you? You just tell her that's what will happen.'

'That's true. But I have some compunction about it. I feel I'm not treating her properly. That it's my side only that counts.'

'And you come back, you the moral being, the man afflicted with conscience, and baldly announce that your marriage is over. Full stop. Take it or leave it. What sort of argument is that?'

'It's more complicated,' he said.

'I'm sure.'

'I'm not so certain that our marriage is doing her any good.'

'Then, if you'd had any feeling for her, the first thing you would have done was to consult her.'

'I didn't up and leave like you. I put my point of view to her. I haven't gone yet.'

'That's it. Abuse the plaintiff's attorney.'

'I was convinced that we had entered on a contract that would not do either of us any good. We feel, perhaps, that all the time we were not being fair to our partners. That we ought, say, to start a family, or spend more time together. What, in fact, we both need is freedom, to do as we like.'

'Lise doesn't think like that. She was quite happy.'

'She has old-fashioned ideas.'

'When you were in Germany, you realised that you ought to be free. To achieve your destiny.' Scorn burnt; sour, acid. 'Now, I realise that things were going wrong for you at the time, that you were feeling the whole world had turned against you, that your luck had run out. That's all right. We can't think straight when we're badly hurt. But my question to you, is this: do you think the same now?'

'Yes.'

'Why?'

'My misfortunes, call 'em what you will, opened my eyes to our true position. And the position is exactly as it was, as it appeared to me then.'

They stared hard at the ground. He laid an arm glumly on the table. He chewed at his lower lip, breathing heavily.

'You haven't consulted Lise.'

'You didn't consult your husband.'

'I'm not claiming I acted properly. I felt so harried,

240

besieged, battered, that I just escaped. Just as I would have run away from a building on fire. I didn't work it out. I reached a stage where I couldn't think any more.'

'Don't you see I'm in the same position? I can no longer bear to accept the constraints of being married.'

'You don't blame Lise. Not once. I blamed John. He was the trouble, I thought. Wrongly, as it turned out.'

'Except that Lise is not the right woman for me.'

'Is any woman?'

'Probably not.'

'You're thoroughly selfish.'

'True. My sort of career demands that.'

'And you'll sacrifice Lise? Don't you realise that she loves you?'

'Now. Yes. That may be so. She may think so. She'll soon lose it.'

A sharp knock on the door interrupted them. Sebastian punched the table under his arm with real violence. Stella rose, opened the door. Her husband stood there, smiling.

'May I have my wife back?' John spoke facetiously to Sebastian.

'Give us two more minutes,' Stella said.

'Right. The kettle has boiled. We're ready to mash.'

'Pour it out,' Sebastian said. 'It won't be cold.'

John made a curious half-bow in their direction, like a comic Chinaman in a pantomime, and withdrew. Sebastian was now standing.

'Thank you for listening to me,' he said.

'But it won't make any difference?'

'Well, no. You can't expect that.'

'Lise is a human being. Don't forget it. She's not a block of wood.'

'Thank you for reminding me.'

Stella bridled at his sarcasm. She made for the door, but he was there first, holding it open.

'I'm as helpless as you were,' he said softly. 'Believe you me.'

She kept her mouth shut as she walked past him.

241

20

The visitors spent another hour with the younger Alexanders. All lacked ease, but remained polite. They drank tea, ate Madeira cake, and soon after four-thirty Michael suggested that they set off for Beechnall. Within ten minutes they were out of the house.

On the way back, Stella gave a brief, neutral account of her hour with Sebastian, and answered their questions.

'You don't think our visit did any good?' Michael asked.

'Not really.'

The men described their glum forty-five minutes in the pub, where Sebastian had been uncooperative and taciturn. John had suggested, it appeared, that Stella should talk it over with Sebastian, who had immediately agreed, though without enthusiasm.

'It's a failure,' Michael concluded, from the back seat.

'You never know,' John argued. 'At least you bothered to turn up. That might mean something.'

The latter part of their journey was completed in defeated silence. Stella invited Michael in for a drink, and to her surprise he accepted.

At first they were constrained until John asked Michael to play the piano. He seemed unwilling, played two pages of Schumann and then a transcription of a gavotte and musette from the Bach D major Cello Suite. He scowled. Idly he picked up a complete Beethoven from the piano, opened it angrily at the first page, shoved it on the stand and began on the first sonata, F minor, Opus 2, No. 1. By the time he had reached the Adagio, he seemed more cheerful, alert, upright. He smiled in the minuet, and rattled through the prestissimo at a good rate.

'Brilliant,' John encouraged.

242

'Hardly,' Michael answered. 'It's years since I played that through. I've heard plenty of pupils struggling with it.'

'It was great.' Stella.

'There's something about Beethoven,' Michael answered, still on the piano stool. 'You can feel the emotion even here when he's limited by eighteenth-century convention.'

'How old was he when he wrote that?'

'Middle, early twenties. It's dedicated to his old teacher, Haydn, though he said some rude things about him. Published 1796, it says.'

'A good period?' John asked.

'Yes. Late Haydn. And Beethoven at the peak of his apprentice work.'

Michael turned pages with apparent approval, refused coffee but accepted whisky. He sat swaying on the piano stool, perhaps working through music in his mind, for he occasionally stiffened, jerked his head as if at some striking harmony, compelling rhythm.

He picked up the whisky, sipped it, held it to the light.

'Just one more slow movement,' he announced. 'But good. Then it's home and duty.'

'What is it?' Stella asked.

'Opus 10, No. 3, Largo e mesto.' He relished the Italian.

'What's "mesto"?'

'Sad. Gloomy. Suits us to the ground.'

'Wasn't Beethoven supposed to be worrying about his deafness?' John asked.

'So they say.'

'Don't you believe them?'

Michael wet his lips with whisky, and began.

This time he played with intense concentration, as if he and Beethoven found themselves of one mind, in the darkness of the world. Sometimes he breathed deeply through his nose, and then shrugged his shoulders as he played, gathering his body together to express the composer's grief by contortion. His fingers rippled, and he concluded the movement with its quiet, broken voice as though he were trying it over for the first time, making it new. The listeners did not move, their attention fastened by the nails of his notes, on the pianist. Michael held his head to one side, his mouth open, his hands eloquent. When he had finished he sat, daring them to speak, amazed at what he had achieved.

Suddenly with a small sweep of the hands he opened into the sweetness of the minuet, stopping, hands on knees at the end of the first section.

'Go on,' Stella almost shouted.

Michael was smiling, and with an exaggerated gesture, began again; this time he played both minuet and trio with repeats. Concluding he clutched his whisky, drained it, said, '*Dolce*.'

John's eyes were wet; Stella clapped her hands.

'Thank you,' she said. 'That made today worthwhile.'

Michael took a step or two away from the piano; his face had resumed its discomfiture.

'More whisky?' John asked.

'No, thanks. I must get back. I've taken up far too much of your time already.'

'What will you do when you get home?' John asked.

'Sit thinking.'

'About what?'

'My son. Me.'

His answer lacked any sign of humour. He took his coat, held out his hand to Stella, who lifted her cheek to be kissed. He bent. John led him out to the car. Michael slouched like an old man along the path. Stella, on her own, sorted out her bag for the next day.

A week and a half later Stella was surprised to meet Michael in the common room of her college. He was there for an examiners' meeting, he claimed.

'Any news from the London end?' she asked.

'Lise rang last night.' He spoke as if he had just remembered. 'They're still together.'

'Do you think that's good?'

'I can't weigh it up. *Oedipus* has only a fortnight, I think, to run and then she'll be at something of a loose end.' He shook his head.

'But they're still together?'

'I don't know if that means anything. They don't seem to think in the way I do.'

'What do you mean?' Stella asked.

'For all I know they're living quite separate lives. The house is big enough.'

'Didn't Lise say?'

'No.'

The head of music breezed over to collect Alexander.

'Let me know,' she called, 'if anything happens.'

He raised a limp hand in acknowledgement.

When she reported the conversation to John he asked her why she hadn't rung Lise.

'Too busy. Book orders. Exams. And besides I'd be frightened of getting Sebastian.'

'You could ask him how he was getting on.'

'He wouldn't thank me for it.'

'You never know.'

'You ring him then.'

They laughed over that, uncomfortably.

After lunch on the following Sunday, Stella telephoned the Alexanders. It appeared from what Sebastian said, they were in the middle of a meal. They both kept well; both were busy. He did not encourage her to prolong the conversation, nor offer to summon his wife. Two days later, she received a letter from Lise. It appeared both humdrum and menacing.

. . . we are both still in the house together. Does this surprise you? I'm astonished, and yet it developed naturally. Or so it seems.

I hardly said anything to Seb at first, but we have had lunch together from day one. He's busy, and rehearsing as usual, like a lunatic. We manage without difficulty now to discuss meals or arrangements. It's odd. We sleep apart, but that doesn't bother me. Sometimes he seems friendly, gentle, thinking of something else. I don't know what to do or say to him about all this, but while we're on the last lap of the opera, I'm not going to rock the boat. (Do rowers have laps?) I feel both uncomfortable and relieved. It's as if we're talking in different languages. I ring

Michael now and then. He seems occupied and distant. Do you come across him much? He saw you once at your college. 'She looked just as beautiful at work as at home,' he said.

As soon as the opera's finished, well, a month after, I'm touring Australia and New Zealand for three weeks. It's the purest luck. Lenka Fischer (the opera queen) is quite ill, and they signed me on in her place. Seb keeps giving me bits of advice, but half-heartedly, as if he's not entitled to. It's all a terrific hard grind. I'm going for consultation lessons again to John Boys; and Fischer's pianist, Terence Quinn, and I have had a shot or two together. I'm really lucky . . .

Stella telephoned Michael for his opinion.

'Probably the best thing that could have happened. Fills in the two months between *Oedipus* and the beginning of our winter season.'

'Has she spoken to you about it?' she asked.

'Yes. She's asked me for ideas.'

'And you obliged?'

'She's a talented girl . . . woman. She's kept herself in shape, while the opera was going on, for recital work. So she's ready. That's the thing about a freelance career. Be prepared to do anything.'

When Stella asked about Lise and Sebastian, Michael seemed less cheerful.

'They're still together. So that's something. But I don't ask. I don't want to stir trouble.'

'Are you going away this summer?'

'Yes. To Cornwall. To help run a music school a friend of mine directs.'

'Hard work?'

'Yes. It usually is. But it's at the seaside.'

He did not ask about her or John's plans for the holiday. They had, in fact, booked a house near Rennes for the last fortnight in August. They would take John's car and sample great meals. They spoke of it in this offhand way, with not a mention of second honeymoons. It made Stella slightly suspicious, of herself, rather than of her husband. She should feel less grudging.

Two days from the end of term Lise, who had again

written, telephoned to ask Stella to spend a few days, three or four, in Kentish Town, if John could spare her.

'I want to talk to you, and shop a bit. I want to be a woman. It's all men, all of them marvellous, since this tour was arranged, and I want a smart, bright ("old-fashioned", Stella interjected) woman to talk me to normality.'

'Will Seb be there?'

'Yes, he will. But you needn't be afraid of him.'

John laughed at all this.

'It'll set you up. I don't want you up at that damned college all the holiday.'

'No, sir.'

He aimed an unconvincing swipe at her. They sounded happy, giggled often.

Lise, forbidden by Stella to use her car, bear-hugged her guest when she arrived by taxi from the station. They stood in the hallway, and stared at each other, then grappled again. Stella was amazed by Lise's sheer physical strength. When she remarked on it, Lise replied that her time as a mythical Theban had strengthened her shoulders.

'They'd no time for delicate wimps,' she said.

'So, hanging yourself every night has improved your physique.'

Lise grabbed her friend again with such violence that Stella felt slightly apprehensive. 'It's marvellous to have you here.'

They drank coffee until Terence Quinn arrived, the only planned interruption to Stella's visit, Lise said. The two practised for little over an hour, while Stella read the morning papers. Quinn, 'he looks seventy but he's fifty-five', a neat grey-haired little man, very dapper, with polished toecaps to his shoes, stayed to eat an omelette with them, primly flashing his cutlery as he ate very slowly, chewing as meticulously as he talked. He described Lenka Fischer as a fat bully. The words dropped with incredible clarity from his thin, precise lips. 'She was a fine singer once, and her voice has lasted well, but she has no ideas now. She sings by rote.' She had married her agent years ago, and he had made her successful, or more successful than she would have been, but she sang too often to think about what she was doing. 'It amazes me,' Quinn wiped his mouth with a napkin, 'the schedule she worked through. Both she and Micky, her husband, are very rich. There was no need for more money. But, no, he found her engagements quite ruthlessly, and she sang them.'

'Will she sing again?' Stella asked.

'I doubt it. Chemotherapy, radiotherapy, the lot, she's having it. Oh, they'll keep her alive for a few years. But she won't sing in public again.'

'How old is she?'

'Forty-nine.'

'Have you played for her all through her career?'

'No. The last ten years, it's been pretty well full-time. I play opera rehearsals with her. Before that, occasionally when Emmanuel Thurn or John Silk weren't available. I was at the Royal College with Micky before he turned to money-making. He was quite a pianist. We did duets together as students. But he soon swapped to management. He was even better at that. And he dropped his first wife to marry Lenka. Quite brazenly. No passion in it. No sex. Money.'

'And what did his first wife say?' Stella pressed.

'Nothing. She was a nice girl. Also a singer, but had given it up to look after their boy. I've not heard of her for years. The son'll be thirty-ish. He's a lawyer. And I hope he's screwing it out of Mick for his mother. But I doubt it.'

Terence Quinn described his serfdom under Fischer. He seemed quite detached, reporting unforgivable insults without resentment. He had not visited Lenka since she was so ill; she had lost her hair and would see no one.

When the accompanist had gone, Lise asked Stella her opinion of the man.

'He didn't seem human. He really is malicious.'

'Terry would claim he spoke nothing but the truth.'

'Then he'd do better to keep his mouth shut,' Stella answered. 'Is he married?'

'Yes. Happily. Four sons. Grown-up now, but two still at

248

home. I think he resented the Fischer's tyranny and is getting his own back.'

'Dining out on his stories?'

'No. It'll be private. He won't blot his copybook in public in case she miraculously revives and reappears on the scene.'

'Is he any good?'

'Good player. And he's accompanied so many he can give you all their ideas. But if it comes to new songs, by contemporaries, he can't help. He can play them well enough, but he groans and says he could alter some of the chords and nobody would know. But he accompanies you up to the full strength of your voice, and knows the halls, the venues and whether to go strong or go easy.'

'Pretty near perfect?'

'For this tour, yes. I'd really like someone nearer my own age. You have to take meals together, and travel together, and Terry does get tiring.'

In the middle of the afternoon Sebastian appeared. He'd rehearsed at the Barbican, lunched out, practised and now was home for an hour or two to bathe and prepare for the concert.

He shook hands solemnly with Stella, then kissed her on both cheeks. He nodded, friendly enough, in the direction of his wife.

'Did all go well?' Stella asked.

'Yes. The Dvořák. I've done it often enough with this orchestra and conductor.'

'Who is?'

'Tabori. Good string man. We hit it off moderately well. Moderately.' He laughed, and sat without invitation, asked a few questions about Beechnall, her new job, his father, her husband. Lise made no attempt to provide him with a drink, but put on an expression of interested alertness. Just as he rose to leave for 'a long soak in the bath' he turned to his wife.

'Did Quinn come?'

'Yes. Right on time.'

'And how did it go?'

'Fair enough. He says he's getting the hang of my style.'

'I don't like him.'

'No. Well.' Lise drawled out her words. 'He plays the right notes.'

Sebastian left, grinning. When the door had closed behind him she said, 'I shall ask Seb to give me a run-through on one or two of my programmes. He hasn't done so since, since . . . Germany. It'll be a sort of test of how we stand. I think he'll do it, and he's usually very helpful. But I'll leave it until you've gone back.'

'How are things?' Stella thought she'd get awkward questions over. That's why she was here, presumably.

'Just the same as ever. We speak. We have a meal together. We tell each other what our arrangements are. We might discuss some point.'

'Such as?'

'How much milk? Or, do we need to set the central heating? That sort of day-to-day thing.'

'You don't quarrel?'

'No. Never. We can even argue about unimportant things. But he's never again mentioned splitting up.'

'When he first told you,' Stella spoke slowly as if to get it exactly right, 'was he serious? I mean, did it convince you? Or was it just, oh, passing bad temper caused by snags on the German trip?'

'I was absolutely convinced. I was sure he'd move out inside a day or two. I'm pretty certain, though he hasn't said so, that he went to consult his solicitor.'

'Do you think that altered matters, that the solicitor raised things he hadn't thought of?'

'I doubt it, I very much doubt it. At least, I can't myself think of anything Herbert could dredge up that could so radically change Seb's mind.'

A little silence fell, fermented.

'Then, why?' Stella asked.

'He's just changed his mind.'

'Well, yes. But why? Is he usually so volatile?'

Lise waited, slightly caressing her right knee with her fourth finger.

'He's a strange man, Stella. Make no mistake.' She shook her head, glanced at the door as if she expected his return. 'He's nervous, and uncertain, like his father, and they both cover it with aggression.' Lise stopped as if she'd lost the drift of her own thought.

'And so?'

'Yes. He must have come back from Germany sore with the whole world, and with himself. And I perhaps didn't put the right face on, was insufficiently sympathetic, and so he turned his bile on me. And it lasted for two or three days until he saw how unfair he'd been. But he couldn't bring himself to apologise.'

'That's poor,' Stella said.

'That's him. But he'll realise he's acted shabbily so that next time we row he'll start in his own mind a few rungs down.' Lise smiled suddenly, broadly. 'He finally decided that he didn't want to leave, that he was better off here. As he is. The house. The space. Me. The convenience. To his credit, he came to that conclusion.'

'What do you mean?'

'Whatever uproar was going on in his head, and uproar it would have been, riot, he still managed to know which side his bread was buttered.'

'But he didn't apologise.'

'That's a man.'

'And you're satisfied?'

'Yes. I know you think I shouldn't be, that I should rub his nose in it, make him squirm. I think that's right theoretically. But we're both busy and successful. And this life here, just the idea of it, keeps us steady. It's somewhere to run to in between bouts of recital lunacy. I know what you're thinking: that we're more like landlady and lodger than man and wife. So we are. But it will change. And you want to ask me what will happen next time he starts an affair with some pretty lady, don't you? And my answer is: I don't know. I hope this little paroxysm', she choked on the word, 'will teach him what's at risk.'

'Do you mind when he goes off the rails?' In for a penny, in for a pound.

251

'Sexually, you mean?'

'Yes. Adultery.'

Lise rubbed her chin, then dabbed at her lips with her finger-ends.

'I don't know. I don't really know. That sounds feeble. And I am feeble about it. I'm not pleased, that's all. But I sometimes think he can't help himself, and I ought to put up with it. Such quietism I don't approve, really, but . . .'

They ate high tea at about six and Sebastian appeared briefly. He drank one cup, but said next to nothing. When he set off soon after, he was casually dressed.

'He was very quiet,' Stella ventured.

'He's at work.' That sounded final. The man looked pale, older, taut.

The women listened to the concert on Radio 3. The Dvořàk followed Brahms's Tragic Overture. Sebastian's tone sounded extraordinarily large, his playing eloquent and spacious.

The audience, to judge from the applause, thoroughly approved.

'He played that remarkably,' Lise said, soberly.

'Is it a favourite of his?'

'He's done it often enough. He really is at the top of his form these days. I can't think of anybody to touch him. Bach, Brahms. Britten.'

'Will that last?'

'That's a good question. He sometimes talks of taking a sabbatical year just to think and study. Just so it won't all grow stale on him.'

'Is that sensible?' Stella asked.

'I've no idea. No, that's wrong. I think not. That's more honest. It would be stupid to stop when he's somewhere near the height of his power. It takes it out of him, I can tell you. You don't do what he's doing without a long apprenticeship and marvellously concentrated practice all the time and tremendous expenditure of energy. He's doing quite a lot of recording, with more to come, and that'll bring in even more business.'

'Did luck play any part?'

'Of course. To be in the right place at the right time. Yes. But Seb has earned this supreme position he has. It's taken quite a time. He's nearly thirty-seven now. It's not been very easy. Nor have fashion, outside considerations, films, clothes, scandals, played any big part. He is where he is because he's made it clear to critics and listeners and impresarios that he handles the cello repertoire better than anybody else.'

'He realises that, I suppose?' Stella ventured.

'You have to believe in yourself in our game. If you didn't, the preparation is so rigorous you'd drop out. And it's not much of a life jetting it round the world. He won't allow his cello in the luggage bays. He buys a seat for it.' Lise stood now, turned the radio, now beginning Brahms Three, off without a word of consultation. 'But sometimes he feels insecure. He doesn't think, for instance, that he's any better a musician than his father is.'

'Then why is he so much more successful?'

'Opportunity. Personality. Ruthless ambition.'

'Have you ever put this to Michael?' Stella asked.

'He won't have it. "Sebastian's in a different class. Always has been" is what he says.'

'And you?'

'That's probably right. Though Michael's a considerable musician. With better chances he might well have ended up as something different from a provincial schoolmaster.'

Stella put out a mischievous finger at Lise.

'May I ask you a tricky question?'

'Go on. I don't promise to answer,' Lise replied.

'Is it because you think Seb's so outstanding that you make all these allowances for him?'

'I suppose that comes into it.' Lise spoke quite deliberately now, fingers together, her head above her companion's. 'It must. But when I think about him I see him as the man I married six years ago. He's a man. With weaknesses and strengths. Like your husband. He can surprise me with the beauty and balance of his playing, even though I have been brought up to music. Sometimes when he's accompanying me he'll make a suggestion, and I'll think how

253

good it is, how he has showed a grasp of a kind of music, and often literature for that matter, that isn't his direct concern. He's way beyond me. I know that. But he's a husband. A man who grumbles because his lunch is late. Who needs his laundry looking after. Who's put up some shelves I wanted. Who lies in bed with me. I nursed him when he had flu. I bundled him in the bath. I've come back from a party or a pub tiddly on his arm. I've admired him for not letting waiters or shopkeepers boss him about, and for being considerate to not very gifted pupils. Well, sometimes.' She smiled to herself. 'I put up with his tantrums at home, and his high spirits. That's the person, the one I bother about.'

'And?' Stella let her word curve, curvet upwards.

'I've got used to him. I don't want to lose him. He and I have a great deal in common though we are so different. It suits him here, as it suits me. He has his little flings, yes.'

'What would he do if you had an affair?'

'I haven't.'

'But if you did?' Stella pressed.

'I don't think I'd have an affair unless I was seriously in love. And that would involve such changes in me and my way of life that I'd be quite different from what I am now.'

'And that's not very likely?'

'I'll touch wood,' Lise said, 'but I don't think so. We live an unusual life. Practising here all day, with little outings and treats and hospitality, and bursts of public appearance. It's been easier for me, in that I trot off to the same theatre night after night. But soon we shall be shooting in all directions. And if this American *Oedipus* comes off, then God knows how long I shall have to live there. Perhaps it's this house that holds us together. We've never considered children.'

'Doesn't he want them?'

'I think he wouldn't mind. But I want to advance my career before that happens. I'm only twenty-nine, so there's time. How about you?'

'Exactly the same,' Stella said. 'I want to make my way as head of department before I start a family.'

'But you want one?'

'I think so. Even these days there's pressure on women to be mothers. It completes you.' She spoke sarcastically. 'Though at some cost I think. But I'd like to when I'm ready.'

'Will John make a good father?' Lise asked.

'I guess so. He'll be very old-fashioned. Just like his parents. And yet he was an only child. Their home was their everything, but they didn't overfill it with noisy, untidy kids. Perhaps that's why it was as it was. And Sebastian?'

'As a father? I don't know. He'll be pleased to be the actual father, I guess, but what part he'll play in the up-bringing is anybody's guess. We'll need paid help, and I'm sure that means a difference. I can't see Michael as a father-figure. Can you?'

'Does Seb never say anything?'

'I think he was a bit afraid of him. Michael had a sharp tongue as well as a short fuse. And I think he and Louise were often at loggerheads.'

'Do you ever see her?'

'Not often. She rings occasionally. And Seb went to call in on her recently. Now I come to think of it, it must be more than twelve months ago.' Lise hesitated, as if she rarely considered these matters.'

'Is she musical?'

'I think so. In an amateur way. She teaches still, though she has said something about retiring. She's just a bit older than Michael. They had the three children close together, in three or four years.'

'The others are girls, aren't they?'

'Yes. Maria and José.'

'Are they musicians?'

'No. Not so far as I know. One's a solicitor, married to a solicitor. The other's married to an engineer, who works abroad a lot. That's José, the youngest. As soon as she got into university, Louise upped and left Michael. She'd been waiting for the day, as far as I could make out.'

'Did they stay with their mother or father in the university vacations?'

'I've no idea. Seb had left home altogether by this time.'

'Where does Louise live?'

'Yorkshire, somewhere. Keighley. Batley. Ilkley. I don't know. She came originally from up there.' Lise came across. 'Would you like just a short stroll outside? I wouldn't go out on my own, but the pair of us will be all right. Ten minutes' exercise round the streets will do us good. It's been marvellous to sit and gossip and answer your questions. I feel like a human being.'

They slipped on light coats and stepped out into the warm night. Few people were about, but one middle-aged man raised his trilby hat, calling out a greeting.

'Oh, oh,' Lise said.

'He must be lonely,' Stella replied.

'Would you like a drink?'

'Not really. Not unless you do.'

Now they marched briskly, a foot apart, each pleased with the other.

They had scarcely done five minutes and were making handsome progress along a street of shops when they paused of one mind to discuss three dresses tastefully arranged in Laura's, though they were certain that the colours were altered by the streetlighting.

'I like the shape of that,' Lise said. 'We'll look at it in the daylight.'

'I don't think I ever consider cut first,' Stella answered. 'It's always the colour in the first place that attracts. It just shows that walking round in the dark gives you new ideas. Does that place usually have good things?'

'No idea. I've not seen it before. It might be utterly scruffy in the broad light of day. On the other hand there are some interesting . . .'

Lise stepped away and almost fell over a pair of outstretched legs on the pavement before her. Two young men, seated on steps in a doorway, avoided their eyes. In front of the legs was the shallow lid of a cardboard box on which was crudely painted 'Hungry and homeless' and at the side of the legend two 2p pieces and three 1p's. Both women, unwisely, they said afterwards, stopped, read,

256

looked. The man with the outstretched legs who perched
on the lowest of three steps was a young West Indian in a
T-shirt and jeans and wearing a baseball cap. In this light
he looked moderately respectable. His companion, two
steps up, feet on the lowest, knees spread, wore black
trousers and an unbuttoned, heavy dark coat. He was white
with his longish untidy hair parted in the middle. He stared
at his hands clasped between his thighs. Neither man
would be more than twenty. They said nothing, seemed
drugged.

Stella felt in the pockets of her slacks for loose change,
which she bent to drop noiselessly into the lid. Lise clicked
open her handbag, extracted a pound coin and quietly
added that, reaching downwards. Neither man said a word
of thanks. The women waited, hesitated shortly, then hurried away, expecting perhaps that the beggars would leap
up, snatch their handbags, molest them. Hearing no sound
they stopped, half-fearfully glanced back over their shoulders. The dark legs stuck forward. Stella thought again of
the doorway, three tall steps, a high wrought-iron gate
behind and the two silent figures.

'They'll spend it on drink,' Stella said.

'They won't buy much for that.' Lise put her hand on her
friend's arm as they walked furiously on again. 'I always
hope they're people doing it for a bet or charity. I mean,
they weren't in rags.'

'I wish I'd given them more.'

'Oh, no,' Lise said. 'I give, but I think it's wrong.'

'They won't do very well there, will they?'

'I shouldn't think so. People go to and from the pubs.
Perhaps that's the spot they've chosen for the night, and
they leave their box out just in case.'

'Won't the police move them on?'

'Not much likelihood of a policeman along here.'

'It must be awful,' Stella said, 'having to beg. And no-
where to live.'

They walked on, but in silence; their spirits had been
knocked out of them. When they returned home they drank
Horlicks and watched a film about hatred between a

deranged mother and her daughter. Just before twelve, Sebastian returned. He joined them, but without a drink.

'Did all go well?' Lise asked.

'I think so. Didn't you listen?'

'We did. And taped it for you.'

'And you should have heard your wife's praise for you,' Stella said.

'But you didn't tape that.'

Their gloom lightened, but they did not stay downstairs for long. They were weary.

21

The next two days of Stella's stay in London passed placidly. After breakfast Stella read the newspapers for an hour or so while Lise practised. On the first day, it rained, the clouds strung low above the housetops, so that they did not go out and Sebastian joined them for lunch.

'This is an unexpected pleasure,' he informed the guest. 'I expected you to be enjoying yourself up in the West End.' It was clear to Stella that Lise had told him she'd prepare lunch for the three. Sebastian spoke with ironical politeness never overdone. He returned to his practice room, warning Stella that he would be out for dinner that evening, and he hoped she would forgive his discourtesy.

'I didn't think you'd want my interruptions,' he said, closing the door.

'He's going out to see Bobby Squires, an old friend. They'll argue and row and Bob will lose his wool, but they'll enjoy it. They'll be in such a bate when Seb comes home, they won't try to get in touch for at least a couple of months.'

'Is it always the same?'

'Invariably. Bob taught Seb when he first came up to London. They've never seen eye to eye. Seb said it was a wasted year, but they've always remained in touch. And in the last two or three years, since Bob retired, they've had these meetings. He's a bit like Michael, is Bob, but even more irascible. Seb says that he resents his success.'

'Was he any good?' Stella asked.

'Oh, yes. He had a respectable recital career, and was a very fine chamber-music player, but he began to suffer from rheumatism or arthritis, some painful complaint that made him finish early.'

'So what will happen?'

'They'll argue and disagree and feel all the better for it, I hope. Then Seb will wheel him out to an Indian restaurant.'

'And they'll heal the wounds?'

'I doubt it. But it will be a few hours' break for Bobby. And he's pleased to be seen in public with Seb. I'm glad Seb puts himself out.'

The two women walked round to the dress-shop. Lise immediately dismissed the window display, but Stella insisted on going inside, where she purchased an embroidered blouse. Pleased with herself, she looked again at the steps and alleyway where the beggars had sat. They had left no signs of their occupation; the speckled mock-stone had been thoroughly scrubbed. At the side of the door were two plaques, a large one for Stokes and Whitley, Solicitors, with a list of partners and associates and their degrees. A smaller oblong on the other side read T.A. Jepson, Engineering Consultant. The iron gate was locked back to the wall.

'I wonder where they are this morning?' Stella asked, pointing to the steps.

'No telling. They say you shouldn't give them money. They'll only spend it on drink or drugs.'

'What should one give them?'

'Food.'

'I don't carry ham sandwiches round with me.'

They laughed and turned defeated into a bookshop where Lise held up a copy of *The Ragged Trousered Philanthropists*.

'Have you read it?' Stella asked. 'It's no laughing matter.'

But Lise almost immediately found *Down and Out in Paris and London*.

They bought neither.

The next day they started late, traipsed round West End shops and wore themselves out at an exhibition of modern paintings of naked figures.

'I feel disappointed,' Lise said. 'Some of these are really good, but I hate the trouble that's been taken. They are not exactly ugly or distorted, but, oh, ill-tempered, painful. As if the artists could take no pleasure in what they see, but must import their own fatigues and hang-ups.'

Lise, though pleasant and lively, seemed determined not to be pleased. That night they drank more than was good for them.

On the next morning, the day Stella was to leave, Lise sounded noisily cheerful as she prepared breakfast.

'Have you got a hangover?' she shouted.

'No. Have you?'

'No. But,' she dropped her voice to a whisper, 'my husband returned last night to my bed.'

They embraced, then jigged round the kitchen floor hugging, laughing.

'Where is he now?'

'Still there. Fast asleep.'

Lise put a finger to her lips to bring the conversation to an end.

They had just started their boiled eggs when Sebastian appeared, unshaven and tousle-headed.

'You didn't wake me,' he said to his wife, roguishly.

'I thought you'd be tired.'

'Our guest is leaving. Our bringer of good luck.'

He rattled a cereal packet.

'At what time are you going?' he asked. When she told him he said very quietly, 'Do you think you could put it back for an hour? There's something I'd like to play to you.' She acquiesced, nodding in silence. 'Stephen Steinberg will be here at ten,' the clock showed nine-five now, 'and we'll do it.'

He finished his cereal, asked to be excused, and walked out with his cup of coffee.

'What's he going to play?' Stella wanted to know.

'I haven't the slightest idea. That's the first I've heard of it.'

'Why does he want me to hear it? I'm no musician.'

'It must run in the family. This attraction of yours', Lise spoke solemnly, 'for the male Alexanders.'

'He hasn't mentioned it to you?'

'Not a word.'

Stephen Steinberg arrived on time and was instructed to find his own way to the practice studio. Ten minutes later, Sebastian appeared to invite, then lead, the women upstairs. Two chairs had been placed for them. They sat, slightly overcome, not talking.

'I want you to hear this,' Sebastian said, resuming his seat and picking up his cello. He rapidly checked the tuning. 'It's an air with five variations and coda, though the variations run into each other, with one exception.'

'Who's it by?' Lise asked.

'I'd like you to try to guess that, if you can. There is some reason behind my making all this mystery.'

The music on his stand had been hidden in a black cover. 'Right, Steve.'

The pianist began with large, soft, odd chords, discordant but not unpleasantly so, delivered as if to put the listeners both at ease and also in a state of puzzlement. The slight jaggednesses of rhythm did not disturb, but were placed as if to catch, maintain interest among the chords which signalled no clear key, only a slow march ahead. At the end of the fifth bar the cello cut in above the still tramping, quietly heavy, chords, like a bright shaft of gold. The melody had simplicity about it, though its rhythm seemed not uncomplicated, but Sebastian played with such ease and amplitude that they were held with its strange beauty. The marching piano, still with its stumbles, seemed less important though the powerful eloquence of the aria, now mounting to a climax of strong plangency, dismissed it as subsidiary. The aria, two sections, both repeated, ended, and there followed a short pause, during which Sebastian hung over his instrument, daring the women to move.

Down he brought hand and bow, leapt for joy, clashing at speed and yet somehow steadily linked with the piano on its shining, virtuoso course at the top of the keyboard. The players opposed each other as they frolicked, made a game of competition, wrestled and caressed, breathless with vigour, lithely stout. Athletic speed in the swoopings and sudden scurries dispersed themselves without ostentation to a pizzicato, running canon, one part to cello, two only to the piano and then accelerating to an inversion and finally to the theme, still at speed, in canon in three different keys, mocking, devilish, quickening by the second until the whole was broken by a great sound, all four strings, on cello only, to introduce five powerful lines of unaccompanied huge chords formed from, upthrust round some shifting counterpoint, adagio, every note wrenched nobly, in arrogant rhetoric, by Sebastian from his instrument. It strangled Stella; nothing should have such knotted strength – such throttling weight, such threat in declamation. She could discern no connection with the aria.

Six chords, smally quiet, called from the piano, unassuming except to suggest a new, or the original key.

Sebastian drew a magnificence of eloquence from this, the climax of the work, the longest of the movements. As the cello began, Stella could make out the aria though its shape seemed more intricately decorated. As though to announce a peace, an order, a calm commentary, the cello sang, soared and dipped with comforting energy until it climbed to the highest register, where it speeded, flying like a swift in brilliant darts. It became passionate, so that Stella lost all connection with the original simplicities but was buffeted, not harmfully, but as on a fairground ride, in scaring safety, until the broad jagged strength of both strings and piano shouted such furious complexity that she was lost, overcome with the wide tract of sound which ended its vertiginous climb with a dive on to the deepest C and its octave, blaring out alone fortissimo, vibrating through her head, stripped of all but brute strength.

There followed a brief hiatus.

Almost at once the cello skipped into semiquavers, as if zestfully parodying Corelli or Vivaldi apart from the truly discordant support. The movement cheered, cleansed, made the moment healthy with direct speed, braced. In this, the fifth variation Stella knew where she was, understood the language, danced with the bow, smiled. The movement, though it had repeats, seemed to last no time, but ended with the brilliant descent down a three and a fifth major arpeggio and without apology sang again a shortened, simple, artless first form of the melody, but once, mezzo-piano, and left it, there, naked, as it were, on their laps.

Sebastian lowered his bow, but still held his cello between his knees.

'What do you think of that?' he asked Stella.

She waved a hand, unable to speak.

'Who wrote it?' he asked, leaning back, smiling, running a passage silently through on his fingerboard.

'Shostakovich,' Stella guessed.

'I don't think so,' Lise said.

'Who then?'

'Somebody I've not heard of. Slightly academic, but . . .'

'But what?'

'Marvellous,' Lise said. 'Full of passion.'

'You liked it?' Stephen was grinning from the piano.

'Oh, yes.'

'And you? You like it?' To Stella.

'I feel . . . overwhelmed.'

Sebastian carefully lowered the cello to its side on the floor, loosened his bow and stood. He lifted the music from the stand.

'Arietta, Variations and Coda', he read out, holding the music spread, 'by Michael Alexander. For Sebastian and Lise and Stella.'

He whirled the music loose to show the inscription to the women.

Stella shook her head.

Lise clasped her hands like a saint in ecstatic prayer.

'Are you going to include it in your recitals?' she asked.

'What do you think?'

'As an encore?'

'It takes ten minutes.' Sebastian bowed. 'Now ladies, thank you for listening. He kissed them both. We must practise.'

'When did you get this?' Lise asked, doggedly.

'The day before yesterday. There's some young man at Dad's summer school who made this beautiful fair copy.'

'That's not Michael's writing?' Stella asked.

'Only the inscription.'

He opened the door for them. They slipped out, and walked hand in hand together down the stairs.

'You'll write and tell Michael?' Lise asked.

'I will. Though I won't know what to say.'

Stella found the words and Michael wrote back by return to say he'd been working on and off with the piece for eighteen months, and that he was glad finally to have done something that pleased his son. That sounded nervous or grudging, but he accompanied them to Birmingham in the autumn for the first performance, which he sat stiffly through.

'Seb made one or two suggestions and alterations that I've incorporated,' he said in the interval. But he was proud. When after the concert they delivered him at his house, it was well past midnight. He said humbly, 'Thank you for this evening. I'll remember this for the rest of my life.' That, they were not to know, was a bare five months. 'I'm working now on a passacaglia for him.'

'Will this arietta be printed?' John asked.

'Yes. It's been accepted, but they'll do it in their own time. They'll let Seb have the first months to popularise it. I think you made me write it,' he said suddenly, in a whisper in Stella's direction. 'You. And you forced it out of me. I'm not prolific. Perhaps I'll do more now. But you made me complete it, and it pleased Sebastian. I'm glad of that. Thank you.'

Five months later he was knocked down and killed instantly by a joy-rider as he waited at his bus-stop. He had that morning received a proof of his music for correction. The manuscript of the passacaglia was found incomplete in his desk. Sebastian played a recital on the evening of the funeral, but could not include the Arietta.

Outside the closed door of Michael's house, John and Stella stood hand in hand.

'A good trip,' John said. 'We're on the up.'

They looked at the cold moon. Before he had gone in, Michael had kissed Stella hungrily, had hugged her.

'We're making progress,' John said.

They walked the short path towards the warmth of the car. John whistled the beginning of the Arietta. She was amazed he could recall it so readily. They stood on the pavement in the moon-shadow of a lime-tree.

All the front windows of Michael's house were lit.